A SUITABLE YOUNG MAN

By Anne L Harvey

Although the town of Horwich is very real, the characters in this book are entirely the figment of my imagination and bear no resemblance to anyone, living or dead, who might have lived in Horwich during the period in which the novel is set.

In order to fit in with the story, I have used what's known as 'poetic licence' by changing certain dates and facts. For the purists, these are listed under Author Notes at the end of the book.

Foreword

Teddy boy: (noun) British (in the 1950s),a young man of a subculture characterised by a style of dress based on Edwardian fashion (typically with drainpipe trousers, bootlace tie and hair slicked up in a quiff) and a liking for rock and roll music. <origin> From Teddy, a pet form of the given name Edward (with reference to Edward VII's reign).
Oxford Dictionary of English

A popular conception of a Teddy boy (every effort has been made to trace the owner of this cartoon, if he or she would get in touch, I will gladly acknowledge)

Acknowledgements

With grateful thanks to my original beta reader, Sheila Morris, and my three later beta readers, Judith Nisbet Lowe, Lynn Lilliman and Sally Jenkins, all of whose input was invaluable.

I would also like to thank successful self-published author and friend, Lizzie Lamb, for all her help, encouragement and self-publishing advice. I'm in good company!

Finally, but by no means least, thanks to my wonderful husband without whose help, support and advice, this book would not have been possible.

CHAPTER 1

Kathy winced as she stepped down from the bus. On a December evening, in court shoes, her feet were numb and she couldn't feel her fingers despite the woollen gloves. But it hadn't been like this when she'd set off for work this morning and pride had conquered common sense. Now, it even smelled cold, with the sharp acrid edge of the ever-present sulphurous-smelling blue haze spewing from the nearby Locomotive Works. Cloth-capped, clog-shod workers still straggled into Horwich from the entrance to the Works over the hump of the railway bridge. Many of the passengers who'd got off the bus with her were mill-workers from either Beehive or Victoria Mills and walked arm in arm, in chattering, cheerful groups, to their various homes.

Before crossing Chorley New Road to take the short cut up Curteis Street, she checked her wristwatch. She would have to hurry to catch the library before it closed. As she walked, the click-clacking of her high heels on the pavements echoed off the darkened gable-ends of the terraced houses that made up the centre of this small Lancashire mill town. In contrast to the busyness of Chorley New Road, the street, apart from a man in a trilby and belted raincoat going in the opposite direction, was eerily quiet. She'd walked these pavements hundreds of times, knew them well, yet tonight she was aware of her solitariness.

Ahead, lit by a solitary gas lamp, was Coffin Alley, the gap between two blocks of houses and, as she stepped into the alley's shadows, she saw, too late, two figures. One of them grabbed her arms from behind then, as she screamed, the other clamped a hand over her mouth. 'Shut up, you stupid cow!' a rough voice whispered. She kicked out but whoever held her from behind laughed and dodged his body out of the way. In the dimness of the gaslight, a face leered close to hers and the hand was taken away from her mouth. Before she could scream again, whoever it was fastened his lips on hers in a mockery of a kiss. The stink of cigarettes on his breath sickened her. She wrenched her mouth

1

away from his and, in the sickly light, saw that it was Jud Simcox. She'd never liked him, had always found him creepy.

From somewhere close by came a commanding voice. 'That's enough, you two. Leave her alone.'

'Who says?' jeered the one who held her, not loosening his hold.

'Nick Roberts.' Kathy's heart leapt in the relief of recognition as a tall young man stepped into the meagre pool of light.

Whoever was holding her let go and she stumbled to the ground. Her rescuer came to stand between her and her attackers. All three, she saw, were Teddy boys. She wondered if, despite recognising Nick, she should be more afraid than ever. The distinctive Edwardian clothing and often violent behaviour of Teddy boys set them apart from the crowd.

'We were only having a bit of fun, Nick,' whined Jud. 'A bit of a kiss and a cuddle.

'Stupid sods! Kathy Armstrong's not that sort of girl.'

The one who'd grabbed her, Bill Murphy she saw now, bent to peer at Kathy's face. 'She were asking for it anyhow, using Coffin Alley at this time of night.' She recoiled, as she caught the whiff of stale cooking from his clothes.

The comment incensed Kathy. 'A girl should be able to walk where she likes when she likes.'

'Ooh, pardon me for breathing,' taunted Jud.

Nick advanced towards them, hands clenched by his side, his body poised for action. 'Bugger off, the pair of you.'

'Why should we?' demanded Jud. 'You're not top dog around here now, Nick Roberts.'

'And you are, Jud? We'll see about that.' The tension almost crackled between them. Any minute now they'd be fighting.

For a long moment, all stood in silence, until Bill Murphy said, 'Aw, let's go, Jud. There's no fun in it anymore.'

'Yeah, you're right.' Jud turned to Nick. 'But don't think I'll forget this.'

The two sloped off, their laughter fading into the distance.

When Kathy tried to push herself up from the ground, her legs seemed to have lost their power. Nick, as if sensing the problem, offered her his hand. She reached up to grasp it, found it warm despite the cold. The feel of it was oddly familiar yet she couldn't remember them ever touching before. 'You OK?' he asked as he pulled her up.

'I think I'll live.'

'Where were you off to anyroad?'

She pulled away from his grasp and stepped back to look at him. Maturity had made a good-looking lad into an attractive young man. His thick dark hair was brushed back from his head and had the beginnings of a Tony Curtis quiff. Black drainpipe trousers encased long legs. The battered leather jacket he wore gave him a careless grace that only enhanced his attractiveness. With a catch in her breath, she said, 'To the library.' She looked at her watch. 'It's too late now; I was cutting it a bit fine anyway.'

'In that case, do you fancy a drink at the Temperance Bar?' He picked up her library books, pushed them back into her shopping bag and handed it to her.

'Thanks. I could do with a bit of a sit down,' she admitted.

She was still a little unsteady on her feet as they set off walking and he touched her arm. 'You sure you're all right?'

'Yes, but I'll be better when we've had that drink.'

'I don't think they meant any real harm, you know.'

She gave a mock shudder. 'I daren't think what would have happened if they'd been serious.'

Harry Stocker's Temperance Bar, an oasis of warmth and light, attracted the younger element of Horwich but tonight there were few customers. The jukebox was playing an old hit of Dickie Valentine's as they sat down on one of the wooden benches. Kathy cupped her hands round the white mug bearing the Vimto logo, breathing in the blackcurrant fumes. 'Mm, lovely,' she said as she took a sip. 'I'd forgotten how good it tastes.'

Nick raised his own Vimto to her. 'Not me usual tipple on a Friday night.' He put the steaming mug on to the pitted table and looked at her. She knew she'd changed from the skinny awkward schoolgirl he'd remember from his youth. 'Haven't seen you around for a long time, Kathy. Must be what – three, four – years?'

3

'About that,' she agreed. 'You've been doing your National Service, haven't you?'

'Just finished, three years. I signed on for an extra year so's I could do a motor mechanic's course. I'm trying to find a job in that line.' He pulled a packet of cigarettes from the inner pocket of his jacket and offered her one.

She shook her head. 'What were you doing before you were called up?'

'Labouring on a building site.' He lit his cigarette and inhaled deeply. 'Good money but not that fulfilling.'

'What did you do in the Army?' Her fingers traced the outline of some initials on the table, scored by countless individuals over the years and wondered how someone had had the patience to do it.

'Worked in MT. Motor transport. I could've signed on as a regular but I'd had enough by then.' He leaned towards her, chin tucked into hand. 'What about you, what have you been doing with yourself these past few years?'

'I went to the Commercial College in Bolton after I left school. Now I'm a shorthand typist at the Bolton Evening News. Nothing very grand but I like working for the newspaper.'

'Are you courting?' he asked, then to her surprise, he coloured a little. She could tell he'd regretted asking. It was the sort of thing elderly aunts asked.

'No.' She squirmed in her seat. Her mother frequently reminded her that, at nineteen, most girls of her age were either courting or engaged. As if it was her fault. 'How about you?'

'I've been out with Jud's sister, Sally, a couple of times since I came home.' He flicked the ash off the end of his cigarette into the ashtray. 'Do you remember her? Small, blonde and bubbly?'

'I do. Always had lots of boys hanging round her. I used to think it was because she was…,' she hesitated and gave him a knowing look, '…more physically mature than the rest of us girls.'

Nick laughed. 'How much do you remember of those youth club days?'

'Too much sometimes.' As an immature and shy 14-year-old attending St Catherine's Youth Club, she'd developed an embarrassing crush on him.

'I don't know.' The way he was looking at her with those dark heavy-lidded eyes was disconcerting. Even more so, was her reaction to him, a sort of melting of her insides, well remembered from those days. 'They were interesting times.'

To cover up the blush she could feel rising, she looked down at her watch. 'I'd better be going.'

'Where do you live? I'll walk you home if you like.'

'Travers Street opposite the Greenwood. But I'll catch the bus from the Black Dog,' she added.

'Then I'll walk you to the bus stop.'

'There's no need. I'm fine now.'

'No, I insist, after the shock you've had.'

On her feet, she was glad of his suggestion; the attack had shaken her more than she'd realised.

As they walked, they talked and she was surprised to find how at ease she felt with Nick when years before, she'd been tongue-tied in his presence. When they turned the corner into Chorley New Road, a bus was already at the stop. She sprinted towards it, just as Nick was saying, 'Kathy, will you...?' On the bus, she gave him a cheery wave, guessing he'd been on the point of asking her out. Would she have gone out with a Teddy boy, though? She grimaced. Her mother would have been horrified at the idea.

* * *

When Nick got home that night, Mary Roberts was asleep in the chair, the wireless playing quietly in the background. Her face in repose looked much less than her forty-one years. Her earlier beauty, seen only in an old photograph, had faded to a soft gentleness, her fair hair wisped with grey and scraped back into its usual bun. Not for his Mam the expense of a permanent wave.

Opening her blue-grey eyes, she said. 'Hello, love, you're home early.'

'Nowt much doing tonight.' He shrugged off the old and much favoured leather jacket he'd bought off an American airman and hung it over the back of one of the rickety kitchen chairs. 'Fancy a brew, Mam?'

'Mm, good idea.' She made as if to get up but he stopped her with his hand.

'I'll do it, Mam. You rest your legs.' He pulled the pouffe towards her and lifted her legs on to it. He knew she'd be tired. Not only did she have three younger children to care for, she worked as a weaver at Victoria Mill part-time. It didn't help that, with his Dad in prison, the family was strapped for cash. Admittedly, his sister Joyce was working now but, as a trainee weaver, her wages didn't amount to much.

As he waited for the kettle to boil, he looked at the old gas cooker encrusted with years of grease. The brown stained earthenware sink with its wooden draining board, was the only place the family had to wash, not only the dishes, but themselves. The spotted and cracked mirror hanging from the net-curtained sash window was all that he, and his father and brother Phil when they were here, had to see in to shave. He wished they could get out of this house but they'd been on the council housing list for years. Of all the similar streets of terraced houses opening straight on to the street in Horwich, Winter Street was considered the worst. It was only in his mother's lifetime that they'd got rid of the bugs and some people still had a problem with fleas. He wondered what sort of home Kathy Armstrong lived in. Travers Street was a mixture of rented and privately owned houses and he was willing to bet hers was one of the latter.

'This is nice, love,' Mary said as she took a mug of tea from him. 'We don't often get chance for a chat on our own without the kids around.'

'Peaceful with the lads in bed, isn't it?' He sat down in the worn easy chair opposite her.

She gave a snort of exasperation. 'Those two lads will be the death of me, always up to mischief.'

'They're lads, Mam, what do you expect?'

'I don't remember you and Phil being half as much trouble.'

6

'Phil and I are as different as chalk and cheese, Mam,' he pointed out. 'We never went around together like Brian and Derek do.' He put his half-empty mug on the hearth. 'Life's hard for you, Mam, isn't it, with Dad being in Strangeways?'

She made a huffing sound. 'It's not that much different if he's here, drinking or gambling his wages away.'

'How long has he got to do yet?' He was ashamed he hadn't thought to ask before but he'd preferred not to think about it. Life was a lot more peaceful without his father.

'About six months.' She sighed. 'If he behaves himself.'

Nick told her about the incident with Kathy and Jud earlier. 'Poor lass. Was she all right?' Mary asked.

'She seemed to be but I went to the bus stop with her to make sure.'

'You're a good lad, Nick, despite what people might say.'

He fidgeted in his chair. 'Best not say that too loud, I've me reputation to think of.'

'What's she like then, this Kathy? Do I know her?'

'Wouldn't think so. She's not from Horwich. Her Dad works at Dehav's,' he said, using the nickname for the large works of Dehavilland Propellers in Lostock.

Later, in the room he shared with the boys and separated from his sister by an old blanket slung over a washing line, Nick lay awake, recalling the time he'd spent with Kathy. Who'd have thought the gawky schoolgirl he remembered from his youth would bloom into such an attractive girl. Then, her hair had been an unruly mop of curls; now it had shiny auburn tints and smelled of something lemony. She wore it longer than was fashionable and caught at the sides with combs, a style reminiscent of the forties, yet it suited her. Her eyes, a startling green, were fringed with long lashes, and had an intensity that spoke to him of hidden depths he'd like to explore. His sleep that night was troubled by disturbing dreams of a young woman in an olive green coat, fitting tightly at the bodice yet flaring over slim hips.

CHAPTER 2

In the rough and tumble of sheets and blankets she'd somehow tangled around her, Joyce was reluctant to leave the only peaceful spot in the Roberts' household. Moments of privacy were rare and you had to grab them while you could. Her brothers, Brian and Derek, had woken her early, fighting over an Eagle comic, resulting in the comic being ripped in two, each blaming the other for its destruction. It had ended only when Mam had called up the stairs, 'Come and get your breakfast now or that comic'll go in the bin.' The two boys had squabbled their way downstairs with frequent demands from their mother to, 'pack it in or you'll see the back of me hand.'

All had gone quiet now. The boys would have given their faces a lick and a promise at the kitchen sink and gone out to play. She pictured them whooping down the back street. The two lived to play out, no matter what the weather. Everything mundane, like eating, sleeping, going to school, they considered interruptions to the serious business of playing out.

Joyce was content to lie there a little longer thinking about Bragger Yates. She conjured up Nick's friend in her mind, blue eyes twinkling beneath blond Tony Curtis-style hair, his tall lean body encased in a burgundy Teddy boy suit. No one, not even her best friend Sheila, knew of her feelings for him. Not for nothing was he called Bragger. He had a reputation for getting, and talking about, lasses but she'd come to suspect it was all talk. For one thing, not one of his supposed conquests was a local girl. Oh no, Mr David – she always called him by his real name to herself – Yates, you don't fool me. For one thing, he was neither a labourer nor a layabout. He was a trainee draughtsman at Dehav's, which had got him deferred from doing his National Service until he'd completed his apprenticeship.

Still engrossed in these delicious thoughts, she didn't hear anything until a voice whispered. 'Joyce, are you asleep?'

Her little sister was standing at the side of the bed, bearing a mug of tea. 'No, Lucy, I'm awake.'

'I've brought you some tea.' The child proffered the mug which had lost about a third of its contents in her precarious passage up the stairs.

'Well, aren't you a clever girl!' She took the mug carefully from Lucy's fingers. The girl's hands were chilly despite carrying the tea. 'You're cold, love. Come in beside me.'

'You don't mind?' The six-year-old's elfin face always looked as if she expected to be told off.

'Course not. Come and cuddle up to me. We'll soon get warm.'

Her small body nestled in the crook of Joyce's arm. After a moment, she said, 'I wish I were able to stand up for meself.'

Joyce pulled the worn, and much-washed, blankets closer round the little girl. 'Has summat happened, love?'

'Promise you won't tell anyone?' she begged. Lucy's face was so pleading, she gave the child her word. 'Some of the bigger boys got hold of me in playtime and dragged me through the boys' toilets. Ugh, it was horrible!'

'The smell, you mean? Boys' and men's toilets always smell.' Joyce was trying not to laugh, relieved it had not been anything worse.

'Not only that but there were a boy in there having a wee,' Lucy whispered, her colour rising.

'He were probably more embarrassed than you.'

She giggled then. 'He were, he put his thingy away quickly and ran out.'

Joyce chewed her lip, trying to find the right words to reassure her sister. 'Look, love, I know it's hard but that sort of thing does go on in the playground. Did the boys see you were afraid?'

'Yes, I cried. I couldn't help it.'

'If it happens again, remember it'll be over in seconds,' Joyce reassured her. 'If you try to show them you're not afraid, they won't be so inclined to do it again. That's what I used to do.'

Lucy gawped at Joyce. 'You mean the same thing happened to you?'

Joyce gave her a hug. 'Of course it did. The second time, I held me breath, stuck me chin out and marched through of me own accord. They never bothered me again. I think they thought I might do it when they were in there weeing.'

Lucy sighed. 'I wish I weren't such a mardy.'

'What are you afraid of, sweetheart?'

'Noise, the dark, big boys – not Nick, though.'

'You're not afraid of Phil, are you?' Joyce queried.

Lucy appeared to be contemplating the question. 'No, not really. He just seems...different.'

And there, thought Joyce, the child had summed up their middle brother, Phil, currently doing his National Service. Even when he was home, he seemed detached somehow. He rarely came home on leave, preferring to spend the time with his RAF mates. Joyce hugged the child's thin body and said, 'Never mind, love, we'll all look after you. Even Brian and Derek.'

They both giggled at the thought of the two lads looking after anyone. They couldn't even look after themselves without getting into trouble.

* * *

Light was beginning to filter through the curtains when Kathy woke. Muffled movements from her parents' room and the smell of cigarette as her father lit up the first one of the day drifted into her consciousness. Moments later, she heard her father's hacking cough as he made his way to the bathroom. Hovering on the verge of wakefulness, in the cosy cocoon of blankets and eiderdown, she remembered that she had seen Nick Roberts again.

In the years since she had last seen him, she thought he would have lost the power to affect her. He hadn't. With maturity, he was even more attractive. And there was that weird feeling, when he took her hand, of belonging. She sighed. Perhaps it was a good job their paths were unlikely to cross again in a hurry.

She reached for her dressing gown on top of the bed and fumbled with her toes for her slippers. Opening the curtains, she saw that frost had formed a lacy network on the inside of the windows. Rubbing a peephole, she could see that the privet hedge of the tiny front garden was rimed with white. Even now a wintry sun was making its appearance and soon the fragile loveliness would be gone. Sighing again, she grabbed a notebook and pencil from the bedside table and padded downstairs.

Immediately, the beiges and browns of the sitting room, stuffed as it was with pre-war furniture, stifled her. Her soul longed for the bright primary colours of the contemporary furniture so fashionable now. The room sparkled with cleanliness for her mother ran the household with methodical precision. The hearth was spotless and the fire dared do no other than burn brightly when the chimney was swept with annual regularity. The encyclopaedias her parents had bought her when she passed her 11-plus stood to attention in the glass-fronted bookcase that gleamed with its daily dose of furniture polish. Her Dad's pride and joy, a 14-inch television, its blank screen not showing a speck of dust, stood in one of the fireplace alcoves. Yet for all the room's pristine appearance, it was warm and inviting. The brown moquette three-piece suite, large and comfy with plumped up cushions, welcomed her as she curled up in the corner of the sofa. In the notebook, she scribbled a few lines describing what she'd seen from her bedroom window, trying to recapture the loveliness in words.

'Are you listening, love?' demanded Vera Armstrong from the kitchen door, through which came the tantalising aroma of bacon cooking.

'Sorry, Mum, I was concentrating,' she said, indicating the notebook. 'What did you say?'

A look of exasperation flitted across Vera's face, a look Kathy knew well. 'You and your scribbling! I asked if you wanted some toast while I'm doing some.' She stood in the doorway, arms crossed over plump bosom, her styled and permed hair as stiff as her demeanour.

Kathy closed the notebook with a sigh. 'Yes, please.'

The door opened between the hall and stairs and her father, a tall, thickset man with thinning hair and a solid dependable face, stepped into the sitting room. 'Morning, Kathy, love.' He rubbed his hands together. 'It looks a bit fresh out this morning.'

'It was frosty last night too.'

Her father took his usual chair and held his hands out to the fire. 'Where did you get to then?'

Kathy remembered the encounter with the two louts but knew better than to mention it or she'd never hear the last of it. Her parents' protectiveness always made her want to do precisely the opposite. 'I went to change my library books but I was too late.'

'You were late home if you only went to the library, weren't you?' Ron asked.

'I bumped into Nick Roberts and we went to the Temperance Bar, then I went to Carole's house.' She hoped she didn't sound as if she was floundering. Which she was.

'Nick Roberts? Isn't he that boy you used to be keen on at the youth club?' Vera had appeared in the doorway again to call Ron to his breakfast and caught Kathy's last words.

'That's right. He's not been long out of his National Service.'

'Didn't I read in the Journal that his father went to prison?' Vera asked.

Here we go, Kathy thought. 'Yes, but that's not Nick's fault.'

'Still, you want to steer clear from the likes of him.'

Stung by the disapproving note in her mother's voice, Kathy retorted, 'Mum, I only chatted to him over a hot Vimto.'

Ron rose from his chair, wagging a paternal finger at Kathy. 'We'll have less cheek from you, my girl.'

The ingrained attitude of not questioning their authority led her to say, 'Sorry, Dad, sorry, Mum.'

'That's more like it,' Vera said. 'Now come and get your breakfast, both of you.'

She rose, taking the notebook with her. 'I'll just nip up to the bathroom. I won't be a minute.' She needed a few moments to get her rioting emotions and rebellious thoughts in check before facing her parents over the breakfast table. Why must it always be like this? She knew they wanted the best for her but she found the constraints they placed on her stifling. It seemed as if their one desire in life was for her to find 'a suitable young man' and settle down. Well, she hadn't had much luck in that direction so far. She'd had a few boyfriends but nothing serious. And Nick Roberts didn't exactly fit the criteria.

CHAPTER 3

A few days before Christmas, Nick had an interview for a job at a small garage in Bolton. He'd been disappointed a couple of times already. It seemed that army qualifications didn't count in Civvy Street. Yet he didn't regret the extra year he'd done. Still, with this job, he was more optimistic because the chap he'd spoke to seemed eager to meet Nick. He'd guessed that they were desperate for someone.

The garage was down a back street behind St George's Road and looked prosperous enough with several cars parked outside either waiting for collection or to be repaired. The blue-overalled man who came out to shake his hand was tall and thin. His short fair hair looked as if he'd run his fingers through it. 'Nick Roberts?' At Nick's nod of assent, the man gave him a sharp look. 'You're a little late.'

Nick's heart plummeted. Not a good start. 'I'm sorry, sir, it took me some time to find you.'

'No need for such formality. You can call me Fred. Everyone else does.' He indicated the two men working on the innards of a car. 'Now come through to what passes as an office.'

As Fred led the way through the workshop, Nick was impressed with the orderliness of the place. In the Army, he'd always had to work in such conditions and he didn't think he could work in chaos. He desperately wanted this job. Would he be lucky today?

The so-called office, up some rickety stairs had room enough only for a desk, piled with grease-smeared papers and a couple of chairs side by side. Fred sat in one and indicated that Nick should sit in the other. 'Now, Nick, tell me a little bit about yourself and why you think you're up to this job.'

'I should tell you right away that I'm not a qualified mechanic.' Seeing the start of surprise on the other man's face, Nick hurried on. 'But I've done three years National Service, mostly in Motor Transport. And I signed on for another year to do a mechanic's course.'

14

'How did you do on the course?'

Nick squirmed. It didn't come easily to him to boast about his Outstanding award. He produced a rolled-up certificate from the inside pocket of his leather jacket and handed it to Fred.

Fred studied it. 'I'm impressed. Did you enjoy your time in the Army?'

'On the whole, yes, though not in the early days.'

Fred grinned. 'I've heard it can be a bit grim.' He looked at Nick's certificate again. 'How come you ended up in Motor Transport?'

'It were a lucky accident. Once I'd been transferred to MT, I found I had a knack for tinkering with cars and wagons. I learned a lot from the older men, regulars all of them.'

'What did you do before you went in the Army?' Fred asked now.

Nick set his lips in a grim line. 'I worked on a building site as a labourer. There didn't seem much point in doing owt else until I'd done me National Service.'

'You didn't fancy the Locomotive Works then? That's where most of the Horwich men are employed, isn't it?'

'I worked there for a while labouring but didn't like it,' Nick said, shuffling his feet.

'Why didn't you try for an apprenticeship?'

'I didn't do well at school, didn't try hard enough, I suppose.'

Fred gave him another of those sharp looks. 'Regret that now, do you?'

'I do. That's what I enjoyed about the Army. There was always summat new to learn.'

Fred waved the certificate at him. 'I guessed as much. You certainly seem to have applied yourself to this.' He stroked his chin. 'Well, Nick, much as I'd like to help you, it's a problem with you not being a time-served mechanic.' Nick shrugged his shoulders; he was getting used to this kind of brush-off. 'I'd like to have taken a chance on you but one of my chaps is leaving at the end of the week and, with everything we have booked in, I need someone urgently. I hope you understand?'

15

Nick stood and, with as much dignity as he could, offered his hand to Fred. 'Thanks for being so honest.'

Fred shook his hand. 'I'm sorry, Nick. I think you have a lot to offer.'

'Thanks for that. Can I ask you summat?'

'Of course.'

'Did me being a Teddy boy put you off at all?' He'd already had one experience where the boss told him to get out before interviewing him because he was a Teddy boy.

Fred looked puzzled. 'Why should it? As long as you're a good worker, that's what counts. Which reminds me...' He handed the certificate back to Nick. 'You might want to think about going to night school, get some accreditation to your name.'

'Thanks for the advice,' Nick said at the door. 'I'll give that some thought in the New Year.'

Once out of view of the garage, he slumped against the end wall of a terraced house and pulled out a cigarette, heart-sick that he'd been knocked back again. What was he to do with himself? Should he have signed on as a regular like they'd suggested? No, although he'd enjoyed his time in the Army, he'd no compulsion to make it more permanent.

Pushing himself off the wall, he meandered in the general direction of the town centre. Maybe he'd call into the Market Hall, get himself a mug of tea and a bacon buttie while he considered his alternatives. With little experience of anything other than labouring, his options were limited. Yet he was desperate to make something of himself.

The void in his belly filled, he decided to walk to Trinity Street to catch the bus back to Horwich. Walking along Newport Street, he came to a fenced-off building site. Maybe he should call in to see if they'd anything available. Picking his way across the frost-filled ridges of the site, he located the site manager's office, a ramshackle cabin, and knocked on the open door. A ruddy-faced man, Nick guessed in his fifties, looked up from the telephone receiver he was holding and waved Nick in the direction of a chair opposite the desk. 'Won't be a tick,' he mouthed at Nick.

Nick sat down and looked round the cluttered office. On the wall behind the man was a blue print of the proposed building, beside it a front and side elevation. It was too far away for him to see what the building was to be but it looked substantial enough to provide work for some months to come.

The man, big and bluff, finished his telephone conversation and turned to Nick. 'Now, young man, what can I do for you?'

'I were wondering if you had any labouring jobs available.'

'Any experience?'

'I worked for a large builder afore I did me National Service.'

'What sort of labouring did you do?'

It seemed so long ago now, he struggled to remember. 'Wheeling bricks, mixing mortar, running errands. Whatever needed doing.'

'Well, we do need a general labourer. When can you start?'

Taken aback that it had been that easy, he said, 'Er – whenever you like.'

'Can you manage tomorrow?' Nick nodded. The sooner the better. 'Be here at half past seven. See me first and I'll take all your details.' He held out a hand to Nick. 'I'm Sid West, by the way, site manager.'

'Nick Roberts, Mr West.'

'Good. Oh, and don't forget to bring your P45.'

As he stepped outside, he couldn't believe it had been so easy. He wasn't that keen to rush back into the building trade but at least it would be something to do till he managed to get work as a mechanic. And there was no doubt his money would help his Mam out.

* * *

That night, Nick decided to walk up to the Squirrel, a pub a mile or so up the road on the way to Chorley. It had been raining earlier but now the rain had cleared and a brisk chill wind was scattering the remaining clouds eastwards. He wished it were light enough to walk up to Rivington at the heart of Lever Park, something he and his mates liked to do of a summer evening or a Sunday afternoon when all the girls were out walking as well.

Round the back of the Crown, he caught sight of three or four youngish lads clustered round what seemed to be a bundle of rags on the ground. They were laughing and pushing at the bundle with the toes of their brothel creepers. 'Now then, lads, what's up?' he asked as he drew near.

'Just some drunk,' returned one of them, a cocky young lad. 'Nowt to worry about.'

'That's for me to decide.' He was up to them now and saw that the bundle was a man, much the worse for drink. 'Let me see'. He bent and touched the man's neck. Possibly the cold of his fingers roused the man for he stirred and mumbled.

Behind him, he heard the lads muttering among themselves. 'Who's that?'

'Nick Roberts.'

'Who's he when he's at home?'

'Heard of the Black Cat Gang?'

'Who hasn't?'

'That's Nick Roberts.'

To Nick's amusement, there was an element of awe in the young lad's voice. Putting on a stern face, he looked up and said, 'You got a problem with that?' The lad in question backed away, shaking his head. 'Then you can all bugger off.'

The cocky one pushed forward. 'What about him?' he asked, indicating the man on the ground.

'It's all right; I'll look after him. I know who he is anyway.' The man was a Scot, a regular in the pub he frequented, a pleasant enough bloke but quiet. 'Mac? Can you hear me?'

There was an answering mumble from the older man but nothing coherent. Nick pulled him to rubbery feet and supporting him as best he could, tried to get him to stand. The Scot wasn't a big man, but he had a solid, stocky body, making Nick's task more difficult. Mac belched a noxious stench of beer, whisky and vomit, causing Nick to turn away in disgust. Bugger! Why had he got himself into this? Because the man reminded him of his Dad and he'd had to do this on the odd occasion for him. 'Come on, Mac, time to get you home. Where do you live?'

Mac seemed to pull himself together. 'Garage. Crown. Chorley New Road.'

Nick remembered now where the garage was but had never connected it with the Scot hanging on to him. 'You live there, too?'

'Over the top.'

Bearing most of Mac's weight, he struggled past the closed doors of Ferretti's Ice Cream Parlour and the adjacent terraced houses till he came to the garage, tucked almost out of sight round the side of the last house. Now in complete darkness, it had a run-down neglected air and Nick guessed that business wasn't so good. 'Keys, Mac? You got any keys?'

The Scot made a futile attempt to reach his coat pocket. Supporting him with one arm, Nick fumbled in the man's pockets and found a bundle of keys, which he tried one by one on the little door inset into the larger double doors. 'No, no, side door,' Mac managed. The side door opened on to a flight of linoleum covered stairs, worn on the treads and with dust balls in every corner. The first door he came to, proved to be an untidy, shabbily furnished sitting room, the second a bathroom badly in need of a clean. The third revealed a bedroom, as untidy as the rest of the flat, but with a double bed, piled with rumpled blankets and an eiderdown.

Nick dropped his burden on to the bed and pulled off the man's shoes and, with some difficulty, his vomit-stained overcoat. And that, he decided, as he pulled the eiderdown up, was as much as he was prepared to do. Still, he thought he ought to stick around for a bit, make sure Mac was all right.

Leaving the bedroom door wide open, he went through to the sitting room, which, he found, had a small scullery attached. This was cleaner and tidier, with only a few pots in the sink. Setting the small kettle to boil, he rummaged in a cupboard and found a clean mug, a tea caddy and an opened tin of condensed milk. Once he'd got a brew, he shifted a pile of old newspapers and magazines off a sagging armchair, settling himself into its surprisingly comfortable depths.

With nothing to do but keep an ear cocked for Mac's breathing, his thoughts drifted back to the whispered conversation of the four lads who'd found Mac. The Black Cat Gang! Now those were the days. As children, he and his mates had swung from lamp-posts on an old piece of rope, cadged old pram wheels to make go-carts or played football in the park. As they'd grown older, but still too young to go in pubs, they'd congregate in the Temperance Bar. Or they'd stroll round the town, talking loudly and eyeing up the girls at every opportunity, the ubiquitous cigarette hanging from nicotine-stained fingers as if to prove they were men. From there, it was a natural progression to adopt the Teddy boy gang culture, developing a cocky, threatening attitude. It was the inevitable call-up papers that had broken up the gang. Some of them, like Nick had completed their National Service, others were still doing theirs. Still others, like Bragger, a latecomer to the gang, having theirs deferred until they'd finished their apprenticeship.

Nick woke sometime later, stiff and cold. Even as he pulled himself upright, Mac appeared in the doorway, undressed now and wearing a shabby dressing gown. His eyes were bleary and unfocused, his thinning hair plastered to his skull in places.

'What the…!' He checked in surprise, seeing Nick.

Nick pushed himself up from the depths of the armchair. 'I brought you home, Mac, after you'd passed out on the street.'

'Oh, hell! Did I make a complete fool of myself?' he asked in a soft pleasing Scottish accent.

'Not as far as I know. Some young lads found you and didn't know what to do till I turned up.'

The older man rubbed his forehead. 'Thanks for bringing me home. It is Nick, isn't it?'

Nick nodded. 'You feeling better now?'

Mac fell on to one of the two chairs pushed up to the scarred gate-leg table. 'Bloody world's stopped spinning, at least.' He saw the empty mug Nick had used. 'Fancy making me a brew, lad? It'd better be coffee. There should be some in the cupboard.'

Nick put the kettle to boil again and found the small tin of Nescafé powder. 'Mind if I have some, too?'

'Help yourself, you deserve it. It was good of you to stay.'

Nick spooned coffee into two mugs. 'Thought I'd better hang on for a while.' He poured boiling water on to the coffee and added a generous helping of condensed milk. 'Not that I'd have been much use. I fell asleep.' He passed Mac a mug and sat companionably at the table beside him.

'I'm grateful, Nick. Fact is, today – yesterday now – was the tenth anniversary of the death of my wife and little girl.'

Whatever else Nick had expected, it wasn't this. 'Hell, Mac, I'm sorry. You don't need to say any more.'

'Probably wouldn't if I wasn't still a bit drunk. I've kept it bottled up too long.' He stared at the contents of his mug, then took a long swallow before carrying on. 'I stayed in the Navy after the war, I was a regular, you see. My wife had coped all through the war, despite me being at sea for long periods of time. Then ten years ago…,' he choked up and cleared his throat as if it were a normal constriction. 'The tenement where they lived…Glasgow it was…caught fire. With the poor state of the building, the fire ripped through…they were on the top floor…they didn't stand a chance.' His description, fragmented though it was, told its own horrific story. Nick remained silent. What could he say that would be of any use?

Mac hadn't finished. Pulling himself together with some effort, he said, 'The funeral was over and done with before I could get back. Her family never liked me, were glad of the excuse to shut me out. I never got to say goodbye to them, that's what hurts.' Mac choked again; this time a definite sob came out.

Nick reached out and touched Mac's arm briefly. 'Your little girl. How old was she, Mac?'

'Seven, only seven! I…hardly saw her during the war, a couple of weeks here and there…that was all.' He drew in a breath and took another long swallow of his coffee.

'I'm sorry, Mac.'

He shrugged. 'Nothing anyone could do, that's what made me feel so helpless…I went to pieces afterwards…had a breakdown, ended up being discharged from the Navy.' He shook his unkempt head. 'Another blow. After my wife and kiddie, the Navy was my life. I didn't know what I was going to do.'

'How did you end up here?'

'Saw the business for sale in a newspaper while I was staying in Blackpool, caught the train here, decided it seemed as good a place as any to start afresh.'

Nick's interest quickened. 'You a time-served mechanic, then?'

Mac shook his head. 'Never saw the need myself, though I've always tinkered with engines. That's what I was in the Navy, an engineer. Most of what I know, I picked up. A lot I've learned as I've gone along.' He yawned, now much more relaxed and a lot less drunk. 'Look, lad, you get off home now.'

'Will you be all right on your own?' Nick stood and looked him in the eye. They both knew he didn't simply mean the drink.

'I'll be OK now.' There was a sudden awkwardness between them. 'Thanks again for taking care of me. I'll not forget that.'

'It were nowt.'

When he was half way down, Mac called out. 'By the way, lad, you'll not repeat anything I've said tonight, will you?'

'Wouldn't dream of it, Mac.' Nick let himself out of the door and into the shivery midnight air.

CHAPTER 4

As soon as Kathy had arrived at this New Year's Eve party, she'd known she was out of her depth. The atmosphere was noisily cheerful, loud music precluding any chance of conversation, and heavy with cigarette smoke, spilled beer and the girls' perfume. The young people here all displayed a confidence and sophistication beyond the scope of her experience. She'd come, in a taxi, with a couple of girls from work whom she didn't know that well. But her best friend, Carole, had the flu and Kathy had been at a loose end. Now the two girls, Rita and Pauline, had disappeared and she didn't know how she was going to get home. She hadn't a clue where the party was being held, somewhere near Moss Bank Park she suspected. Not an area she was familiar with.

A well-spoken voice near her ear said, 'May I get you another drink?'

She looked to the young man accompanying the voice then down at her empty glass. 'Er...no, I don't think so.'

He grinned at her. 'I don't bite, you know.' As the inevitable blush rose to her cheeks, he said, 'you looked as if you were wondering how soon you could leave.'

She gaped at him. 'How did you know?'

'Probably because I'd been thinking the same thing.'

She laughed then. 'This isn't my sort of party.'

'Nor mine. Can't think why I came. Except that I know the bloke who's throwing it from my rugby club.'

He looked a rugby club sort of a chap. Not too tall but stockily built with fair hair, slicked into a short back and sides. The blue of the shirt he was wearing matched the intense blue of his eyes. Round his shoulders was slung a soft grey jumper, 'I'm John Talbot, by the way.'

'Kathy Armstrong.' She made a move to shake his hand but saw that he had a glass in one hand and a bottle of straw-wrapped Chianti in the other.

He saw her puzzled glance and said, 'If I put it down anywhere, I'll never see it again.'

23

'I did wonder.'

He raised the bottle as a questioning gesture. 'Can I tempt you to share it with me?'

She held her glass out to him, deciding she might as well enjoy his attention while it lasted. 'OK, I'll try some.'

'Would you mind holding my glass while I pour it?' He poured a measure of Chianti into her glass. 'What do you think?' he asked as she sipped.

'It's a little rich for my taste. I'm more of a Babycham person, really.'

He laughed. 'We'll soon have you educated in the finer things in life.'

The superior tone in his voice stung a little. 'I know what I like.'

He gave her a rueful grin. 'Sorry. I sounded priggish, didn't I?'

'You did rather.'

'I promise I'll behave from now on.'

It was her turn to laugh. 'We probably won't see each other again after tonight.'

A serious expression came onto his face. 'We will if I have anything to do with it.'

He was older, a man really, around 23 or 24, and she liked his assured, confident manner. She smiled. He would certainly meet her mother's definition of 'a suitable young man.'

The noise level of the party dropped a little as someone put Al Martino's 'Here In My Heart' on the record player and dimmed the lights. A few couples started shuffling round to the music. 'Shall we dance?' John asked.

'OK then.'

He pulled aside a curtain to put the bottle and both their glasses on the window sill and placed his arm round her waist and pulled her close to him, her hand in his.

After a few minutes, he said, 'Did you come with anyone, Kathy?'

'I did, two girls, but they seem to have done a vanishing trick.'

He grimaced. 'Not a nice thing to do to a so-called friend.'

'I'd hardly call them friends. They're work colleagues.'

'How are you getting home then?'

'I was planning on getting a taxi.'

He looked down at her, his face pale in the subdued lighting. 'I doubt that you'd find one, being New Year's Eve.'

Her heart sank. 'I hadn't thought of that but you're probably right.'

'May I give you a lift home? My car's only a dilapidated old Ford Pop but you'll be safe enough.'

'That'd be lovely. Thank you.'

The music came to a halt but he stood, still with his arm round her waist, her hand clasped in his. 'When do you want to leave?'

'Could we go before midnight? I'd rather not be here for the midnight scrum.'

He laughed. 'You mean for the kissing?'

'Especially when they're all strangers.'

'Then, as it's turned eleven, shall we go now?'

'What about your wine?'

H shrugged. 'The bottle was all but empty anyway.'

After the warmth of the party, the night air was so crisp and cold, she shivered and pulled her coat collar higher.

'Cold?' he asked.

'A little.'

'Come closer to me then.' He placed his arm around her shoulder and she huddled into his warmth.

When they reached his car, he opened the door for her, shutting it only when she had settled herself. When he was in the driver's seat, he turned to her and gave her a rueful look. 'I never thought to ask where you live.'

'Horwich.'

He pulled out the choke and turned the key in the ignition. 'That's a relief then. I was hoping it wasn't Chorley or Bury.'

She laughed. 'What would you have done if it was?'

'I'd have taken you because I promised but I'd have had to walk home,' he said, a rueful smile on his face. 'I don't have enough petrol to go much further.'

25

The old car had an inadequate heating system and she was glad of the thick coat she was wearing. During the journey, she learned that he was a newly qualified chartered accountant and, in turn, she told him a little about her job at the Bolton Evening News.

As they turned left into Travers Street, she said, 'Will you stop near the top of the street?' She certainly didn't want him stopping outside her house in case her mother was peering out of the window. 'I live a little way further down.'

When they stopped, he turned to her and said, 'I'm glad you came to the party, Kathy. May I see you again?'

His remark gave her a warm glow. 'I'd like that.'

'I have rugby training Tuesdays and Thursdays so what about Wednesday? We could go to the cinema. Or out for a drink, if you'd prefer.'

'Go for a drink somewhere, I think,' she replied. It would give them more time to get to know each other. And she knew she wanted that, very much.

They made arrangements when and where they would meet then, as Kathy went to open her door, he said, 'Allow me,' and shot round to open the door for her. 'I'll walk you to your front door.' He did too, walking on the outside of her even though there was no traffic.

At her door, he didn't try to kiss her, merely squeezed her hand and said, 'See you Wednesday.'

* * *

Wednesday hadn't been a good day for Nick. He had overslept, been late for work and earned a ticking-off from Sid, with his pay docked by half an hour. And it had rained. Not the driving heavy kind that would stop all work on the building site and leave them all in the prefabricated hut designated the canteen, chain-smoking cigarettes, moaning about the weather and drinking endless cups of tea. No, it was that damp dreary drizzle that seemed peculiar to Lancashire and through which they were expected to work. At dinnertime, he discovered he'd left his jackbit at home and had only enough money on him to buy a packet of crisps and a small bottle of Tizer. He didn't know his work-mates well enough yet to ask if anyone would lend him some money for a bacon buttie.

And tonight was the night he was due to start night school at the Mechanics Institute. He'd enrolled before Christmas, even though the school year had started in September. It hadn't been easy. He'd had to argue his case, to convince them that he could cope with the academic side as easily as the practical. Most of the lads on the course were in the second year of an apprenticeship, he was told, and he wondered what they'd think about an older lad joining them and a rookie at that. Still, he was nervous as he walked into the classroom on that first evening, to be faced with a group of sixteen and seventeen-year-old lads. Everybody looked up but nobody spoke to him.

Much as he would like to have seated himself somewhere near the back, the only available desk was near the front. Knowing the others would be whispering about him behind his back, he twiddled with the pencil and exercise book he'd brought with him. Just then, the door opened and the instructor walked in. To Nick's surprise, it was Fred, the garage owner who'd interviewed him before Christmas. Nick half-raised a hand in greeting but seeing the blank look on the other man's face, dropped it as quickly. Did he really not remember Nick? Or simply choosing not to acknowledge him? Probably the latter. Fred shuffled a few papers on the dais, then looked up. 'Good evening, gentlemen. Are you all raring to go?'

Mock groans and laughter came from the lads behind him and Nick smiled. He'd been dreading the strict classroom regime he remembered from his school days but it looked like this was going to be much more informal and he relaxed a little.

Fred peered at Nick as if seeing him for the first time. 'It appears we've been joined by a newcomer. Brave soul that he is. Would you like to tell us a little about yourself so that we can get to know you? Come and stand out here so's we can all hear you.'

Heart sinking, Nick rose and faced the class. 'Me name's Nick Roberts and I've recently finished me National Service. I've already got an Army qualification but it don't count on Civvy Street. Now I want to get proper qualification.'

Was he imagining it or was that a snigger from someone in the back? He gritted his teeth and clenched his fists. If he was going to do this, he'd have to put up with this kind of attitude but it wasn't going to be easy.

Fred waved him back to his desk. 'Thanks, Nick. Very commendable. Now, lads, shall we get started?'

What followed was an hour of purgatory, much of it going over his head. He wondered if he could ever cope with the sheer volume of facts and figures. He tried his best, jotting down in his notebook the bits that did make sense and hoping that, with sheer determination, he'd come to understand the rest of it. At the end of it, to his relief, Fred announced that they'd all be doing some practical work. This he could handle.

In the well-lit workshop in the basement, stood two engines on blocks, chains hanging above them for ease of movement. Nick's hands itched to get at them. 'Now, you lot,' Fred said. 'I want you to imagine that you're out in the middle of nowhere and your battery has died. Someone stops and offers to help but he doesn't have any jump leads. Can any of you think what you can do to get the car started enough to get you home?'

Silence descended, with the younger lads looking at each other, as if for inspiration. Nick almost felt like laughing. This was a doddle. He'd been shown what to do in his first year in MT by an older, experienced regular. Fred looked at the group clustered round the two engines. 'No? No-one? What about you, Nick? Had any practical experience like this?' Nick knew then that Fred did remember him and was offering him a way of integrating him into the class.

Nick walked round the outside of the first of the engines and, grabbing a couple of spanners off a nearby bench, unscrewed the so-called dead battery. Then he whipped out the battery from the second engine and fitted it to the first engine. Turning the ignition key, the engine started straight away. Leaving the first engine running, he swiftly unscrewed the battery, fitted it back into the second engine then fitted the so-called dead battery back into the first engine. Just to be on the safe side, he started the second engine too, leaving both engines running sweetly. Behind him, he heard gasps of amazement and someone say, 'It's like bloody black magic!'

'Well done, Nick. I thought you might know that trick. Now what should you do next?'

Nick grinned. 'Jump in the car smartish and be on your way so's the battery will charge up. Not forgetting to thank your Good Samaritan, of course.'

Turning back to the group of lads clustered round the engines, Fred said, 'Just remember, you lot, that while it's essential these days to have the paper qualification, a bit of practical know-how never comes amiss. It's not going to be easy for Nick, picking up when you've all done the theory, but perhaps you can all learn from each other. That ok?' There were several nods of assent and one or two of the younger lads looked at Nick with something like awe.

Fred set them all to one or two other tasks on the engines and, while they were occupied, he took Nick to one side. 'Glad to see you've followed up my suggestion. I think you'll do well, lad.'

'I'll try, Fred, but I might struggle with the paperwork.'

'You can only do your best. I'll let you have copies of any hand-outs from last term.'

Later, on the way out of the workshop, one of the older lads came up to Nick. 'That was a neat trick, mate. I were well impressed. Me name's Roy, by the way.' He held out a greasy hand which Nick shook. 'If you want to borrow me notes some time, you're welcome.'

'Thanks, that'd be good.' He left the Mechanics Institute that night, feeling he was at last getting somewhere.

CHAPTER 5

Waiting for John to collect her on Wednesday, Kathy was jittery with nerves. What had John Talbot seen in her to make him ask her out again? He was so self-assured and, compared to the young women she'd seen at the party, she was naïve and inexperienced. Her apprehension about the evening had been aggravated by her mother's warning not to seem too eager. 'It wouldn't do to let him see you're interested in him.'

'Mum, it's too soon to be thinking along those lines,' Kathy had sighed. 'I've only just met him.'

She heard the sound of a car outside and, though she desperately wanted to peek through the curtains, made herself sit still. Vera, hearing it too, jumped up and snatched the Bolton Evening News from Ron's hands, placing it in the newspaper rack.

'I hadn't finished with that,' Ron protested.

'You can go back to it once he's gone.'

Kathy rose as she heard the doorbell. 'Stop fussing, Mum. I'm not inviting him in.'

Vera plonked down in the armchair. 'Oh, aren't you? I was looking forward to meeting him.'

She gave her mother a look under raised eyebrows. 'Don't you think inviting him to meet my parents might seem a bit premature?'

John stood on the doorstep, wearing a thick overcoat and scarf around his neck. Above it, his face was pink with cold.

'Hello, Kathy. I'm not too early, am I?' he said, rubbing gloved hands together.

'No, you're spot on.'

He gave her a rueful grin. 'Actually, I arrived about ten minutes ago and I've been parked at the top of the street waiting.'

It warmed her to think he'd allowed plenty of time. 'You must be cold then.'

'Just a bit. It's bitter out there so you'd better wrap up.'

She reached for her winter coat from the old-fashioned coat stand that stood in the hall but he was there before her. 'Allow me,' he said, holding it out for her put her arms in. 'And is this your scarf?' He picked an old brown scarf of her mother's off the coat stand.

She laughed, shaking her head. 'I keep telling my Mum should treat herself to a new one. Mine's the pink fluffy one.'

He held it up to his cheek. 'Mmm, nice,' he said and before she could stop him, he'd draped it round her neck and, with both hands, cuddling it close to her cheeks.

She flushed at the intimacy of the moment and reached into her coat pockets for her gloves.

'Ready? Let's go then.' He stopped on the doorstep. 'I don't know Horwich that well. Where did you have in mind?'

She pondered for a few seconds. 'There's the Yew Tree in Anglezarke. It's a decent pub and they usually have a log fire.'

'That sounds good on a bitterly cold January night.' Again, he opened the car door for her, made sure she was seated, before going round to the driver's side. 'You'll have to direct me. I've been before in the summer but it's a different proposition in the dark.'

The run to Anglezarke from Horwich could be a pleasant one on a lovely day but bleak during the long winter months. She stared out of the car window and wished they were already at the Yew Tree, with its homely old-world atmosphere and the smell of wood-smoke emanating from the log fire.

As they walked into the pub, she sat down at a table close to the fire while John went to get some drinks. He turned sideways to speak with someone standing next to him and his face broke into a smile at whatever was being said to him. She chose to be deliberate in her perusal of him, liking what she saw. As he came towards her with their drinks, his face lit up with another smile. 'You're right about this place, Kathy. We'll definitely have to come here in the summer.' He put the drinks down, slopping a little over the sides. So he, too, was nervous. 'I'm sorry, I shouldn't assume...' He hesitated, choosing his words, '...that we were meant to meet. That it was at the end of the old year and

31

the start of a new one.' He raised his glass to her. 'Here's to what I hope will be the beginning of…?'

She picked up her Babycham glass. 'A happy friendship?'

He touched her glass with his. 'That sounds like a good start. For both of us, I hope.'

'Tell me about…' John began.

'What do you…' Kathy said, at the same time.

They laughed then he said, 'you first. Tell me what you do at the Bolton Evening News. It sounds exciting.'

She pulled a face. 'My job is hardly that. I work in the Advertising Department as a shorthand typist in a small typing pool. We share the work of a few managers in a dismal office at the back of the building. Hardly essential to the running of the newspaper.' In fact her job, which at first had seemed perfect, had become increasingly mundane. She longed to be more involved in what she thought of as the buzz of the place, would love a job on the editorial side.

He cocked his head to one side. 'I think it is. I mean, without the advertisers there wouldn't be a newspaper.'

'I hadn't thought of that.'

He laughed. 'Being an accountant, I would think of the money side first.'

She took a sip from her Babycham, the bubbles making her nose tickle. 'Your turn now, tell me a little more about your job.'

His face lit up. 'I know accountants have a boring image but if you love figures the way I do, it's the only job to be in. The initial training was for three years working for a firm of accountants, then an additional two years to become a Chartered Accountant.'

Kathy couldn't imagine anything worse. 'Wouldn't do for me. I'm hopeless with figures. English was my best subject at School.'

'Which school did you go to?'

'Rivington and Blackrod Grammar School.'

'Isn't that the lovely old building on the way to Rivington?'

'Yes, that's the one.' She took a sip of her Babycham. 'What about you? Where did you go to school?'

32

'Bolton School,' he said. She was impressed but not surprised. You had to be clever – and comfortably off – to go to Bolton School, a huge red brick building on Chorley New Road.

'Not far for you to go, then.' He'd already told her he lived in Heaton where the school was located.

He looked uncomfortable. 'My parents had had my name down since I was little.'

'What does your father do?'

'He's a GP in Bolton; he has a surgery on Chorley Old Road. My mother stays at home but does a lot of charity work.'

She thought his mother sounded a little daunting. 'Do you have any brothers and sisters?'

'Just one sister, Madeline. She's married and has a little one. What about you?'

'I'm an only child,' she sighed. 'Unfortunately, it makes my parents over-protective.'

'Yet they let you go to the party,' he pointed out.

'They don't mind me going out, within reason, but they like to know exactly where I am and what time I'll be back,' she said. 'Like most mothers, mine doesn't go to sleep until she knows I'm safely home.'

He laughed. 'Is that why you asked me to park at the top of the street when I took you home from the party?'

She nodded. 'As it happens, they were up anyway, waiting to see the New Year in.'

He gave her a quizzical look. 'Did they want to know all the ins and outs of your evening?'

'Exactly,' she laughed, 'though I was selective in what I told them. I certainly didn't tell them I'd been abandoned and that you'd had to rescue me.'

'I'm glad I did,' he said seriously.

The evening seemed to go quickly and almost before they knew it, it was time to go. As John was helping her into her coat, he said, 'I've really enjoyed this evening, Kathy.'

As she snuggled deep into the coat in preparation for venturing into the cold, she said, 'So have I.'

'Enough to come out with me again?'

'Definitely.'

'I'm not sure what I'm doing over the next few days. Are you on the phone?' he asked.

'Yes, Dad had one installed to keep in touch with our relations in Cheshire.'

'Is it all right if I ring you then?'

They were mostly silent on the way back to Kathy's home but it was an easy companionable silence, allowing John to concentrate on driving in the icy conditions. Occasionally, a flurry of snow showed up in the headlights of the car and appeared to be dancing in the glow. The effect was hypnotic.

Minutes later, they were drawing up outside the house. The sitting room lights were on but when she looked at her watch, she saw that it was only quarter to eleven. The snow was coming down harder now and she guessed that he would want to be on his way home. 'Thank you for a lovely evening, John.'

'I'm already looking forward to the next time.'

Again, he came round to her side of the car and opened the door for her. This time he reached inside and helped her out with his gloved hand. 'Before you go…,' he said, and pulling her towards him, kissed her. As kisses went, it didn't raise her pulse but was an echo of the enjoyable companionship they'd shared. A brisk wind sent the snow skittering around them and reluctantly, he released her. 'I'd better let you get inside before you freeze out here.'

'And you need to get home while you still can.'

'Until next time then, Kathy.' He waited with her till she'd opened the door and with a quick wave, stepped into the car.

* * *

Friday night saw Nick and his mates in their favourite pub. Everyone knew it as The Long Pull, though its proper name was the Old Original Bay Horse. He was coming out of the toilets when, in the corridor outside, he found his way blocked by Jud Simcox, and his crony, Bill Murphy.

'Well, if it isn't Errol Flynn!' Jud stood with hands tucked into waistband.

'Eh?' Nick stared at Jud blankly.

'Coming to the aid of a damsel in distress,' Jud sneered. With Nick still in a fog of puzzlement, Jud continued, 'Kathy Armstrong. Were she suitably grateful?' Behind him Bill was smirking.

'None of your business,' Nick retorted.

'It is when you're supposed to be going out with our Sally.'

Nick sighed. That was the trouble with Horwich. Being such a small town, everybody always knew everyone else's business. 'I've had a couple of dates with your sister, that's all. We're not going out.' He went to push past the pair.

'That's not what she thinks.' Jud shoved Nick hard on the shoulder.

Jud wasn't very tall but he had a wiry strength and Nick didn't underestimate the veiled threat in Jud's behaviour. Nick knew he had to take a chance and charged, head down, into Jud. Then the two of them were tussling, each trying to get close enough to land a punch, while Bill was egging Jud on. When Nick managed to hit the other in the stomach, Jud wheezed to Bill, 'Don't bloody stand there! Give us a hand.'

'Oh, no, you don't, laddie.' Nick heard Mac's voice before he could see him but, getting the better of Jud, he could see that the Scot had a tight grip round the neck of Bill, struggling ineffectually to free himself. Nick managed to get Jud in an arm-lock and frog-marched him to the back door of the pub. He was followed out of the door by Bill, propelled by Mac.

'Don't try and come back in, either of you,' Nick called after the pair, 'or we'll be waiting for you.'

'You and whose army?' jeered Jud from the safety of the back gate.

'You'll stay away if you know what's good for you,' growled Mac, taking a step forward.

'Aw, Granddad, I'm scared,' crowed Bill.

'Leave it, Bill, we'll get our own back some other time,' came Jud's voice as they disappeared through the back gate.

Nick reached out and grasped Mac's hand. 'Thanks, Mac, you came at the right time.'

'More by good luck than good management,' the Scot said. 'I was on my way for a pee. And that's where I'm off now.' He reached in his pocket and handed over a ten shilling note. 'Here, get yourself a drink on me. I'll have one too.'

Nick tried to push the money back. 'It's me what should be buying you a drink.'

Mac closed Nick's fist over the money. 'Least I can do after what you did for me a few weeks back.'

By the time he'd got the drinks, Mac was back and gestured to Nick to join him at the table in the corner where he usually sat. 'What was all that about?' he asked, as Nick sat down. In between gulps of beer, he outlined what had happened with Jud which led to explaining Kathy to Mac. 'You really like this lass, don't you?' Mac said. The statement fell into the conversation like a stone.

'So what?' Nick gave a derisive laugh. 'She wouldn't want owt to do with a bloody labourer on a building site.'

'Haven't you ever wanted to do anything else?' Mac pulled a battered pipe out of his pocket and tamped down its contents with a finger before attempting to light it.

'When I were 15, there didn't seem much point, getting an apprenticeship, having to put off doing me National Service,' Nick explained. 'It seemed easier to get it over and done with. Short-sighted, I know.'

'And now?' Having given up on the pipe, Mac was now pulling threads of fresh tobacco from a pouch and packing it into the bowl of his pipe.

'I want to work in the motor trade but the garages I've tried only want time-served mechanics.' Nick took another gulp of beer.

Mac, having got his pipe going, nodded sagely. 'I'm not surprised. The old days of enthusiasm and experience have long gone. Have you thought of going to night school to get a qualification?'

Nick grinned. 'I started this week at the Mechanics Institute but it'll take a while.'

'Couldn't you take a labouring job at one of bigger garages in the meantime? It might lead to other things.'

'I'd thought of that but Dad's in prison and Mam needs me to help out with money.'

Mac considered Nick's statement then said, 'You could give me a hand in the garage from time to time.'

Nick gaped at him. 'You really mean that?'

'Why not? My eyes aren't what they used to be, I could do with a bit of help with the fiddly jobs. Come round tomorrow morning and I'll see what you can do.'

'Thanks, Mac. That'll be a great help,' Nick said. He'd missed tinkering with engines and couldn't wait to get started again.

CHAPTER 6

'I don't know what John Talbot sees in her.'

'She's nothing but a jumped-up little shorthand-typist.'

The voices came to Kathy clearly, as they were meant to do, from an adjacent table in the canteen. They belonged to Pauline and Rita, the two girls who'd invited her to the New Year's Eve Party.

'Take no notice of them,' Linda hissed across their table. A little older than Kathy, she was good-natured and with a ready laugh. 'Just because they're news typists, they think they're someone special.' News typists were the select few who typed up reports dictated to them over the phone by reporters. Usually editorial didn't mix with the admin staff but news typists fell somewhere in between. Quite why they'd invited her to the party in the first place, she didn't know, she only knew that they'd been spiteful ever since. One of them, Rita, had actually said to her, 'You're not backwards at coming forward, are you?'

'What do you mean?' she'd asked, puzzled.

'Setting your cap at John Talbot.'

'If you'd been watching as closely as you're making out, you'd have known that he approached me in the first instance,' she'd retorted and walked away.

Now she turned back to Linda. 'I'm going out for some fresh air.'

'Good idea. I'll come with you.' Linda pushed herself up with her hands on the table. 'There's a nasty smell in here,' she said as the two of them passed the table where Pauline and Rita were seated.

Kathy suppressed a giggle as the other two girls glared at Linda. 'And what do you mean by that?' demanded Pauline.

Linda wafted her hand in front of her face and, with a look of innocence, said, 'Cigarette smoke, boiled cabbage and stale cooking fat. What else?'

The laughter bubbled over in the corridor outside the canteen. 'Priceless,' Kathy spluttered. 'I wish I could think of clever remarks like that.'

Linda gave a snort of disgust. 'Their sort aren't worth bothering with. Now, where did you have in mind?'

Kathy glanced at her watch. 'We haven't got time for much else other than a short walk around the block.'

'Ah, well, it'll blow the cobwebs away for the afternoon, Miss Armstrong,' Linda said.

Kathy laughed and linked the other girl's arm. Their boss, Mr Mansfield, was fussy and most particular about manners, calling his staff 'Miss' at all times. Despite the appearance of being almost comically old-fashioned, he could be a sweetie sometimes.

Outside the front doors of the newspaper building, a brisk wind skittered round their legs as they clutched their coats more tightly around them and set off walking in the direction of Deansgate. Coming towards them were two head-scarfed elderly ladies looking around them in bewilderment. As they drew abreast, one of them said, 'Excuse me, love, can you tell me where the Bolton Evening News office is now?'

'Just in front of you, to the left,' Kathy indicated, half turning to where the recently-installed plate glass windows were.

'No, that's a grocer's shop now,' one of them said.

Kathy and Linda looked at each other, puzzled, then Linda said, 'Why would you think that?'

It was the turn of the two ladies to look to each other for enlightenment. 'Well, it's got a display of coffee in there now,' one offered.

Kathy laughed. 'It's still the Evening News offices. The coffee display is in advance of an advertising campaign that's running at the moment.'

The two women started laughing and one nudged the other and said, 'Aren't we daft, not realising?'

'It's the new windows,' Kathy explained. 'You're not the first people to be confused.'

'Well, thank you so much for your help,' one said. 'We'd gone past them a couple of times without realising.' The two set off, still tittering.

'You know, that would make a good item for Town Topics,' mused Kathy, 'if it was properly written up.' Town Topics was the nightly gossip-type column that featured short snappy pieces.

'Why don't you write it then?' Linda countered.

'Doesn't the features editor write the column?'

'Not all of it. He relies on other contributions. That's just the sort of thing he'd like,' Linda explained.

With a surge of excitement, she turned to Linda. 'What would I have to do? Do you know?'

'I'd suggest you write it up first, make it as amusing as you can, then go and see Mr Bleakley.'

Kathy spent that evening writing up the episode, altering, deleting, adding, until it was as nearly perfect as she could make it. And she loved every minute of it. Although she'd scribbled in her notebook for years, it felt good to be structuring a piece she hoped would be suitable for the newspaper.

The following day, during her lunch break, she knocked on Mr. Bleakley's door. From inside came a cough then a deep voice said, 'Come in.'

Mr Bleakley rose to greet her as she entered. He was thin with the sloping shoulders of tall man trying not to be so, with a mop of unruly white hair and a pipe in his hand with which he indicated a chair by his desk. 'Yes, young lady, what can I do for you?' he said, as he sat down himself.

'I've heard that you're always on the look-out for amusing pieces for Town Topics,' she said.

He gave a deep laugh. 'Desperate, more like. Do you have anything for me?'

By way of reply, she handed him the neatly written piece she had composed and waited while he read it. In the couple of minutes it took, no expression crossed his face and she wondered if perhaps he didn't like it or think it worthy of inclusion.

When he looked up, he was smiling. 'But this is excellent stuff, just the thing to amuse the readers.' She breathed a sigh of relief. 'Do you have anything else like this?'

Her heart leaped with excitement. 'Not at the moment but I'll keep my eyes and ears open from now on.'

He pulled a sheet of foolscap paper towards him, possibly a list of what he was including over the next couple of nights. 'I'd like to put this in Thursday's paper, if that's OK with you.'

'Really? Oh, that's brilliant.'

'We don't pay anything for these pieces but you'll have the satisfaction of seeing something you've written in print,' he explained.

'That's all right, I wasn't expecting payment.'

'Have you done much writing previously?' The scribblings in her notebook didn't count, did they? She shook her head. 'You should. You've a certain flair for it. What's your name, by the way, and where do you work?'

'Kathy Armstrong and I work in Advertising.'

'Well, Kathy, I shall look forward to anything else you can unearth for me.' He held out a surprisingly strong hand and she shook it.

Outside, she was tempted to do a little jig but one of the newsboys was just coming towards her with an early edition of the paper. Instead, she made do with a wide grin on her face. She couldn't wait to tell Linda.

* * *

When John came to pick her up that night, she'd hoped for a quiet drink somewhere. Instead, he wanted to go to Fanny's, a pub on Markland Hill. It was someone's birthday, he said, and he'd promised they'd be there. 'What do you think?' John asked, as they entered Fanny's.

She looked round, taking in the plain wooden floors, tables and chairs. Not that there were many of them for nearly everyone was standing. 'It's certainly different,' she conceded.

'Great atmosphere, isn't it?' he enthused.

'Why's it called Fanny's?' She had to raise her voice above the chorus of Happy Birthday ringing out. 'I noticed its real name is the Victoria Inn.'

Keeping hold of her hand, he edged his way to the bar. 'I don't really know but I guess it's after a former landlady.' At the bar, he said, 'I should warn you, they only serve beer.'

'I'll have half a shandy then.'

A young man, leaning on the bar next to her, one foot on the brass rail beneath, said in mock horror, 'A shandy? You're ruining the finest of cask ales, woman.'

She stuck her chin out. 'If I can't have a shandy, I won't have anything.'

John put an arm round her shoulders. 'Take no notice of Nigel. He's just being bloody superior.' The young man laughed and raised his glass to her in a mock salute.

All the seats were taken but they managed to squash themselves into a corner by the window. 'It's obviously very popular,' Kathy said, 'everyone seems to know one another.'

'A lot of us went to the same school. Or go to the same rugby or cricket clubs,' he explained as someone came up to him and started chatting about some rugby event.

Kathy took the opportunity to look around her. The typically middle-class young crowd here exuded the same carefree confidence John displayed. Then, as the crowd shifted and parted, she saw, on the opposite side of the pub, Rita and Pauline. In the same instance, they saw her and, with a glance at each other, made their way over to her. Her heart sank.

'Hello, Kathy, haven't seen you here before,' Pauline said, implying that they were regulars.

The young man John had been talking to walked away and John turned. 'Hello girls. That's because I haven't brought her before.'

Rita leaned forward and kissed John on the cheek. 'Hi, John, how are you?'

'Ok. You?'

'Yeah, fine. Are you going to the cricket club dance on Saturday?' Rita looked up at John with doe-like eyes and Kathy suddenly realised the reason for all the bitchiness. Rita fancied her chances with John. Or had done until Kathy came on the scene. The realisation gave her confidence.

John gave Kathy a questioning look. 'Fancy going to the Cricket Club dance on Saturday, Kathy?'

'A cricket club? In the depths of winter?'

Rita gave a patronising laugh. 'The cricket pavilion is heated, you know.'

'Well, I wouldn't be expected to know that, would I?' Kathy returned.

'Sorry, I'm sure,' Rita said, a superior smirk on her face. 'Come on, Pauline, let's find someone to buy us a drink. The two girls wandered off giggling and Kathy gritted her teeth.

'So, how do you feel about it, Kathy?' John asked again. 'The club holds a dance there every couple of months or so. We – that is, the crowd I usually hang around with – go regularly.'

'Would that be the Fanny's crowd?'

'Does that bother you?'

'They are a bit intimidating,' she admitted.

'You'll soon get used to them. Which reminds me,' he said, 'I shan't be able to see you at the weekend in a couple of weeks. Every winter we have a rugby match at a Welsh club. To make a weekend of it, we usually stay over.'

She had a suspicion that such weekends would end up being rowdy drunken affairs. He was welcome to them. 'Aren't you rather taking it for granted that we'll still be seeing each other in a couple of weeks?'

He gave her a look of surprise. 'I'm sorry if I am but I thought it was what you wanted too. Am I wrong?'

'No. I would like to keep on seeing you but it's perhaps too early to be thinking too far ahead,' she hedged.

He reached for her hand. 'I should warn you that I am serious about you, Kathy.' His words thrilled her, making her heart beat faster.

It wasn't until they were in the car on the way home that Kathy had a chance to tell John about being featured in Town Topics.

John interrupted her. 'Isn't that the column that appears daily in the Evening News with the illustration of the Town Hall?'

'That's the one. Because it appears every night, Mr Bleakley, the Features Editor, is always on the lookout for interesting snippets that people have seen or overheard.'

'Oh, I never read that,' he said, his voice dismissive. In the face of her stricken silence, he hurried on, 'What I really should have said, with not having much time to read, I tend to skip items like that and concentrate on current affairs and the business pages. Please go on.'

Mollified, she continued, 'I went to see the features editor, and he was quite encouraging. And well,' she drew a deep breath, 'it's going in Thursday's paper.' She sat back and waited for his reaction.

'Is that it?' he said finally.

Hurt by his dismissive tone, she said, 'Well, Mr Bleakley seemed to think it was amusing.'

He changed gears as he slowed to turn into Travers Street. 'I'm sure it will be fine and I will make a point of reading it, I promise. Only...' he hesitated

'Only what?'

'You won't let it go to your head and start fancying yourself as a reporter, will you?'

She didn't know whether to laugh or cry. In the end, she chose to laugh. 'Oh, John, it's only a piddling little piece in Town Topics.'

* * *

Nick was smoking an after-dinner cigarette one Saturday morning in February. He'd been working at Mac's garage a couple of weeks now and thoroughly enjoying it. He guessed that Mac was in his mid-forties, perhaps a bit older, but despite the difference in ages, he and Mac got on well. Taciturn in company, Mac had opened up with Nick and kept him chuckling with his escapades from his Navy days. The Scot treated him as an equal, unlike his father who, before he went to prison, had blustered and shouted in his dealings with Nick. The difference between the two men could not have been more marked and Nick knew he could talk to Mac about anything.

His Mam broke into his thoughts. 'I wonder where those two lads have got to,' she said. 'They're late today.'

He looked at her over the fish and chip papers strewn over the table. 'They'll come home when their stomachs tell them it's dinnertime.'

Joyce nodded to the window overlooking the back yard. 'They're here now.'

The two boys pushed and shoved at each other as they tried to clatter in through the back door together.

'Where've you been?' Mary eyed them suspiciously.

'Here and there,' replied Brian in an offhand manner.

'Not up to owt, I hope?'

'Us, Mam? Never!' said Derek.

In spite of her doubts, Mary laughed. 'Your dinners are warming in the oven. Be careful when you take them out.'

'Not so fast, Mam,' Nick said, 'I want a word with these two afore they have their dinners.'

'Aw, Nick, we're hungry,' protested Brian.

'You can't be that hungry or you'd have come home afore now.' He rose, still in his work clothes. 'Into the front room, the pair of you.'

In the cold and dismal atmosphere of the front room, the two boys stood before Nick. In ripped short trousers, too small jumpers, socks round their ankles and scuffed shoes, they had an apprehensive look on their mucky faces. He had to suppress a smile and to remind himself that in their Dad's absence, he was the acting head of the house.

Brian was the first to speak. 'What's up, Nick?'

'I might ask you the same thing. Have you owt you want to say to me?'

'Like what, Nick?' said Derek.

'Like what have you been up to this morning?'

The two boys looked at each other but it was Brian who spoke. 'Playing out.'

'And where'd you get the money for those sweets you bought?' At their stunned silence, Nick smiled. 'You were seen by Mrs Fishwick from Summer Street.'

'It were our spending money, Nick,' said Brian.

'Don't lie, Brian. Mam told me she hasn't given you any yet.' They looked at each other again as if searching for answers, excuses, or even more lies. He made them wait a few seconds before he said, 'It wouldn't have owt to do with nipping over the wall of the chippie in Dixon Street to nick a couple of empty bottles from the back yard then asking for the money back on them?'

As one, their mouths fell open and before Brian could say anything, Derek blurted out, 'How did you know?' Brian gave him a furious look, which promised retribution later.

'Again you were seen, this time climbing over the back wall.'

'Didn't you ever do owt like that when you were a lad, Nick?' was Brian's last attempt at wriggling out of the situation.

'None spring to mind right now.' Nick paused. 'Anyroad, what you did was stealing, whichever way you look at it. It's bad enough for Mam with one convicted criminal in the family without you two starting young.'

'Sorry, Nick. We didn't think of it like that.' Brian hung his head.

'Since Dad's been in prison, lots of people are saying we're no better than we should be,' Nick went on. 'You know what I'm saying because you've had to put up with some stick at school. You've had the bruises to prove it.'

'I'm sorry, too,' Derek said in a small voice.

'Off you go for your dinners then.'

At the door, Brian, fair hair tufted in different directions, blue eyes endeavouring to look innocent, gestured to the garment hanging on the picture rail. 'Is that me Mam's new coat?'

'Cheeky little bugger!' Nick playfully cuffed Brian about the head. 'You know damned well Mam hasn't had a new coat for years. It's me new suit.'

'Then how come you've got one?'

'Because I've saved up for it meself.' He shooed the pair out of the room. 'Go on with you!'

Alone in the front room, dark with brown paint and faded flowered wallpaper of uncertain vintage, he lovingly fingered the new Edwardian suit he'd collected that morning from the tailor's. Of the finest midnight blue gabardine with hand-stitched lapels and pockets and a peacock-blue lining, it'd taken him several weeks to save up for it and he was looking forward to wearing it tonight when he went out with his mates.

Someone knocked on the front door and Nick opened it to find Bragger Yates on the pavement. 'Is Nick…? Oh, hiya, Nick, I didn't expect you to answer the door.' He, too, had been working this morning and was still wearing his work suit. Tall and rangy, he had laughing blue eyes and blond hair combed into the ubiquitous DA and Tony Curtis quiff.

'I happened to be in the front room when you knocked.' Nick opened the door wider. 'Come on in.'

Bragger stepped inside, rubbing red hands together. 'It's a bit cowd out there.'

'Aye, it's brass monkey weather, that's for sure.' Nick indicated the front room with a wave of his hand. 'It's not much warmer in here. Come through to the kitchen and have a brew with us.' He led the way through to where the boys had demolished their dinner in record time and were once more heading for the back door. Mam and Joyce were still sitting at the table and Lucy was in her favourite place, the pouffe by the fire, reading a book. 'Any chance of a brew, Mam?'

'I'll do it, Nick.' Joyce jumped up and busied herself filling the kettle.

Mary smiled up at Bragger. 'Hello lad, come and sit down. Sorry about the mess.' She indicated the dirty plates, vinegar bottle and assorted newspaper wrappings on the table.

'Hello, Mrs Roberts. How are you?' Bragger sat down in the place vacated by Joyce and pushed a plate to one side.

'I'll move that lot while I'm waiting for the kettle to boil.' With sure movements, Joyce collected the remains of their recent meal.

'I'm fine, lad. How's your Mam?'

'All right, as far as I can tell,' he replied.

'It can't have been easy for her, losing your Dad like that,' commented Mary. Bragger's Dad, Bill Yates, had died of a heart attack only weeks ago.

In the small silence that followed, Bragger turned to Nick. 'I've come to see where you fancy going tonight.'

'What about the Barn?' Rivington Hall Barn was located in the pretty village of Rivington and held dances every Saturday night, patronised by youngsters from miles around.

Bragger looked surprised. 'Last time we went there, you said it were too boring. "Never again," you said.'

'Ay well, that's a bit since and happen it'll be a different crowd by now.' He grinned. 'Besides I want to show me new suit off.'

'Not seeing Sally tonight?' Joyce asked as she passed Bragger a mug of tea and sat down beside him.

'We're not courting, you know that,' Nick retaliated.

'I'm sure she'd like it if you were,' his mother pointed out.

'I'm not ready for settling down yet. Anyroad,' he turned to his younger sister, 'what about you? Any boyfriends?'

To his amusement, she blushed a deep red. Her mother, seeing her embarrassment, was quick to defend her. 'She's too young for a serious boyfriend.'

He took a good look at Joyce, noting how much more grown up she seemed since starting work last summer. Of the whole family, she was the one most like him in looks and temperament. They had the same wavy hair but hers, being longer, seemed to have a mind of its own. Her eyes were dark brown set in a face similar to his own, yet there was a subtle difference. Her face was lively to the point of always seeming on the verge of laughter, as if she didn't take life or herself, too seriously. Tall with slim hips and girlish breasts, there was no doubt that she was going to be the beauty of the family. 'But she's sixteen next month, Mam.'

'Time enough for boyfriends then,' Mary remarked calmly while Joyce squirmed on her chair.

Taking a sip of her own tea, Joyce turned to Bragger and Nick. 'So you're off to the Barn tonight, then?'

'We'll see what the rest of the lads say when we meet up later, but all being well, yes,' confirmed Bragger, looking at her over the rim of his own mug.

'How come you haven't got a date for tonight then?' she asked, a warm colour rising to her cheeks. Nick looked at her in surprise. She wasn't usually as forward as this, especially in company.

Bragger grinned at her. 'What, on a Saturday night? That's the big night out with the lads. Unless of course, you fancy coming to the Barn with us tonight, Joyce?'

'No, she is not,' Mary remonstrated. 'She's far too young.'

'Then how about you, Mrs Roberts?' he teased.

She gave him a friendly tap on the face. 'Go on with you, lad.'

CHAPTER 7

Kathy stood in front of the age-speckled mirror in the stonewalled, whitewashed cloakroom at Rivington Hall Barn, a nervous excitement making her stomach flutter.

'Why is it always so cold in here?' Carole rubbed her arms to rid them of the goose pimples that had risen unbidden as another group of girls entered on a blast of cold air.

Kathy, who'd been trying to ignore the chill that threatened to creep into her bones, looked at Carole's round dimpled face with affection. The two girls had met when they were both doing the same secretarial course in Bolton and had been going around together ever since. 'Something to do with the building being so old, I expect,' she said, wishing she hadn't worn something warmer for a freezing February night than her short-sleeved, sweetheart-necked dress. Except she knew she'd be more than warm enough on the crowded dance floor. 'Time we were getting out of here, I think.'

The two girls pushed their way to the door, bracing themselves for the cold of the lobby beyond, leading to the dance floor. The double doors opened as a group of lads laughed their way to the Gents' toilet in the courtyard. The gust of hot air from the dance floor was redolent of cheap scent, warm beer and cigarette smoke. A twirling, fast-moving crowd was quick-stepping on the dance floor while around the perimeter boys and girls were standing three and four deep. 'Phew! It's packed in here tonight,' breathed Carole.

Kathy was already feeling a flush of heat rise to her face. 'Let's go over to that corner, see if we can squeeze in there.' She indicated a space close to the group of middle-aged dinner-jacketed men who made up the band.

The quickstep finished and couples were leaving the dance floor, wedging the two girls in even tighter under the beams of the 14th century Barn. The MC announced a waltz and boys began walking around, eyeing the girls up and down before asking any of them to dance. She and Carole were giggling over the ritual, likening it to a cattle market, when a tall, gangling boy with ginger hair asked her to dance. He led her to the dance floor, to be followed shortly after by Carole and a short, dark-haired boy. From then on, the two girls were whirled into dance after dance by different partners until they were hot and dizzy.

Kathy was dancing again with the ginger-haired lad when she saw Nick Roberts, glass in hand, standing near the bar. Her heart started to pound and her breath caught in her throat. She would have stumbled had not her partner held her in a firm grip. A moment later, they'd reached the same spot again. Nick raised his glass in greeting and she gave him a quick smile, hoping he'd put her sudden colour down to the heat of the room.

At the end of the dance, she thanked her partner and made her way back to Carole. When the music started up again, this time for a waltz, and Carole was once more partnered on to the dance floor, Kathy heard a deep dark voice at her elbow. 'All alone, Kathy?'

She knew from the way her stomach fluttered who it was and, drawing a deep breath, turned to face him. 'Hello, Nick. I wouldn't have thought the Barn was your sort of place.'

He gave a nonchalant shrug. 'Makes a change, I suppose. Come to that, I haven't seen you here before. Decided to slum it, have you?'

She flicked her eyes away from his face. His dark, heavy-lidded eyes were playing havoc with her insides. 'Something like that.'

'In that case, care to lower your sights a bit more and dance with a Teddy boy?' he asked.

She indicated the half full glass in his hand. 'What about your drink?'

'No problem.' With a couple of gulps, the beer had gone and he put the empty glass on a table behind him. The dance floor was, by this time, crowded but Nick led her straight to the middle where couples, taking advantage of the close quarters, were smooching. Nick put both his arms round her and bent his head to whisper, 'You don't mind, do you?'

His high-handed attitude and her own physical reaction to him annoyed her. Did he expect her to fall at his feet in gratitude? 'What if I said I did mind?' she asked.

He gave her a calculating grin. 'You don't, though, do you?'

Almost unwillingly, her body relaxed into his and they swayed to the rhythm of the music. Too soon, that particular tune finished and almost immediately the band started another waltz but she didn't notice. The lights, the noise, the slightly tinny instruments, the press of bodies close by, all receded, leaving her isolated in the island of Nick's arms. She'd never experienced anything like this feeling before and the knowledge shook her.

As the dance ended, he dropped his arms reluctantly and they began to walk away. As they did so, the MC announced that, by special request, the band would play 'Rock Around the Clock.' This was a departure from the unaltered fare of quickstep, waltz, and foxtrot, with only the occasional Gay Gordons or Valeta. The announcement caused excitement for those who loved the brash sound of Bill Haley and The Comets and consternation for those more conservative dancers who wanted none of this new rock and roll. Couples thronged on to the floor, anticipation on their faces as the band started to play a plodding and barely recognisable version of 'Rock Around the Clock'.

He indicated the dance floor. 'Shall we?'

Already the music was pulsating in her blood. 'Why not?'

She started off tentatively, then with more confidence as her movements followed Nick's sure guiding hand. She ducked and twirled, both of them moving their feet in precise time to the music. As it stopped, there was thunderous applause from the dancers and calls for more.

'It's not often I can find someone to follow me. That was great.' His arm was still round her as they walked off the floor. He turned to her, his flushed face serious. 'Dance with me later?'

Before she could reply, from the direction of the bar, came the sound of breaking glass followed by shouts and screams. A whisper went round. 'A fight!' 'There's a fight at the bar.'

'It'll be those damned Teddy boys,' came a clear voice not too far away. 'Always looking for trouble.'

She half expected Nick to round on the person who had spoken. Instead he gave her hand a quick squeeze and said,

'Must be the lads. I've got to go but save the last dance for me, ok?'

Before she could reply, he'd gone and she was left staring after him.

* * *

'Bugger!' Nick said as he and his friends were dumped unceremoniously outside the entrance to the Barn by door staff doubling as bouncers. 'That's five bob down the plughole!' He straightened his suit jacket on to his shoulders, inspecting it for damage. Thankfully, there was none though his face was smarting where someone had landed a punch. His knuckles, too, stung where he'd had to retaliate. 'What the bloody hell happened there?' he demanded of no one in particular.

Bragger, who had a trickle of blood where his lip had been cut, said, 'Some lads behind us mouthed off about Teddy boys. You know the sort of thing, calling us hooligans and layabouts.'

'Ay, and it were really getting to me,' said Ray Brown, whose truculent attitude and cocky manner often riled Nick though he couldn't have said why. Ray had what promised to be a beautiful black eye, the flesh around it purpling and puffing even as he spoke.

'Then someone knocked into him, spilling beer down his suit,' explained Ken Johnson. He and Ray were cousins but they couldn't have been more different. Ken was a tall, stick-thin lad with red hair while Ray was small and sturdily built. 'Ray turned and thumped him,' continued Ken, his face showing an angry redness in several places and his pocket had been ripped away from his suit jacket.

'Then of course everyone around pitched in…' added Bragger.

'Just waiting for the opportunity, they was.' The interruption came from Ray, as if trying to justify himself.

'Bloody fools, the lot of you,' said Nick. 'You know us Teds are always the first to be blamed if there's any trouble.'

'What's up, Nick? Going soft, are you, now you're interested in that snooty-looking girl you were dancing with,' taunted Ray.

Nick grabbed hold of Ray's lapels, thankful that none of them stitched razor blades into their lapels as many Teddy boys did, and lifted him off his feet. Shoving his face close to Ray's, he said, 'Don't push your luck or you'll find out.'

Ray attempted a weak grin. 'Only kidding, Nick, only kidding.'

Nick let him down, none too gently, so that Ray staggered and almost fell. 'And leave Kathy Armstrong out of it!'

'What we going to do now, Nick?' ventured Ken.

Nick looked at his wristwatch. 'It's too late to go to another dance but if we're lucky, we might get last orders down the pub.' He strode over to the bus but in the all-knowing way of bus drivers, the bus pulled away before they could reach it. 'That's all we bloody need!' Nick turned to Ray, who visibly cowered. 'And stay out of me way, you miserable little git, or I might just black your other eye.'

The walk along dark country roads did little to cool Nick's temper but maintaining a fast pace helped, especially as the other three struggled to keep up. He grinned. They must look a sorry bunch as they walked, virtually in silence, the couple of miles from the Barn to Horwich. Not that they minded the walk too much. They were too used to missing the last bus from Bolton, Chorley or Wigan, depending on which dance hall they'd patronised.

Nick's mood lightened a little when they were able to get last orders in The Long Pull. 'That's better.' He licked the foam that had accumulated around his mouth from the good head on his pint of bitter.

'After the route march we've just endured, it tastes bloody marvellous,' said Bragger, downing his pint in one.

'It'll be good practice for when you do your National Service,' retorted Nick, with a grin.

Bragger laughed. 'Busy in here tonight,' he said, as he offered Nick a cigarette.

'Reckon they've all come in tonight instead of last night.' Nick gulped another swig of his beer and lit their cigarettes.

Bragger nodded to a large and noisy group of boys and girls seated by the window. 'Sally Simcox's in. You could always improve matters by taking her home.'

Nick followed his glance. 'Not while her bloody brother's with her.'

As if knowing they were talking about her, Sally was making her way towards him. 'Hiya, Nick. We don't usually see you here of a Saturday night.'

Although she was a pretty curly-haired blonde with a well-developed figure, covered at the moment in a tight pencil skirt and a body hugging black jumper, Nick couldn't help thinking that she looked common in comparison to Kathy. 'That's because we don't usually come in,' he replied, then regretted speaking so sourly. 'Sorry, Sal, I'm not in such a good mood tonight.'

'Got thrown out of the Barn, didn't we?' Ray crowed. He and Ken had re-joined the group after taking themselves off to the Gents to clean up.

'Leave off, Ray,' begged Ken.

'Ooh, you do look a bit the worse for wear.' Sally ignored both Ray and Ken and reached up to touch the redness of Nick's face.

Without thinking, he backed away from her touch and was sorry when he saw the hurt look come into her eyes. He couldn't help it. The thought of Kathy, the way she had fitted so well into his arms, filled him with an unexpected warmth. With her slenderness accentuated by the kingfisher blue dress and her hair caught up on top of her head, she'd appeared older that the nineteen he knew she was. Abruptly, knowing those thoughts would lead him nowhere, he gave Sally what he hoped was a warm smile. 'If you think we look a mess, you should have seen the others.'

'Will you be at the Fling tomorrow?' she asked.

'I expect so, not much else to do of a Sunday night,' Nick said in response to the naked hope in her eyes. 'That OK with you, Brag? No dates tomorrow?'

'Might have had if we'd stayed at the Barn,' Bragger said, digging Ray in the ribs.

'Weren't my fault, Brag,' Ray retaliated in a surly voice.

Nick turned to the other boy. 'Ken? You on for the Fling?'

Ken indicated his torn jacket. 'Don't think so, I've nowt else to wear.'

'Come round to our house tomorrow dinnertime. Me Mam'll fix it for you.'

'Sure she won't mind?'

'No, she's a dab hand with a sewing machine.' Nick turned to the girl. 'See you there then, Sally.'

'OK. Better get to the Ladies, or else our Jud'll want to know why I've been so long.'

Nick didn't miss the glare in his direction on Jud's pockmarked face. 'Don't know why you let him boss you around like he does.'

'He takes the role of big brother seriously since me Dad died.'

'Above and beyond the call of duty, if you ask me,' muttered Nick.

Sally, pushing her way out of the throng at the bar, heard him. 'Aye, well, it helps keep the peace in our house,' she said. 'See you tomorrow.'

'He's certainly a funny bugger, that Jud,' said Ken, finishing off one pint and reaching for the other. 'Don't know what's come over him this last couple of months or so.'

'It's since Nick came out of the Army. Jud isn't top dog around here anymore.' Bragger was also on his second pint.

'It's not only that,' mused Nick. 'It's since I've been seeing Sally.'

'Are you saying he's jealous?' Ken asked. 'But he's her brother!'

'Since when did that stop someone like Jud Simcox,' sniggered Ray.

For the second time that evening, Nick grabbed Ray by the lapels. 'I didn't mean owt like that and I don't want you even thinking it.' He shook the smaller lad then dropped his hold. 'I don't know why I bother with you. In fact, if it weren't for you being Ken's cousin, I wouldn't.'

With Ray, and inevitably Ken, in a more subdued mood, the evening fizzled out, much too early for a Saturday night, leaving Nick feeling flat and disgruntled.

* * *

On the Sunday afternoon following John's rugby weekend, Kathy had a phone call from him. 'Kathy?' he croaked.

'Hello, John. What's the matter with your voice?'

'I'm hoarse from singing.' She grinned. No doubt of the bawdy kind. 'Would you mind if we give this evening a miss? I'm afraid I over-indulged this weekend and I feel rough.'

She was disappointed. She'd been looking forward to seeing him, needed to see him after her disturbing reaction to dancing with Nick Roberts.

'I'm sorry to let you down like this but I really need to recuperate ready for work tomorrow,' he continued.

'That's all right, John. I do understand.' She didn't really though. After he'd rung off, she sat on the bottom step of the stairs. Resentment simmered in her that he'd been away all weekend, enjoying himself, probably behaving badly, but couldn't pull himself together enough to see her.

Popping her head round the sitting room door, she told her dozing parents she was off to see Carole. Although they were lucky enough to have a telephone, albeit a party line, Carole did not.

It was Carole who opened the door to Kathy's knock. 'Oh, hello, Kathy. Come in.'

As she followed her friend into the hall, she said, 'Do you fancy going out somewhere tonight, Carole?'

'I thought you were seeing John.'

Kathy grimaced. 'He's suffering from a hangover.'

Carole laughed. 'Serves him right.' She hesitated. 'What about going to the Fling?' Officially called the Sunday Club of the Prince's School of Dancing, everyone in Horwich knew it as the Fling.

'I've never been but I know you have. What's it like?

'Well, it's not much to look at,' she warned, 'but it's got great atmosphere.'

'If it's a club, how would I go about getting in?'

'You'd have to become a member but that's just filling in a form and paying your entrance fee.'

Kathy reflected for a moment then said, 'OK, let's give it a go.'

Intimate would have been a kind description of the Fling. The dim lighting softened the dinginess and shabbiness and chairs were scattered around its perimeter, interspersed here and there with a dilapidated sofa. She'd been able to make out several couples necking there. The music, though, was something else. The pulsating repetitive sound of 'Rock Around the Clock' and others by Bill Haley and the Comets, some she'd never heard before, sent her senses racing and her feet itching to bop. When the music had slowed right down and the record, 'Earth Angel' sung by the Crew Cuts, came on, the lights dimmed to almost blackness. Bodies welded together, arms twined round each other, cheek bonding to cheek, becoming mere silhouettes, only the occasional iridescence of moth-like pale colours illuminating the scene. The atmosphere was faintly decadent, almost dangerous, and she was stirred in a way she couldn't put a name too.

After one such smooching session, she saw Nick Roberts. He was sitting on one of the sofas with Sally Simcox, left arm around her shoulder holding her close to him, right hand most definitely up the other girl's jumper. Shock hit Kathy almost physically and for a second, she felt sick. He, startled into looking up as the lights went on, saw Kathy and snatched both his hand and his arm away from Sally, leaving her slumped awkwardly on the sofa.

Reeling as if she'd been slapped in the face, Kathy stalked over to where Carole was just coming off the dance floor. 'I've seen enough, Carole, I'm going home.'

Her friend's face dropped in disappointment. 'But we've only just got here. Can't you wait a bit longer?' She made a slight gesture with her head, indicating her partner who, Kathy saw, was the small dark-haired lad from the night before at the Barn. 'I'm beginning to enjoy myself.'

Anger at herself and Nick made her voice sharper that she intended. 'Sorry, but I want to go home.'

The dark-haired lad, who still had his arm round Carole, spoke up shyly. 'If it will help, I'll walk Carole home.'

'Are you sure?' Carole asked, giving him a winsome look. As he nodded his agreement, she turned to Kathy. 'But what about you?'

'Don't worry about me, I'll be fine,' her voice fizzed. 'It's still early.'

Grabbing her coat from the cloakroom, she almost ran out of the club, glad to be out of the stuffy atmosphere and into the clean night air. Drawing deep breaths, she calmed down enough to realise it was cold and frosty again and pulled up the collar of her coat. A voice called out behind her. 'Kathy, wait!'

Ignoring his voice at first, she kept on walking until he caught up with her and stopped her in mid-stride by taking hold of her arm, the warmth of it seeping through her coat sleeve. 'Let go of me, Nick Roberts,' she said, her mouth tight.

He didn't loosen his hold. 'Not until you listen to me.'

'What could you possibly say that would interest me?' she said in what she hoped was a superior tone. 'And let go of my arm.'

He dropped his hold on her but, for some reason she couldn't explain, she chose not to walk away. 'I wanted to say I'm sorry about that.' He indicated with a nod of his head, the direction of the dilapidated Arcade where the Fling was situated.

She tossed her head. 'What makes you think I care?'

'Come on, Kathy, I saw your face when you saw me with Sally'

'Almost on her, more like,' she said through gritted teeth.

He held his hands out palm upward and gave a slight shrug of his shoulders. 'So what? I told you I'd been out with her a few times.'

'Yes, but I didn't know you were so…intimately acquainted,' she parried.

For a short space of time, there seemed to be a spark arcing between them, heavy with unspoken feelings and hidden meanings, a brief moment which passed when Nick spoke again. 'Am I forgiven?'

'It's nothing to do with me what you do. But if it makes you feel better, yes.'

'So can we at least be friendly when we bump into each other?'

'If we do that as often as we have this weekend – twice in two days – I don't think I could stand the strain,' she pointed out.

He laughed and the tension between them eased. 'Probably won't see each other for months now. Come on, I'll walk you to the bus stop.'

'No, you go back to Sally.' She had a vision of Sally sulking in the Fling, wondering where Nick had dashed off to and it gave her some satisfaction knowing Nick would have some explaining to do.

Later that night, she lay sleepless, going over the conversation in her mind again and again. She knew she would have to put up some kind of defence against this unwise attraction she had for Nick Roberts. But what? It was still early days with John and she daren't put all her hopes in him. It was too soon in their relationship but she clung to thoughts of him anyway.

CHAPTER 8

Never busy at the best of times, Travers Street was quiet on this late Sunday afternoon. Kathy's mother was knitting as usual but the clacking of needles was spasmodic as Vera looked up from time to time, peering out of the window. Her father was having a post-lunch nap on the bed upstairs, while Kathy waited for John to collect her. He was taking her to have tea with his parents and she didn't know who was more apprehensive about the occasion, she or her mother.

'Are you nervous?' her mother said.

'A bit,' Kathy conceded.

'Well, it's a big step forward.'

'I'm only taking tea with John's parents, Mum. You can't read too much into that.'

'We both know it's more than a piece of cake and a cup of tea,' Vera said, her excitement showing in the increased speed of her knitting needles. 'How long have you been going out with John now?'

'Just over two months.'

'And already he's taking you to meet his parents. It's obvious that his intentions are serious.'

'I'm not sure I'm ready to settle down yet, Mum.'

The knitting went down mid-row in Vera's lap. 'Don't be ridiculous!' she snapped. 'You're twenty next month and you should be seriously courting by now or you'll be left on the shelf.'

Irritation surged in Kathy. 'But I don't want to tie myself down yet. I'd probably be expected to give up my job after I'm married, become a stay-at-home wife.'

'And what's wrong with that?' Vera snapped. 'It's what most girls hanker after.'

'I'm not most girls, Mum. I want more than that.'

Vera shook her head in despair. 'I don't understand you. Any other girl would be only too glad to be going out with such a nice young man as John seems to be.'

Her mother was right, of course. What was there not to love about John? He was always kind and courteous, treated her like a grown-up, had a good secure job with good prospects – good heavens, she was beginning to sound like her mother!

Vera picked up her knitting again. 'Speaking of which, when are we going to meet John?'

'There's plenty of time for that, Mum.' Kathy sighed with relief as she heard John's car outside.

A short time later, John pulled up outside the large Edwardian terraced house and turned to her. 'Apprehensive?'

She gave him a quick smile. 'Terrified, more like.'

'Are you ready to enter the lion's den, then?' John was looking at her, amusement written on his face.

She sat up straighter and heaved a sigh. 'As I ever will be.'

He led her up the path, bordering a winter-dreary lawn and empty flower beds and opened the stained-glass front door. Inside, the weak winter sun sent reflections from the door onto the tile floor of the hall, making it a riot of assorted colours. 'Mum, Dad, we're here,' John called as he helped her out of her coat and hung it on a huge Victorian hallstand. With his hand behind her back, he ushered her into what she would have called a sitting-room but which she guessed they might call the drawing room.

A portly grey-haired man, wearing a dark blue, slightly disreputable cardigan, rose from a chintz-covered armchair and extended a hand towards her. 'You must be Kathy. I'm Marcus Talbot,' he said. She liked him immediately.

John turned to the slim, elegantly-dressed woman who had also stood to greet her. 'And this is my mother, Celia Talbot.'

'Hello, my dear. We've been so looking forward to meeting you.' She shook Kathy's hand and waved them both to the matching sofa. 'Do sit down, Kathy. And you, John. We'll have tea shortly.' She sat down too, tucking her royal blue dress under her as she crossed her legs at the ankle. Her corn-coloured hair, streaked here and there with grey, was pristine. 'Now, my dear, tell us about yourself.'

Instantly disadvantaged, a feeling she was not unfamiliar with, she truly did not know how to begin. 'Well, I live at home with my parents …'

'What does your father do, Kathy?' Mr Talbot interrupted.

'He's a draughtsman at Dehavilland Propellers.'

'Has he always worked there?

'Only for the past fifteen years or so. Before that he worked for a large national company in Manchester, I can't remember which one. I was only five at the time.'

'So you haven't lived in Horwich all your life?'

'No, I was born in Cheadle, Cheshire.' Kathy was uncomfortable under the questioning but she supposed it was natural for John's parents to be curious about her.

'John's told us you work for the Bolton Evening News as a shorthand typist. What department do you work in?' Mrs Talbot asked now.

'In Advertising. I'm one of four shorthand typists and we work for several people doing a variety of jobs.'

'I understand that you've had something published in Town Topics,' Mrs Talbot continued.

'I showed you, Mum. A couple of weeks ago.' This time it was John who spoke. 'Don't you remember?'

Mrs Talbot gave him a reproving glance. 'Of course I remember. That's why I'm asking.'

Kathy squirmed for him. 'Actually, I have another piece going in this week. Wednesday, I think.'

'Is it something you'd like to develop, do you think?' Mrs Talbot quizzed.

Kathy looked for support to John and he gave her a quick, encouraging smile. 'I haven't given it much thought though I do enjoy doing it.'

Mr Talbot must have thought the questioning had gone on long enough for now he rose and said, 'Time for tea, I think. Celia?'

She, too, stood and, smoothing down her dress, said, 'If you'll excuse me, I'll just go and make the tea.'

Mr Talbot led the way into the dining room while they followed. John caught hold of her hand saying, 'Sorry about her giving you the third degree. She's usually more subtle than that.'

'It's all right. I don't mind.' She did but what could she say?

Tea consisted of boiled ham, salad, finely cut bread and butter, cake, washed down with copious amounts of tea. All served on the finest bone china, as she'd expected. 'I do like your tea service, Mrs Talbot,' she said. It had a delicate pattern of what looked like ivy leaves.

'Thank you, dear. It was a wedding present, wasn't it, Marcus?'

'If you say so, Celia,' Mr Talbot said as he put his own cup down onto its saucer.

'You should have remembered seeing as it was a present from your own mother,' Mrs Talbot said, with a slight exasperation in her voice.

Kathy smothered a giggle in her starched white napkin. It was obvious who was boss in this house.

After more penetrating questions that Kathy thought verged on nosiness, she was grateful to sink against the shabby old leather of the seats in John's car. He climbed in his side and leaned his head back against his own seat. 'Oh, that was simply awful. Mother excelled herself today.'

Despite feeling drained, Kathy started giggling. 'Just wait until it's my mother's turn to grill you.'

'Ah yes, I still have that pleasure to come, haven't I? Is she as much of an ogre as my mother is?'

'I don't know. You'll have to form your own opinion.'

He winced. 'I can't wait. Seriously, though,' he said as he pulled out the choke and turned the engine on, 'I hope my mother didn't frighten you off coming again.'

'Of course not. Your Dad was a sweetie. I bet he's a lovely doctor.'

With the engine ticking over, he turned towards her. 'I thought you coped well. You didn't get flustered by all her questions.'

She smiled. 'I was inside, believe me.'

Placing his hand against her face, he pulled her as close to him as the gear stick would allow. 'You know I'm falling in love with you, Kathy.'

'And I feel the same,' she whispered as their lips met in a kiss that left her feeling weak and trembling. She knew that, with this visit to his parents, they were making some kind of commitment.

* * *

Two weeks after her 16th birthday, Joyce was a disappointed young woman. True, she'd been given her own set of three looms, meaning that she'd be earning more money. Or she would be when she became more confident and didn't have to stop the other two looms while she dealt with a problem on the third. And she'd got a good weaver next to her, Sally Simcox. She'd proved to be kind-hearted and, as with most of the older weavers, always willing to help Joyce if she got stuck.

But she hadn't noticed any difference in people's attitudes towards her, more particularly, Bragger Yates. To her regret there'd been no repeat of the camaraderie of that Saturday afternoon a month or so ago. Did she really believe that being 16 would be different? Perhaps she'd been unrealistic to expect things to change overnight. A birthday was, after all, just another day.

She was thinking all this as she lay in front of the fire drying her thick wavy hair. This part of the Sunday night bath routine, she hated. It meant scorching her face or her back according to which way she was facing. Come to that, having a bath wasn't much fun either, lugging the tin bath that hung from a hook in the yard into the house and filling it with bucket after bucket of hot water. They were fortunate they had a back boiler for this. The drawback of a back boiler, though, was that you had to have a fire blazing all day, no matter what the weather was like outside. Still, it was a good feeling to be clean with freshly washed hair, sitting cosily by the fire in her pyjamas. Mam was curled up in one of the easy chairs, in a threadbare cardigan over a winceyette nightdress. The younger children, with school tomorrow, were in bed long since and it had now gone ten o'clock.

The back door opened and Nick appeared, bringing in a blast of cold air and a not unpleasant whiff of cigarette smoke and beer. 'By heck, it's cowd out there.' Pulling the pouffe closer to the fire, he sat on it and rubbed his hands together and spread them to the warmth of the fire. 'Do you think it'll ever warm up this year?' he said to no one in particular.

'It's still early yet, only the middle of March,' Mary reminded him.

He grabbed the poker and stirred the fire so that the flames leapt higher. 'Ay, I suppose so. Any tea left in the pot, Mam?'

'It might be a bit stewed by now. Boil the kettle up and add a bit of water to it.' As he rose and wandered over to the cooker, she added, 'While you're on your feet, Nick, will you empty the rest of the bath? Joyce has done most of it with the bucket.'

He set the kettle to boil and dragged the bath to the back door, emptying the contents down the drain. 'Do you want me to hang it up again, Mam?'

'No, leave it; I'll give it a good swill in the morning.'

'Anyone would think we were mucky,' he called from the back door as he propped the bath against the wall to drain any residue away.

'Wouldn't it be lovely to have a proper bathroom?' Joyce scrunched her fingers through her hair and turned again as she found a damp bit.

'If wishes were horses, then beggars would ride.' It was one of their Mam's favourite sayings.

'Is there any use getting on to the Council again, Mam?' Nick wandered over to the sideboard and pulled the old pre-war Bakelite wireless towards him.

Mary shook her head. 'I went to the Public Hall a couple of weeks ago but were told there were more deserving cases than ours.' She sighed. 'Mind you, when I told your Dad, he said he'd heard that we might stand more of a chance when he comes out of prison, daft though it might sound.'

'It's worth a try, I suppose.' He began twiddling the knobs on the radio in the usual Sunday night search for Radio

Luxembourg, with the signal fading intermittently between stations. 'How did he seem when you saw him yesterday, Mam?' 'Same as always, subdued. He says it doesn't pay to draw attention to yourself.' She gave a deep sigh. 'Reckons he just keeps his head down and gets on with it.'

Joyce laughed. 'That doesn't sound like Dad.'

They fell into a companionable silence, interspersed with foreign sounding voices, snatches of music and various crackles. Suddenly Nick hit a clear signal and a moody voice rang out in the cosy room, a voice that seemed to jerk from phrase to phrase. The dark bluesy voice sang of finding a new place to dwell in Heartbreak Hotel with a sob on the last two words.

Joyce sat up higher, intrigued. She'd never heard anything like this before, not even when Johnny Ray had toured Britain the previous year. 'What's that, Nick?' she asked as her brother's hand poised over the dials, not daring to touch them now in case he moved it off station.

'I don't know,' he admitted. 'It could be Radio Luxembourg or that American Air Base you get some times.'

'Sounds like cats on the lavvy roof to me,' harrumphed Mary.

'Mam!' exclaimed Joyce, still trying to listen to the fascinating sound coming, for once, clearly from their old wireless.

Nick, too, was silent, listening as the sobbing voice dipped and crescendoed. When the song finished, brother and sister sat in stunned silence apart from Joyce's whispered, 'Wow!' Then the announcer, an American, came on to say 'And that, folks, was the rockabilly singer Elvis Presley's new record, 'Heartbreak Hotel', now storming up the Hit Parade.'

'Who did he say it was?' asked Joyce, still bemused.

'Some bloke, American by the sound of it, Elvis Presley.'

'He'd have to be American with a name like that,' Mary commented.

It was a name Joyce was to become familiar with as the record became the sensation of the spring. Though Mam tutted and shook her heard in disapproval, Joyce and her friends loved this new sound they could appropriate for their own. It made such a change from the post-war big bands and crooners her mother liked to listen to on the wireless. She was eager to see what Elvis looked like. Much as Bill Haley's music made her toes twitch, as a sex-symbol, the slightly podgy man with the ludicrous curl in the middle of his forehead, was a disappointment. When someone at work showed her a photograph in a newspaper, she gasped, for Elvis was incredibly handsome with jet black hair and lips that quirked into a knowing smile. The weedy Anglo-Saxon looks of most of the boys she knew bore no comparison to Elvis's swarthiness. Among her acquaintances, only her brother Nick compared favourably.

* * *

One evening in late March, Nick and his mates were laughing and jostling each other in an enormous queue in front of the Capitol cinema in Bolton to see the X-rated American film, 'The Blackboard Jungle.' It had been on general release since the previous year but because of its violent nature and the near-riots that had occurred whenever the Bill Haley number, 'Rock Around the Clock' was played, several cities and towns had opted not to show it.

Queuing for the pictures didn't bother Nick. Queues were all part of the experience. He didn't feel quite so happy, as they reached the head of the queue for the cheapest seats, to see, on the opposite side of the cinema entrance, Kathy Armstrong queuing for the more expensive seats. But who was the young man beside her? Was he her boyfriend? With straight blond hair cut in regulation short back and sides, dressed soberly in grey slacks and a thick tweed jacket, Nick took an instant dislike to him.

Bragger nudged him. 'Seen who's in the other queue?'

'Yes,' he said through gritted teeth.

'The bloke looks a right prat, doesn't he?'

'I'd like to wipe that superior look off his face.'

'You and me both,' was Bragger's comment.

He had no more than a brief instant to acknowledge Kathy's presence with a nod and a slight raising of his eyebrows as their part of the queue was ushered into the foyer by the commissionaire.

The cinema was filling up rapidly, a large contingent being Teddy boys. From the cheaper seats near the front, he kept glancing round in the hope of seeing Kathy and the boyfriend. Would they be on the back row as most couples would be, to kiss and cuddle throughout the film? He found his teeth clenching and made a deliberate attempt not to look behind again.

They had to sit though the usual short travel film that always ended with a glorious sunset over a deep sapphire sea. Everyone talked through it, despite the determined efforts of the usherettes shining their torches on the culprits and 'ssh-ing' loudly. Next was the Pathé Newsreel. Nick lost interest and let his mind wander again until Bragger nudged him. 'Nick! Look, it's Elvis!'

And there on the screen before him was the real-life Elvis Presley, inordinately handsome and unfailingly polite to the interviewer. The interview showed a clip of him singing, 'That's All Right, Mama,' and there was an audible gasp. His body flowed in provocative yet graceful movements. He pouted, he smirked, he grinned, he sulked, and all in the space of a few bars of a song.

When the lights went up for the interval and the ice cream vendors appeared, their trays laden with an assortment of Lyons Maid goodies, Nick volunteered to go. Laden with his bounty, he didn't see Kathy, in the queue behind him, until she spoke to him. 'Hello, Nick.'

Simply the sound of her voice, especially when he wasn't expecting it, sent a shiver of excitement through him. 'Hello, Kathy. What did you think to Elvis?'

'Wonderful, isn't he?' she said. 'I'm not sure about 'Heartbreak Hotel' though. It's so different. Perhaps it'll grow on me.'

'Come on, mate, get a bloody move on,' someone said behind him. 'Me ice cream's melting while you stand here chatting.'

'Alright, mate, keep your hair on,' Nick replied as the man shoved past.

Then it was Kathy's turn to be served and as she gave the vendor her order, he said, 'I'd best get these back.' He moved on and so did she, widening the gap between them.

When Bill Haley's 'Rock Around The Clock' was played during the opening credits, the audience went wild, singing along with the words. The same thing happened whenever the track was played. The film itself passed in a haze. The music thrummed in his head as he dutifully stood and sang the National Anthem. It stayed with him as he and his mates struggled out through the crowd into the foyer.

Ahead of him, he caught a glimpse of Kathy standing to one side and with a quick word to Bragger, the others being some way behind them, he pushed his way forward. He saw, with relief that she was waiting, as were a few others, for the boyfriend to come out of the Gents' toilet. 'Did you enjoy the film, Kathy?'

Her face came alive and her olive eyes sparkled. 'I'll say, especially when the music came on. I wanted to jump up and dance. Instead, I jogged about in my seat and sang along.' She giggled in remembrance. 'Much to my boyfriend's disgust. He hadn't wanted to come. It was me that insisted.'

'Are you courting now, then?' He hated himself for asking but he had to know.

'Yes. It's been three months now.' She looked towards the door of the 'Gents' as the boyfriend appeared, running a hand over his already immaculate hair.

'Sorry I was so long, Kathy. Bit of a queue,' John said, in a voice with barely a trace of Lancashire in it.

She turned to Nick who stood his ground. 'John, this is Nick Roberts. We've known each other for years.'

Nick forced himself to stick out his hand which John took as reluctantly. 'Pleased to meet you, John.'

70

'Likewise, Nick.' John turned to her and put a proprietary hand on her arm. 'Come on, Kathy, we'd better get going if I'm to get you home at a reasonable time.'

So he had a car as well, did he? Nick hated him even more. Deliberately, he turned his back on the pair but over his shoulder said, 'See you around some time, Kathy,' and joined his mates, who were waiting for him outside. He wished it wasn't too late to go to the pub. He wanted to down pint after pint to sublimate the feeling of jealousy as he saw her walk off with this John, her arm tucked protectively through his.

Kathy haunted his dreams that night. Using only a go-cart, he'd been chasing her round Horwich but every time he tried to catch up with her, she'd disappeared.

CHAPTER 9

'Is it time to go yet, Mam?' Brian asked while Derek jogged up and down with excitement at his side. It was Good Friday and both of them were eager to be off on the annual pilgrimage to Rivington Pike. Ostensibly, the purpose of the trek was to visit the fair, clustered at the base of the hill on which the 18th century tower stood, if you could call a few ice cream vans and the odd hoop-la stall a fair.

'Not yet. It's much too early. Nobody'll be up there yet,' Mary snapped. 'Besides, you're not going out while it's chucking it down.' She pointed to the window where a sudden shower cascaded down. 'Look at it, you'll be soaked through in minutes.'

'We'd put our wellies on,' Brian reasoned.

'You'll do that anyway, even if it stops raining. It'll be like a swamp up there.'

'Ay, and the alligators'll get you,' teased Nick.

Derek's eyes narrowed. 'There aren't any alligators up Rivi. They only live in hot swampy lands.'

'Oh, so you are learning summat at school.' Nick's remark earned him a scornful look from Derek.

'Couldn't we go and wait at Bernard's until it stops raining?' Brian wheedled.

'No, because the minute you're out of the house, I know you'll be off,' Mary said, in the no-nonsense voice they'd all learned to ignore at their peril.

Eventually, the sun came out, a gusty wind dried the pavements and Mary was able to let the lads off the leash, heaving a sigh of relief as she did so. Lucy set off with the parents of her best friend from school while Joyce went with a group of her own friends, leaving Nick and his mother relaxing with a mug of tea and a yearned-for cigarette. Mary pulled the pouffe towards her, easing her legs onto it and sighing as she did so. 'When are you off, Nick?'

'Want to get rid of me, do you?'

'Ay, I'm looking forward to spending some time on me own, summat I seldom get chance to do,' she quipped back.

He glanced at the old clock on the mantelpiece. 'In about another half hour. I'm waiting for Bragger to call for me.'

'Not wearing your Teddy boy suit, I see.' She nodded to the black drainpipes he was wearing and the leather jacket hung on the back of a chair.

'No, I don't want it to get muddy.'

She put her head on one side as if taking a critical look at him. 'You've certainly filled out since you've been in the Army. You used to be shaped like a sauce-bottle before you went in.'

Nick laughed and they sat in companionable silence for the length of their cigarettes. 'Are you off to see Dad this weekend, Mam?' he asked finally.

He was surprised to see a troubled look pass over her face. 'Yes, tomorrow.' She leaned forward to stub out her cigarette in the overflowing ashtray. 'I still feel so bloody angry that your Dad got himself banged up for summat he passed off as a bit of harmless fun. And just as our Joyce started work.'

'What do you think will happen when he comes out, Mam?'

She gave a deep sigh. 'I don't know. He says he's changed. But then, who wouldn't, being in prison with thieves and murderers. He might be a gambler and like the drink a bit too much but he's no villain.'

Nick hoped his Dad had indeed changed because, with all that she'd had to put up while he'd been in prison, Mam was a lot stronger and he had a feeling things were going to be very different when his Dad came out. Mam roused him from his thoughts by saying, 'There's the door. It'll probably be Bragger.'

By the time Nick, Bragger, Ray and Ken had reached the summit of the hill on which the Pike stood, Nick was glad he hadn't worn his Teddy boy suit. Bragger, like him, had worn his second-best suit, while Ray and Ken bemoaned the mud that covered the trouser bottoms of their good Teddy boy suits.

Breathless from the last steep climb, lungs searing with the effort, they looked about them. A considerable number of people were already there, standing close to each other in the buffeting wind, or sheltering in the lee of the building. From where he stood, Nick watched a steady stream wending its way up the path to the Pike. Many more would only now be setting off up the path by the side of Rivington and Blackrod Grammar School or the alternative route round by the back of Rivington Hall Barn and through the Bungalow grounds. Before the end of the day, hundreds if not thousands would have made the trek, until the Pike would seem indivisible from the crowds around it to people like Mam back in Horwich. Nick leaned against the rough-hewn blocks of soot-blackened stone that constituted the Pike's structure. Over the years, thousands of visitors had carved their names and the date into the stonework, so that now there was hardly space to add more. 'Remember how, as kids, we used to try and scratch our names?' Bragger asked.

'Ay, using whatever was to hand, a stone or a penknife,' Nick replied. 'And we barely scratched the surface with our efforts.'

Nearby, a gang of boys were trying to do just that and Nick recognised Brian and Derek among them. He had to laugh. They were all muddied up to the top of their Wellingtons and beyond. Probably pretending to fall, mud had crept onto bottoms, hands, faces, even into their hair. They seemed to be ignoring the cutting edge to the wind, though nearly all of them wore only thick jumpers over frayed shirts.

Again, he was reminded of his own childhood when he and a few other lads had made the trek. At the base of the Pike, one of them would cry, 'Race you to the top! Last one's a cissy!' They'd take off up the last and steepest slope to the top of the hill, scrabbling up, laughing as they got in each other's way, chests heaving with the effort. Later, they would all wander down to explore the Bungalow grounds. He recalled Mam telling him that the Bungalow had been the country residence of the late Lord Leverhulme, who had so loved the area that he had later donated it to the people of the locality as a country park. The Bungalow had been demolished some years before but the much overgrown gardens were a paradise of hidden nooks and crannies for youngsters like Brian and Derek. Even as he was thinking about it, he saw the gang of boys scamper down the path in the direction of the pigeon tower on the road which circled the Pike and guessed that they too were on their way to the Bungalow grounds.

It was then that he saw Kathy standing alone, a hand up to her hair to stop it blowing in her face, and his heart beat quickened.

* * *

As the boys were scrabbling down the deeply rutted track, Joyce and her friends were struggling up the last steep slope to the Pike. Hampered by their impractical but fashionable tight skirts and high heels, Joyce, Sheila, and two other girls, Maureen and Brenda, were making slow progress. Joyce's new black and jade green duster coat, purchased from the recently opened Richard Shops in Bolton, flapped wildly in the wind and threatened to take off with her. They were all four laughing helplessly and holding on to each other for support, taking a few steps then halting as one or the other of them got a heel stuck.

'Look at me shoes!' wailed Sheila, whose tight skirt and jumper topped by a short boxer jacket did little to hide voluptuous curves. 'They're ruined.'

'You and me both.' Joyce looked down ruefully at her black court shoes, scuffed after contact with numerous rocks and stones.

'And I've cricked me ankle,' added Maureen, bending to rub the offending joint. A small slight girl with an underdeveloped figure whose clothes looked too big for her, she pointed to a stony outcrop by the side of the path. 'Can we sit down for a while?'

'Good idea, it'll give us chance to catch our breath,' agreed Brenda. With her angular face topped by short feathered brown hair and a similar figure to Maureen but taller, she reminded Joyce of a twig. The four girls huddled together on the outcrop, not only for warmth, but because it wasn't really big enough for them.

'I wish now I'd put me wellies on.' Sheila indicated her once white shoes, now stained with grass and mud.

'They'd look a bit daft with that skirt,' commented Joyce.

'But a lot more practical.'

'Why do we put ourselves through this, anyroad?' asked Maureen, still rubbing her ankle.

'To be seen by the lads, of course.' Brenda pointed to a group of lads about their own age coming abreast of the girls.

'Not by that lot, I hope. I prefer someone a bit older meself.' Joyce bit her lip, hoping she hadn't given herself away.

'Anyone in mind?' queried Sheila.

Joyce shrugged. 'Not particularly.' The other two were exchanging remarks with the gang of lads and hadn't heard the conversation between Joyce and Sheila. 'Come on, let's get to the top. It's freezing sitting here.'

They struggled to their feet, laughing again as Joyce's duster coat blew up like an umbrella. With aching calves and ankles and huffing with exertion, the four girls finally reached the summit, crowded now with people. Joyce looked across to the horizon. From being a little girl, she had loved this view when, as today, the wind blew away any clouds or mist and she could see as far as the Welsh hills of Snowdonia.

'Marvellous, isn't it?' came a voice at her shoulder. Her heart thudding, she turned to face Bragger Yates.

The sun, which had been shining fitfully for the past hour or so, glinted off something in the far distance. 'Is that the sea?' she hazarded.

Shading his eyes, he looked in the direction she pointed. 'Think so. And I can see Blackpool Tower.'

'Where? Where?' She tried in vain to follow where he was pointing.

He pulled her directly in front of him where, tall herself, she came up to his shoulders, and pointed again. 'There, to the left of where you saw the sea.'

'Yes, I see it now.' She was desperately conscious of his nearness but he made no indication of moving away and neither did she.

He leaned in close to her ear and whispered, 'Joyce, will you come out with me some time?'

She half turned to him, thinking perhaps she'd imagined it. 'You what?'

'You heard.' He grinned wickedly. 'Surely you didn't think I kept coming round to your house to see Nick?'

At the moment when the dream she'd nurtured for so long seemed about to come true, reality intruded. 'Is he here?' she asked nervously and moved away from him.

He indicated with a nod of his head where her brother was standing some distance away, talking to a tall, slim, attractive girl wearing black slacks, a warm jumper topped by a neat short jacket and, she noticed enviously, flat pump-like shoes. 'Who's the girl?'

'Kathy Armstrong. Nick fancies her like mad but she's got a boyfriend. Anyway,' he said, turning her attention back to him, 'you didn't answer me question.'

'I can't,' she said.

'Because of Nick? Do you think he wouldn't approve?'

'I know he wouldn't. He still thinks of me as his little sister. And,' she glanced up at him impishly, 'your reputation doesn't exactly help.'

'My reputation?' He looked puzzled.

'If I went out with you, how do I know that you wouldn't talk about me?'

Bragger's own face was serious. 'Hell, no, you're special in my eyes, you always have been.'

'I don't think Nick would see it that way,' she said ruefully.

'It's because you're his sister that I've not asked you before though I've fancied you for ages.' The quiet, steady tone of his voice told her more than anything that he was serious in his invitation.

'He'd need a bit more convincing than that. Me too,' she said, in an attempt to be flippant. Much as she wanted this, she was a little out of her depth.

'If I can prove I've reformed, will you think about it?'

'I might,' she conceded, not wanting to seem too eager.

'Is that your best offer?'

'Afraid so,' she laughed.

The other girls, having been waylaid by the gang of boys they'd seen earlier, came up to Joyce. 'We're all off down to the

77

Great Barn for some pop. Are you coming?' Sheila asked, glancing quizzically at Bragger.

'OK, why not?' She linked her arm with Sheila's and stepped away from Bragger. 'See you around, Br...Dave,' she said, enjoying the look of amazement on his good-looking face.

'I see what you mean about someone older,' Sheila whispered.

'Not that much older. He's only nineteen.' Suddenly afraid that again she might have given herself away, she went on, 'But he's just one of me brother's mates.'

* * *

Kathy's heart fluttered when she saw Nick Roberts at Rivington Pike. But then why shouldn't he be here too? It was what people who lived in Horwich did on Good Friday. Oh, but he looked good in that leather jacket! His dark eyes told her that he was glad to see her and there was a flirtatious note in his voice when he said, 'We'll have to stop meeting like this.'

'Why, afraid people might talk, tell Sally perhaps?' was her swift retort though she couldn't help laughing.

'I'm more concerned about you.' He glanced round and she knew he was looking for John. 'Is the boyfriend with you?'

'He's round the other side of the Pike trying to find the oldest date. I stayed here to look at the view.' She pointed to where the moors swept past the recently erected commercial television mast on Winter Hill, on towards Scotchman's Stump, the memorial commemorating the murder of a lone traveller in the early 19th century, and the village of Belmont. The sun, hidden occasionally by clouds, caused a subsequent play of light and shadow on the long grass undulating in the wind. 'I love the wildness of the moors, like they're stretching into infinity.' He followed the sweep of her arm.

'I see what you mean,' he said quietly. 'You know, I've been here scores of times yet I've never really appreciated it before.'

'This kind of view always makes me want to see what's beyond the horizon.' Their eyes met and suddenly that spark of electricity was there again, arcing between them. And there was something more, a kind of yearning, like there was a whole world out there, inviting them to explore, to become part of it, together.

'Walk with me across to the television mast?' he asked. 'I've never seen it close up.' And in that moment, she wanted nothing more than to run hand in hand across the moors with Nick.

She shook her head regretfully. 'I'm with John, remember? Besides,' she laughed, breaking the tension between them, 'it's further than you think and it's boggy. I tried it once and got sludge up to my knees.'

'Is he bothering you, Kathy?' John's voice came from behind them.

She bit back the retort that sprang to her lips. Instead, with coldness in her voice, she replied, 'Of course, he isn't. We're just talking, like old friends do.'

'If he's such a good friend, how come you never mentioned him before that night at the cinema?' John came to stand at her side, throwing one arm around her shoulder in a proprietorial way.

Biting her lip, she shrugged her way out of his arm. 'Because he's only recently finished his National Service.'

This seemed to sting John into jeering at Nick. 'Think you're a toughie, do you, now you've been in the Army?'

Nick's fists clenched as did his jaw. 'I've done my stint but I'll bet you've still got yours to do,' he said.

Kathy flinched. John was sensitive that he'd failed his own National Service medical because of some problem with his feet, for which he had to wear special insoles. She put out a hand to stop him but he brushed her gesture away. A look of fury filled his eyes and he thrust his face close to Nick's. 'You fancy yourself as James Dean in that get up, don't you?' he said, flicking his fingers against Nick's leather lapel.

'At least I don't dress like me Dad,' Nick retorted, his own fingers flicking the coarse tweed lapel of John's sports jacket.

'Why, you cheeky bastard!' John lunged closer but Nick, wiser in the ways of the street, sidestepped and, as John staggered, put his foot forward and neatly tripped him so that he sprawled to the ground.

79

Kathy was appalled. 'That's enough, the pair of you,' she said, her voice shaking. 'Bickering like a couple of school kids. You're both as bad as one another.'

'Owt wrong, Nick?' Bragger Yates appeared at Nick's side, backed up by Ken Johnson and the lad she didn't know, the latter looking as if he would relish a fight.

'Not now, there's not.' Nick squared his shoulders. 'I think I've made my point.'

'You certainly have,' Kathy bristled. 'I hope you're proud of yourself.' Her attention was solely on Nick now.

'He needed showing up for what he really is, a stuffed shirt,' Nick said, bravado in his voice. 'It's about time you got yourself a real man.'

John made a threatening move but this time Kathy put a hand on his arm. 'Someone like you, I suppose? Never in a hundred years,' was her parting shot as she and John walked away, her hand now tucked in his arm, towards the path that led to the Bungalow grounds and Rivington Hall Barn.

Once out of sight of the group of Teddy boys, Kathy, her throat tight from a myriad of emotions, removed her arm from John's and withdrew slightly to one side.

'You're angry with me, aren't you?' he asked.

'More than I can say. Whatever made you pull a stunt like that?'

'He's so bloody cocky. I wanted to take him down a peg or two.'

'You realise he could have beaten you up if he'd wanted to?' she pointed out.

'Don't forget, I play rugby,' he boasted.

'And I doubt he'd have played fair. Why do you think his friends turned up then? You know how Teddy boys stick together.'

The two were still walking down the rough track and as Kathy stumbled, John put out his hand to steady her. 'I'm sorry, Kathy, the last thing I wanted to do was upset you.'

She snatched her hand away. 'Upset me? That's a bit of an understatement. I don't know when I've been so annoyed. I sometimes wonder if we're suited after all.' She drew in a deep breath, dismayed at what she had said. Now where had that remark come from? She'd had no idea she was going to say it.

He stood still, a look of alarm on his face. 'Don't say that, Kathy. You know I'd do anything to make amends.'

'Well, you're going the wrong way about it,' she snapped, tossing her head. 'At the moment, I don't care if I never see you or Nick again.' She stalked on, taking care now to watch every step but holding herself away from him. There were people approaching them, climbing up the path from the Bungalow Grounds, but she didn't care.

'You're not lumping me with that Teddy boy, are you?' he demanded, catching up with her.

'Why not? There wasn't much to choose between you.' She turned to him again. 'And it was you who started it, taunting him about the Army.'

'Why are you leaping to his defence all of a sudden? Is there something you're not telling me?'

She chose not to reply, merely giving him a cold look and started down the track. 'I've decided I've had enough for today. I want to go home now.'

He trotted after her. 'But I'd booked us a meal this evening at the Black Dog at Belmont, as a surprise.'

'Why is it that whenever we go anywhere, it's always your choice? If I so much as suggest anything, you generally pooh-pooh the idea.'

'I do not,' he exclaimed. 'We went to see that stupid film, didn't we, because you insisted?

'And moaned all the way through it.' She didn't care that people were staring at them arguing.

'It didn't help matters when you were chatting to that big-headed Teddy boy,' he retaliated.

'Are you going to take me home or do I have to walk?'

'Of course I'll take you home if that's what you want,' he said, 'but what about the meal?'

'You'll have to cancel it, won't you? I couldn't face a steak, having been made to feel like a prize cow.'

CHAPTER 10

After the incident at the Pike on Good Friday, Nick tried to blot out Kathy's last remark, which had seared into his brain, by drinking more than usual. On several occasions, Bragger had to take him home drunk, often bruised and bleeding from fights he'd become involved in. Nick knew his mother feared he was taking after his Dad. She'd tried to talk to him but he resented her interference and they ended up rowing more than they'd ever done.

Mac stopped Nick in the Long Pull one night as he was passing on his way to the bar. 'I want a word with you, lad.'

'Can't stop now, Mac. On me way to get some drinks in.' He tried to pull away but the Scot laid a restraining hand on his arm.

''Your mate here'll do that.' Something in Mac's voice told Nick he'd no alternative. A little mutinously, he passed a ten shilling note over to Ken, who'd offered to go to the bar with him.

Mac gestured to Nick to sit down and, without preliminaries, said, 'You haven't been to the garage this last couple of weeks.'

'I thought it were only a friendly arrangement.' Nick drew on the last of his cigarette and, with an exaggerated gesture, exhaled noisily.

'I took on extra work on the understanding that you'd be there to help.'

Nick stubbed his cigarette out. 'I did intend coming only...'

'You'd had too much to drink the night before,' Mac finished for him. 'What's up with you lad?'

It was the concern showing on Mac's dependable face that finally got through to Nick. He rubbed his temples with circular movements of his fingers. 'I don't know where to start.'

Mac sat back in his chair and pulled his glass towards him to take a drink. 'I've all night.'

Ken approached, carrying four pints of beer by the handles and stopped by the table, his eyebrows raised quizzically. Nick took one of the pints from him and dismissed him with a shake of his head. He took a long swallow, giving him time to order his thoughts, before answering. 'I'd been so looking forward to getting back to Civvy Street but now – what is it? – four months on, it all seems to have gone sour. I thought going back into labouring, having a bit of money in me pocket, would help, at least until I finish night school. But, when the weather was so bad in January and February and me hands were freezing to the shovel, I found myself wondering what the hell I was doing there. There's no challenge in it, you see, that's one thing I've to thank the Army for.'

'Did coming to the garage help?'

'Oh, yes. I was in me element. The only trouble was, it showed the labouring up for what it was, a dead end job. In the building trade, it's the tradesmen who get the money and the satisfaction.'

'If you enjoyed coming to the garage so much, why miss those last few Saturdays?'

'I told you, too much drink.' He looked down at the rings their glasses had made on the plain wooden table, unable to meet Mac's eyes.

Mac puffed on the pipe he'd refuelled while Nick was speaking. 'Drinking's an effective way of not having to think too much. I've done it myself. For the first few months after my wife and kiddie died, I was permanently sozzled.' As Nick lifted his head, Mac looked him pointedly in the eye. 'Are you sure you're not doing the same?'

'What do you mean?'

Mac gave him a quizzical look. 'Couldn't be anything to do with that girl – Kathy – you told me about, could it?'

'Happen you're right.' Nick shifted uncomfortably in his seat. 'The thing is, she made it clear last time I saw her that she didn't want owt more to do with me.' Then he grinned. 'Mind you, I did show off a bit in front of her fancy boyfriend. Not that he was much better behaved. I don't think she were too impressed with either of us.' His mood lighter now, he told Mac what had transpired at the Pike on Good Friday.

'And you've not seen her since?'

Nick shook his head. 'No, I've deliberately kept out of any place I thought she might be.'

'Chances are she regretted the remark as soon as she said it,' Mac suggested. 'I'll bet next time you see her, she'll be as right as ninepence.'

It amused Nick that the Scot often used certain Lancashire expressions. 'She still has the boyfriend,' he pointed out.

'Nothing to stop you being her friend.' He picked up his now nearly empty glass. 'In the meantime, I'd be glad if you'd keep coming to help me out. And work hard at night school.'

'I will, and I'm sorry I let you down, Mac.' He lifted his glass to the Scot who acknowledged the pact by raising his own.

In the week or so that followed, Nick, seeing sense in the advice Mac had given, had toned down the drinking and managed to avoid any fights. Until the last Saturday night in April, when they went to Bolton Palais, a dance hall they hadn't been to for some time.

By the time they got in, the ballroom was crowded, so much so that it was almost impossible to move. Round the perimeter, groups of girls chatted, skirts awhirl with starched petticoats, wafting 'Evening in Paris' or 'California Poppy' as they did so. Although there were a few Teddy boys dotted around, the lads at the Palais were mostly non-Teds, dressed in suits reminiscent of their Dad's demob suit and clearly unhappy at the invasion of yet more Teddy boys.

The girls didn't seem much happier with their presence either, more often than not refusing when asked to dance. Nick and Bragger laughed the rejections off and headed for the bar but Ray, becoming more infuriated with every brush-off, was not so inclined. The last straw for him came when a lass with bubble-cut hair and large earrings, looked him up and down and said, 'I'm not that hard up.'

A non-Ted standing nearby laughed and taunted him. 'Who knitted your face and dropped a stitch?'

Within minutes, a fight developed and Nick and Bragger were forced reluctantly to back Ray and Ken. Hopelessly outnumbered, even though some of the other Teds joined them, they had to retreat, still defending themselves, in the direction of the foyer. By that time, pockets of other fights had broken out as people shoved and pushed and girls screamed in panic. As the four reached the relative safety of the foyer – no sign of the door attendants now, they must have gone into the ballroom to try and stop the fight – Nick heard the clanging bell of a police car. 'Quick!' he said, 'downstairs to the cloakrooms. There might be a fire exit there.'

Thankfully there was, of the push bar kind, and as they burst into a back alley, two police cars pulled up outside. Staying where they were till the coppers had gone inside, they moved to the front of the building. By that time, many people were leaving and they were able to mix with the crowd until someone spotted them and shouted, 'There they are! The ones who started it!'

As attention turned to them, Nick yelled, 'Run! Don't stay together!' Blind to the direction he was running in, he twisted and turned down back streets until he found himself at the top end of Bradshawgate. Winded and with a stitch in his side, he bent, hands on his knees, as he struggled for breath, wondering if the others had got away too.

Glancing at his watch, he saw, that if he hurried, he'd be able to catch the last bus to Horwich but by the time he reached the terminus, the bus had gone. In any case, it had been full, he was told by a morose and unsympathetic inspector. Putting two fingers up behind the man's back, he made his way over to the taxi rank outside the station, an expensive option but perhaps he'd find someone willing to share the cost at least part of the way.

Trinity Street was surprisingly busy, with people crossing and re-crossing the thoroughfare, some running for buses, others swearing in despair as they realised, like Nick, that they had missed the last one. A formidable queue for taxis had been swollen by people pouring out of the station, perhaps from one of the Saturday night excursions to Blackpool. There seemed to be few taxis about and accepting that he was in for a long wait, he joined the queue. Despondency, a usual reaction to the adrenaline rush during a fight, set in and he sagged slightly into himself.

After half an hour or so, the queue was only slightly smaller and that only because people had left to walk home. He was contemplating doing the same when some people in front of him left the queue and he caught sight of a tall slim figure, wearing a familiar olive green coat, a few paces in front of him. Disbelieving at first, he straightened up and moved slightly to one side to see better. 'Kathy?'

She turned at the sound of his voice. 'Nick!'

His spirits soared as he realised she actually looked pleased to see him. So Mac had been right. He left his place in the queue to join her, to remarks such as, 'Oy, you, get back in line,' to which he gave a swift riposte. 'So you missed the bus too?' he asked as he reached her side.

She shifted her weight from one foot to the other as if to ease the discomfort. 'No, I was in time but the bus was full. I'd arranged to meet Carole here in case we became separated so I'm assuming she managed to get on even though I couldn't see her.'

'How come you weren't together?'

'We'd been at the Palais but it was so crowded, we made this arrangement just in case. Then, while Carole was dancing, a fight broke out. The police came and I left as quickly as I could,' she explained.

'You were at the Palais tonight? So was I.'

'I didn't see you.'

'Not surprised with the crowd in there.' He was jostled to one side as some drunk barged past him.

'Were you involved in the fight?'

'Not willingly, I can tell you,' he said ruefully.

'Did you get hurt?'

Was he imagining the note of concern in her voice? He put up a hand to his face, rubbing his jaw. 'A bit battered and bruised but nowt I can't handle. I'm more bothered about the others.'

'Perhaps they managed to catch a bus,' she reasoned.

'Let's hope so.' He gave her a quizzical look. 'How come you're not out with the boyfriend? Another rugby weekend?'

'No, he had to go down to London for some award ceremony with his boss.' The tightness in her voice told him it was a sore subject with her so he said nothing.

They stood for some moments in silence before Nick spoke again. 'Look, we're getting nowhere fast here. How do you fancy walking home?'

'Walking?' she squeaked, looking down at her high heels. 'But it's about five or six miles.'

'It's better than standing here half of the night with no guarantee of a taxi,' he reasoned. 'There's only been a couple in the last half hour or so.'

'I'm not sure if I can do it.'

'Me and the lads have done it a time or two, usually from Wigan or Chorley. It's not bad if you've got company.'

Still unsure, she hesitated, then seemed to make up her mind. 'OK, let's go.'

Peeling away from the queue, they set off in the direction Nick had indicated, with Kathy muttering under her breath, 'I must be mad.'

Elated that he was going to spend the next hour or so in her company, he said, 'Join the club!'

* * *

Back in Winter Street, Joyce was warming her cold toes at the remnants of the fire when she heard a subdued knock at the front door. She rose quickly, not wanting to wake the rest of the family. Her mother was always tired out, physically as well as emotionally, after the trek to Manchester to see Dad in Strangeways. Thinking perhaps Nick had forgotten his key, she opened the door to find Bragger on the doorstep. 'Hello, Joyce. Sorry to bother you at this time of night but is your Nick in?'

'No, he's not back yet.' She drew a deep breath in an attempt to still her pounding heart.

'Bugger! I hope that doesn't mean he's got caught.'

'What do you mean, caught? He's not in trouble, is he?' she said, a clutch of fear making her voice rise.

'Not as far as I know.' He hesitated. 'Can I come in for a few minutes and I'll tell you all about it without half the neighbours knowing.'

She held the door open for him. 'Go through to the kitchen,' she whispered, 'but don't, for goodness sake, make a noise or we'll have me Mam down on us like a ton of bricks.'

'Why? We're not doing owt wrong.'

'She may not see you sneaking round here so late in quite the same way,' she warned.

'She wouldn't mind,' he grinned cheekily. 'By now, she's used to me bringing Nick home the worse for wear. She's even let me sleep on the sofa in your front room a time or two.'

'Cold comfort there, then,' she quipped to cover up the fact that, whenever he had done so, she had been all too aware of his presence. 'Do you want a brew? There's still some in the pot.'

Settled with a mug of tea in the opposite chair to Joyce, Bragger recounted the story of the fight.

'How did you get away?' she said when he'd finished.

'I belted hell for leather up St George's Road and hopped on the first bus that came. It happened to be the Chorley bus so it dropped me at the Craven Heifer,' he explained. 'I don't know what happened to Ray and Ken.'

'When did you last see Nick?' Although she knew her older brother was well able to take care of himself, she was still concerned.

'Running in the opposite direction, towards the town centre. Happen he were hoping to catch the last bus.'

She noticed, for the first time, the dried blood above Bragger's left eye-brow. 'Let me wash that cut for you.' She fetched a chipped enamelled bowl from under the sink, filled it with the remainder of water from the kettle and a drop or two of Dettol. With a clean piece of rag, she dabbed at the cut. As she got through the congealed crust, the warmth of the water started it bleeding again, though not profusely. 'It's a nasty cut. You could have done with a stitch or two.'

'Not a good idea under the circumstances,' he said, giving her a rueful grin. 'Have you got any sticking plaster?'

'With two young lads in the house? What do you think?'
Patting the wound dry and applying a plaster, she stood aside to admire the effect. 'There, a proper wounded hero.'

He took her hand and turning it palm upwards, kissed it. 'You've gentle caring hands, Joyce.'

'Comes in handy with younger brothers.' She tried to pull away but he tightened his hold.

'But have you got a gentle caring heart?'

'That's for me to know and for you to find out.'

'I'd give owt to find out.' He placed her hand on his chest. 'Can you feel me heart beating, Joyce?'

'You'd be in trouble if I couldn't.'

'Oh, Joyce, what am I going to do with you?'

'You could kiss me.' She couldn't believe afterwards she'd said that but when he placed his lips on hers, in a feather-light kiss, she was glad she had.

* * *

Despite her aching feet, Kathy was surprised to find she was enjoying the walk home with Nick. The night was cool rather than cold, with a refreshing breeze that rustled the trees and privet hedges of the large, privately owned houses lining either side of Chorley New Road. The sky above was clear with only a few scudding clouds playing hide and seek with the moon. She and Nick had talked and laughed almost non-stop which stopped her from thinking of the distance they still had to go. So far, they had walked with a respectful distance between them but as they crossed the cobbles of Beaumont Road, she went over on her ankle. She would have fallen had Nick not grabbed her arm and steadied her. Wincing with the pain, she stooped to rub it, still holding on to Nick and glad of his support. As she straightened up, he said, 'Your feet are suffering a bit, aren't they? Why don't you hold on to me? I promise I'll behave meself.'

'You'd better.' She put her weight tentatively on the offending foot.

He tucked her arm into his and pulled her closer to him, a gesture she appreciated. 'We'll help each other along.'

They reached Lostock before Kathy began to flag again, every step now becoming an agony, as much because she needed to relieve herself, as her feet hurting. Nick suggested they sing to while away the remaining miles, which they did, singing quietly so as not to disturb any householders. It was Nick's exaggerated rendition of 'Heartbreak Hotel' that reduced Kathy to hysterical giggles and forced her to stop as the pressure on her bladder increased. 'Stop it, Nick! I'm dying to...'

'To pee?' he finished for her. As she nodded, he pointed to what looked like an unmade lane. 'If you want to nip up there, I'll keep watch for you. Not that there's anyone about.' The roads, apart from the odd car, were quiet and since leaving the boundaries of Bolton, there'd been no other pedestrians.

Not sure which was worse, the discomfort she was feeling or the disquiet at having to relieve herself behind a convenient bush with Nick only feet away, she did as he suggested.

'Better?' he said as she reappeared. 'Do you mind keeping watch for me?' Nodding her agreement, she stood with her back to the lane, looking across at the darkened golf course opposite. As he joined her, moments later, he turned to her and took hold of her hand, squeezing it gently. 'Not too embarrassed, I hope?'

'A little,' she admitted, liking the feel of her own hand in his, 'but I'm more comfortable and there's only a mile or so now.'

She was aware of a different feeling between them, a yearning similar to that she'd experienced at the Pike. Her heart was pounding and her throat was tight with emotion. Why did this keep happening to her, whenever she was near Nick?

He must have sensed it too for, before they set off again, he turned to her. 'You know, Kathy, in spite of having to walk home, I've really enjoyed being with you tonight,' he said. 'I wish we could do it again.'

'I wouldn't mind but I think my feet might have something to say on the matter.'

'I wasn't meaning the walk necessarily, simply being with you...'

'Please don't say such things, Nick,' she pleaded. 'You're putting me in a difficult position.'

'I don't mean to but when I'm with you, it seems the most natural thing in the world.' The look he was giving her made her heart flutter and her stomach churn. Before she knew what was happening, he pulled her hard against his chest and his lips descended on hers. She was not prepared for the strength or depth of feelings his kiss aroused in her. As they drew apart, he said shakily, 'Oh, Kathy! I...'

She put her fingers to his lips, feeling their tempting fullness and wishing they were still on her own. 'We mustn't let that happen again.'

'You're right.' He loosed her and, drawing a ragged breath, said, 'Come on, I'd better get you home.'

Although they walked on, at a distance now, Kathy's senses were whirling, knowing that if he had reached out for her again, she would have gone into his arms gladly. With that kiss had come a sudden and demanding flare of passion that shook her and bore no resemblance to mere friendship.

Then, into the silence, he said, 'Are you and John serious now?'

Startled, she turned to look at him. 'I think so.'

'Then there's no chance for me?' His voice was grim.

'We're too different, you and I,' she prevaricated. 'We've nothing in common.'

'It wouldn't have owt to do with the fact that I'm in a dead-end job and can't offer you what he can?'

'No!' she burst out. 'I'm not like that.'

'Aren't you?'

'If you think that, you don't know me very well,' she snapped.

'As I'm beginning to realise,' he said bleakly. He didn't speak again until he said goodbye to her at the top of Travers Street.

Her sleep that night was fitful, troubled as she was by this fascination with Nick Roberts.

CHAPTER 11

The day after walking home with Nick – and that kiss – was the day John was to meet her parents for the first time and she was dreading it. Tea at the Talbots had been bad enough; tea with her parents – well, her mother – would be purgatory, if not for John then for her. Ten minutes before John was due to arrive, her mother was flitting round the room, plumping up the cushions again, tweaking ornaments another half inch or so and standing back to judge the effect. Finally, her father said, 'Vera, love, will you please sit down. You're making Kathy and me as twitchy as yourself.'

'I just want to make sure everything's perfect,' she huffed.

'Mum, John's not going to run his fingers across the top of the sideboard to see if you've dusted,' Kathy pointed out.

Vera did sit but kept stretching her head up so that she could see out of the window into the street beyond. When eventually the doorbell rang, she shot upright and patted her hair. Kathy made her way to the front door trying not to smile. She didn't know who was more nervous about this visit, she or her mother. Although he hadn't said anything, she knew that John had wondered why it had not taken place before now. After all, it was now the end of April and the meeting with his parents had taken place in early March. She'd been a few times to the Talbots but with each meeting, she had the feeling she was being evaluated and found wanting.

She opened the door to John, smiling a greeting. For this first meeting with her parents, he had chosen to be formal, with a suit and subdued tie. Yet she could tell he was nervous by the way he touched his already neat hair. As if sensing her assessment of him, he said. 'Will I do?'

'Mum and Dad will definitely approve,' she said. 'Dad's one of these old-fashioned men who believes that a man isn't properly dressed unless he's wearing a tie.'

'It's a good job I decided to wear one, then, isn't it? I nearly didn't.' As he stepped into the hall, he whispered, 'Do I get a kiss for luck?' and slid his arms round her. As his lips claimed hers, the memory of Nick's kiss last night caused her to draw back a little.

John seemed not to notice. 'That's better,' he said. He let her go, then pulled down the cuffs of his jacket down over his shirt cuffs. 'I'm ready.'

Drawing a deep breath, she opened the door into the sitting room. 'Mum, Dad, this is John.'

Both her parents rose from their seats but it was Ron who said first, 'Pleased to meet you, John,' and shook his hand.

'It's good to meet you both too,' John said, turning from her father to her mother.

As John shook her mother's hand, she simpered, 'Come and sit down here, John,' she said, patting the seat of the sofa nearest to her. 'Kathy, do sit down. You're making the place look untidy.' Kathy bit her lip to silence the retort she wanted to make but sat down obediently at John's side.

Seated once more but leaning forward a little, Ron said, 'I understand you're an accountant, John. Do you enjoy the work?'

'Very much so, Mr Armstrong. Some people think accountancy boring but I've always had a passion for figures.'

'Better than our Kathy then. She was always hopeless at maths,' Vera said.

'Kathy's strength was in her English,' Ron said, with a glance at his wife. 'Always got top marks, she did. I suppose you've seen the pieces she's been writing for Town Topics?'

'Yes, they're very good,' John agreed. 'She's seems to have a way with words.'

Kathy looked at John in pleased surprise. He'd said little to her about her writing and she'd assumed that he didn't think much to it, perhaps considering it not worthy of his notice.

Vera stood, smoothing down her skirt. 'Are you ready for some tea, John?' she asked. 'If so, I'll go and put the kettle on.'

'May I do anything to help?' John asked.

'No thank you, our Kathy will do that. Come along, Kathy,' she said, as she bustled into the kitchen.

Kathy followed her. 'Why are you doing this, Mum?' she hissed, filling the kettle up at the sink to cover her words.

'What are you talking about?'

'Trying to humiliate me in front of John,' Kathy retorted.

'I'm sure I don't know what you mean.' Vera had her back to Kathy and was busy rearranging the plates on the table, tweaking them here and there, as if they weren't already pristine neat.

Seething, Kathy turned to concentrate on warming the teapot and putting the tea in when the kettle had boiled.

'He seems a polite young man, with good manners,' Vera commented brightly, as if to break the tension between them.

'You should listen to yourself sometimes, Mum. You sound like he's being interviewed for a job,' which, in a way, he was, as a prospective husband for Kathy, albeit some time in the vague future. 'And you're putting on your posh telephone voice with him.'

'I am not,' her mother protested. Kathy sighed and said no more, busying herself instead with the preparations for tea.

By the time they were all seated round the kitchen table, the atmosphere had lightened enough for them all to converse naturally. Even Vera relaxed her 'on my best behaviour' mode enough to laugh at some tale John was relating. A couple of hours later, when it was time for John to leave, the atmosphere was comfortable enough for Kathy to know that her parents liked and fully approved of John. Despite this, when Kathy prepared to leave with him, her mother could not resist one last remark. 'Think on, Kathy, don't be late in. You've got work tomorrow.'

Only when she was seated in the car did she allow herself to relax. 'I'm sorry about my Mum, John. She was every bit as bad as I expected, treating me like a child.'

He put the car into gear and pulled away from the kerb, heading towards the bottom of the street where there was ample room for him to turn round. 'Who am I to judge with a mother like mine?'

She started to laugh. 'We're well blessed between us, aren't we, with our respective mothers?'

'Let's just forget them and start to enjoy our evening,' he said, as he manoeuvred the car round to face up the street. 'We've done our duty.'

'Above and beyond the call of, I think,' she giggled. 'One thing I would say is that you seem to have created a favourable impression on Mum and Dad.'

He risked taking his left hand off the wheel to cover hers where it lay on her thigh. 'It's important to me to know that, feeling as I do about you. And the future belongs to us, Kathy, not our parents.'

Driving round Anglezarke and Rivington in the pleasant evening sunshine, she settled down to enjoy John's company, putting thoughts of Nick the night before to the back of her mind with fierce determination.

* * *

Saturday morning chaos reigned in the house in Winter Street, with Nick dodging round bodies as he tried to get ready to go to the garage. Mam was trying to write a list of items she wanted Brian and Derek to get from the grocer's while the two boys pushed and shoved each other. Joyce was yawning as she made herself some tea and toast and Lucy was doing her best to ignore everyone by losing herself in a book.

'Will you two shut up?' Mary yelled, driven to the last of her patience. 'I can't think straight with you mithering me.'

The two lads looked to one another and subsided into an armchair, the springs groaning in protest under their joint weight. 'Sorry, Mam,' muttered Brian, nudging his brother and giggling as he did so. The two continued to shove each other but at least they did so in silence.

'Do you want me to go instead, Mam?' said Joyce. 'I'm off out later but I can go up the Lane first.'

'No, these two do precious little to earn their pocket money. It's the least they can do to run a few errands for me. Besides, you and Nick have done your share in the past, still do come to that.' Mary turned back to contemplating the list before her. 'There, I don't think I want owt else. Now you do know where you're going, don't you?'

Derek smirked. 'To the Co-op so's you'll get the Divi.'

95

Mary opened her purse and gave them a ten-shilling note. 'Mind you don't lose it now. If you do, you'll get no pocket money until it's all paid back.'

Brian carefully folded the note and put it into the top pocket of his shirt, under his Fair Isle pullover, handing the list to Derek to look after. 'We won't, Mam, we'll be careful.'

'Aren't you forgetting this?' Mary called as they reached the back door and held out a battered and much used shopping basket.

Nick dug into his own pocket. 'Here's a bob between you for being good lads and not grumbling.'

'Thanks, Nick, a tanner each'll buy some sweets and a couple of marbles.' Brian pocketed the shilling piece.

The two left, banging the back door as they did so, and the instant silence was more noticeable than the noise preceding it. Mary heaved a sigh of relief and started clearing the pots from the table.

'Where you off to then, Joyce?' Nick asked as he shrugged on his work jacket. Although Joyce turned away quickly, he couldn't help noticing the colour rise to her cheeks and wondered if he was missing something.

'Bolton. We've heard about a shop where, for a shilling in the pound deposit and a small weekly payment, you can buy the hit records.' She was fiddling with something on the sideboard and still had her back to them.

'What's the use of that?' Mary sprinkled some soap powder in the washing up bowl and turned the hot tap on. 'You haven't got a gramophone.'

'But we can listen to the records in the soundproof booths,' she pointed out. 'Anyway, Maureen's Dad's bought a new radiogram and says we can play our records on it.'

'There's a coincidence, Bragger was saying his Mam's bought one out of his Dad's insurance money,' Nick commented as he too left by the back door.

In the alleyway between Winter Street and Abraham Street, the sky above Nick was a clear blue with only a few clouds, promising a fine and reasonably warm day. On days such as these even the back street, with its broken-down gates, crumbling brick walls, bits of old prams that boys had discarded after using the wheels to make go-carts, didn't look as grim. Climbing the slight incline that led to Lee Lane, he could see up Albert Street and beyond to the Pike. It helped focus his attention away from the grey monotony of tightly packed terraced houses, the smoke issuing forth from mill and domestic chimneys and the foul smelling blue haze from the Works.

Over a brew at the garage, he told Mac about his walk home with Kathy. He'd thought about her a lot this past week.

'You are keen on this lass, aren't you?' Mac said now as Nick finished telling him.

Nick pondered the question. He'd tried to analyse his feelings for her. He only knew he'd never been this comfortable with anyone before. 'I don't rightly know what I feel about her, if I'm honest,' he admitted. 'When we're together, it seems so right, so natural. Yet there's this other chap, John.'

'She might be as confused as you are.' Mac picked up his pipe and starting tamping its contents down.

'If her response to me were owt to go by, then yes, you're right.' Nick drained his tea down to the last dregs. 'But what's the point, Mac? She's made it clear she doesn't feel the same. And there's no way would it work even if she were free. Her parents wouldn't approve of her going out with a Teddy boy. She's another year to go before she's 21 and can please herself.'

'I've always thought it a bit daft to have a 'coming of age' when you get the key of the door and supposedly more freedom,' Mac said, using his pipe as a pointer. 'I mean what can you do the day after you're 21 that you can't do the day before?'

Nick was struck as always at the older man's common sense. He'd come to value his friendship. 'You've got a point but I think her parents are a bit old-fashioned.'

'And probably over-protective with her being the only one.' The pipe was waving about again.

'Aye, Mam's a bit more lenient, especially with Dad being away. She'd be forever on to us, otherwise. Tell you what, though, Mac,' Nick mused, 'I don't enjoy me nights out with me mates like I used to though I don't mind going out with Bragger.'

'What happens when he meets a girl and wants to settle down?'

'Bragger? Settle down? No chance!' Nick scoffed.

* * *

Early one morning in mid-May, with the sun shining higher in the sky and a warm breeze chasing the litter across Victoria Square, Kathy stepped off the bus opposite the Town Hall. Like many of the other buildings in Bolton, the Town Hall's imposing architecture was soot-blackened from a century of domestic and factory chimneys.

It had been a difficult couple of weeks. She hadn't been able to forget what had happened during that walk home with Nick. It didn't help that she hadn't seen much of John as he'd had to work late almost every night. On the nights he hadn't worked, he'd been training. When she was with John, she felt safe, protected against any threats. And Nick definitely posed a threat to her peace of mind. Immersed in her thoughts, a piercing wolf whistle caused her to turn even as she blushed.

It was Nick, grinning as he caught up with her. 'Kathy! Didn't you hear me shout?'

'Sorry, I was miles away.' She hoped the breeze would cool her burning cheeks. 'Are you working near here?' She indicated the shabby, clay-caked trousers shoved into sturdy boots and the disreputable wind-cheater open at the front to display a check shirt beneath. His face had taken on the ruddy glow of the outdoor worker and his hair, normally immaculate, was ruffled by the wind. This workaday Nick had about him a dry, dusty, faintly oily smell and she tried to quell the tingle of excitement it gave her.

He nodded in the direction of Newport Street where she could see some hoardings round a building site. 'I've been running a few errands for the lads, bacon butties, baccy, cigs. You off to work?'

She glanced at her watch. 'Yes. I'd better be going or I'll be late. My boss is a bit of a stickler about punctuality.'

As she edged away, he sidestepped so that her way was blocked. 'Meet me at dinner-time for a chat?'

'I don't think that's a good idea.'

'Come on, Kathy, a cup of tea and a sandwich. There's no harm in that,' he pleaded. 'I have me dinner about 12-ish. Can you manage that?'

It wouldn't be wise; they might bump into John. Then she remembered that he was at a mill in Egerton and unlikely to make the trip into town during his lunch break. 'I can't promise but I'll see what I can do.'

'What about meeting in that new coffee bar in Old Hall Street?'

'OK. Now you'd better get going or you'll have everyone complaining about their bacon butties being cold.'

'Bugger! I'd forgotten about them.' With a quick wave of his bag-laden hand, he set off at a run.

Nick wasn't there when she got to La Casa Blanca coffee bar and she tucked herself in a corner till he arrived, taking in her surroundings. It hadn't been open long and this was the first time she'd been in. She liked the bamboo screens, the empty Chianti bottles hung in pairs on the walls and the posters advertising Spanish bullfights, while the Italian coffee machine hissed and steamed like some instrument of the devil. It was so far removed from somewhere like the Temperance Bar as to seem exotic.

She shook her head at the invitation to order from the red-faced waitress, saying that she was waiting for someone. 'Oh, that explains it,' the girl said, her face red from the heat and exertion, 'there's a lad outside says he's meeting someone only he's not allowed in because he's in work clothes.'

Nick didn't see her come out. He was jigging up and down in front of the window, trying to peer into the dimly lit interior as she joined him. 'Waiting for someone, Nick?'

'Kathy! They wouldn't let me in.' He'd cleaned himself up a little but there was no mistaking his workman-like appearance. Again, there was that absurd tingle of excitement.

'Never mind, let's go to the Market Hall. They'll serve us there and it's cheaper, too.'

99

As he turned, Nick collided with a middle-aged lady coming through the doorway, followed by a younger woman. Although he apologised immediately, the woman said in a well-modulated but loud voice, 'What you could do with, young man, is a spell in the Army. That'd soon knock some manners into you.'

Kathy's cheeks burned and she couldn't stop herself from saying, 'My friend has done his National Service and more besides.'

'I do beg your pardon,' the woman said but in a condescending manner.

Looking uncomfortable, the younger woman said, 'Come along, mother, before you say anything else.'

As Kathy and Nick made their way to the solid Victorian edifice of the Market Hall, Nick said huffily, 'I can stick up for meself, you know.'

'I'm sorry. I shouldn't have said anything but she reminded me so much of John's mother, with her middle-class accent and superior attitude.' She knew that by speaking of John's mother, she'd reminded them both that she had a life that didn't involve Nick and never would. It was as if they were circling round each other, seeking boundaries for this strange relationship.

It was only when they were seated in one of the tea bars with their mugs of tea and plate of sandwiches that they begin to relax. 'It's a bit different than…,' she began.

'Not the same as the Casa Blanca,' he said at the same time. They both laughed. 'Sorry about not being able to get in there.'

'It doesn't matter. We'll be more comfortable here.' She indicated their companions in the small tea bar, almost all middle-aged ladies wearing hats or headscarves and clothes of a pre-war vintage.

'What have you been doing with yourself?' he asked as he spooned sugar into his tea.

'Writing bits for Town Topics,' she said mischievously.

'Really? Any luck with them?'

'A few have been published.'

His face lit with a beaming smile, and he said, 'Kathy, that's brilliant. I can't believe I'm in the presence of an author.'

'Hardly that,' she protested.

'Well, a writer then.' He drained the last of the tea in his mug. 'Is there any chance of you taking it further?'

'It's not something I've given much thought to but I do enjoy writing them.'

'Could you do it for a living though? All day and every day?'

She pondered for a few seconds then said, 'I think so.' She was conscious of the notebook, now nearly full of her scribblings, in her handbag.

'Then maybe it's summat you should follow up,' he said.

'I'd have to think about it,' she said, glancing at her watch, amazed at how quickly the time had passed while she was with Nick.

As they walked towards Victoria Square where they would separate, he turned to her and quietly said, 'Meet me again sometime, Kathy?'

For an instant, she allowed herself a tantalising glimpse of the two of them, at the pictures, walking up Rivington. Then she clamped down on the thought and shook her head. 'I'm sorry, Nick. I can't do that. It wouldn't be fair to John.'

'The boyfriend? I wish you luck with that one,' he said and stalked off.

She gazed after him in astonishment then shrugged and walked on, feeling suddenly deflated.

101

CHAPTER 12

'I'm not sure about this,' John said, as they got out of the car in Mason Street.

'I know the Picture House isn't exactly the Odeon in Bolton but it's not a flea pit either. And besides,' she reminded him, 'you were the one desperate to see this film.'

'You think I'm being a snob again.' He tucked her hand into his as they walked round the corner. 'And perhaps I am.'

She laughed and squeezed his hand. 'You'd have something to complain about if it was the Palace. There, if it's raining, you can't hear the film for the drumming on the tin roof. And Johnny's, now that really is a flea pit.'

He gave a mock shudder. 'OK, I take your point. I won't say another word.'

'And it's the last chance we'll have to see this film. By the time films are shown in Horwich, there's nowhere else for them to go,' she reasoned. 'Now we'd better hurry, we're a bit late as it is.' A dwindling queue was snaking through the foyer to the ticket office.

As they settled themselves in their seats towards the back of the cinema, Kathy was glad of the easy companionship she had with John. It probably wasn't the most exciting of relationships but then too much excitement wasn't always a good thing, as she knew only too well after meeting Nick Roberts again. Thankfully, she hadn't seen him since that lunchtime in Bolton a couple of weeks ago when he'd walked off in a huff and she'd been able to put him to the back of her mind.

With an effort, she concentrated on the Pathé Newsreel. The continued bombings and ambushes in Cyprus were the main item. There were rumblings from Egypt over the fact that the United States had refused to help with the financing of the Aswan Dam.

As the lights went up for the interval and John rose to buy ice-creams, Kathy looked round at their close neighbours but didn't see anyone she knew. In any case, these seats were mostly taken up with courting couples. Everyone else was likely to be in the cheaper ones lower down. Or was she subconsciously looking for Nick? She knew he visited the cinema a couple of times a week. Most young people in Horwich did, with the programme changing every few days.

The main film, 'The Seven Year Itch,' followed and despite her initial reservations, Kathy became engrossed in it. She was comfortable with John holding her hand, glad that he restrained from trying to kiss her as so many courting couples did, so that she could concentrate. Seemingly all too soon, the film ended, the lights came on and they all stood for the National Anthem.

'What did you think to the film, after all?' John asked as they made their way to the exit. He knew she hadn't been particularly keen on seeing it.

'I enjoyed it, much better than I expected,' she admitted. 'Bet I know which part you liked the most,' she teased. 'You and the rest of the men in the audience.'

A hand firmly in the small of her back, he guided her towards the exit. 'You mean when Marilyn's skirt blew up around her waist as she walked over a subway grating?' He grinned. 'That was a classic cinema moment, I reckon.'

'It was certainly tastefully done,' she agreed. 'She is beautiful, isn't she?'

'She certainly is. Didn't think much to the bloke playing opposite her though. He seemed a bit dopey to me.'

'I think that was the part he was playing. He's probably not like that in real life,' she reasoned.

'That's my girl, always thinking the best of people.'

She wished he wouldn't sound so patronising but she suspected he didn't realise he was doing it. 'Better than always thinking the worst of people.'

Concentrating on getting out of the cinema and engrossed in their conversation, they weren't taking any notice of anyone around them until a voice reached them as the last of one-and-ninepennies met up with the people from the more crowded cheaper seats in the foyer.

'Well, well, look who's here. Slumming it, are we?' It was Nick, arms folded across his chest, legs apart, blocking their way. Sally Simcox was by his side, a mulish look on her heavily made-up face, and wearing a tight black skirt and a mannish-style black coat that almost drowned her small frame.

John dropped his arm from Kathy's back and stood up to Nick, his face stormy. 'It's nothing to do with you,' he retorted.

'Don't come the high and mighty with me, mate! You're the one who's intruding here. I'm on me own territory,' Nick's own face was set in angry lines and Kathy's heart sank.

'Don't, John,' she said, plucking at his arm.

John drew himself up to his full height and squared his shoulders. 'Look, you – thug – I've paid good money to take my girlfriend to see a film. You've no right to butt in.'

'Oh, don't I? Bet you don't know what your girlfriend were up to a couple of weeks ago,' Nick taunted.

The shock of what Nick had inferred hit Kathy like a blow and she took a step back, her heart hammering. Was he going to mention their walk home? And that kiss?

'What on earth are you talking about?' John's curiosity was aroused.

Kathy knew that she had to do something to avert the pending disaster. 'I've had enough of both of you sparring like a couple of kids, I'm off home,' she retorted and stalked off towards the bridge that crossed over the railway tracks.

John caught up with her as she reached the brow of the hill and pulled at her arm. 'Kathy! Where are you going?'

She shrugged his hand away. 'Leave me alone! I'm going home.'

'But we came in the car,' he reasoned.

She stopped then. 'I don't care. I'll walk.'

John tentatively reached for her hand. 'I'm sorry about the scene back there,' he said. 'I don't know what it is about that Teddy boy. He riles me up every time I see him.'

'He had no right to say the things he did. Even for a Teddy boy, he's not usually so badly behaved.' She knew why, of course. He was jealous but she could hardly tell John that.

'No matter what you say, I'm guessing he'd like to be more than friends with you. He's no chance,' he scoffed, 'the two of you have nothing in common.'

104

This was a bit too near the truth for Kathy and she chose not to say anything.

John stopped and half turned to her. 'Anyway, what did he mean when he asked if I knew what you'd been up to a few weeks ago?'

She'd been hoping he'd forgotten the taunt and was glad it was nearly dark now to cover up the colour on her cheeks. 'Oh, I saw him in Bolton one lunchtime and we went for a cup of tea.' She hoped this would be enough to satisfy him.

He looked at her sideways. 'You never mentioned it.'

'Why should I? It meant nothing to me,' she was quick to say.

He raised her chin with his fingers. 'Am I forgiven for letting him get to me?'

'There's nothing to forgive,' she said and raised her lips for his kiss.

* * *

'I want a word with you, young lady.' Vera was standing, arms folded tightly under her bosom, in the doorway between the sitting room and the hall.

As she hung her coat up, Kathy knew from long experience that she was in for a telling-off. It was the last thing she needed. She was tired, hungry and had been looking forward to getting home. Now she wanted to walk out again. Instead, she sighed and said, 'What have I done now, Mum?'

'Don't come that tone of voice with me, young lady.' Her mother's voice began to rise. 'You know very well what you've done.'

'I don't, Mum, I swear I don't. Now can I go and at least sit down? I've had to stand all the way home.'

Despite the belligerent stance, Vera stepped aside to let Kathy pass into the sitting room. She sank into the comfy depths of the sofa while her mother perched on the edge of her chair, knees and feet tucked together, hands clasped on her lap.

'Now are you going to tell me what this is about?' Kathy asked, trying not to let her annoyance show.

'Mrs Westbury saw you outside the Picture House the other night.' The statement came bursting out as if it had been fermenting in her mother's mind for the best part of the day.

'That nosy old biddy!' Mrs Westbury lived on the opposite side of the street and made it her business to know everyone else's.

'That's no way to speak of your elders.'

'But not betters,' she muttered.

'I'm warning you, Kathy!'

She took a deep breath, knowing they'd get nowhere by yelling at each other. 'Calm down, Mum, and tell me what you think you know.'

'That you and John were involved in an argument outside the Picture House with a Teddy boy.' She ticked her fingers like items from a list. 'Then Mrs Westbury said she saw you having words with John as the bus passed.'

'I wasn't involved in the argument outside the Picture House. In fact I walked away from it, which is why John came after me.'

'You don't deny that there was some sort of row?'

'There's no point, is there?' Kathy pushed the shoes off her feet, one after the other. 'I was seen and that's all there is to it.'

Vera sank back into the depths of the chair, her whole demeanour one of dejection. 'Oh, Kathy, how could you show yourself up like that? And with a Teddy boy? What will people think?'

'Mum, I don't care what people think. It's nothing to do with them. It was a bit of confrontation with Nick Roberts and I walked away from it.' She knew her voice had a hard edge to it but now that she'd turned twenty, surely she had the right to speak out?

'That was Nick Roberts?' Vera almost squeaked. 'But he's a Teddy boy!'

Kathy reached out to touch her mother's arm in the hope of calming her down. 'Nick might be a Teddy boy but he's not such a bad lad, Mum, when you get to know him.'

'But his father's in prison,' Vera wailed.

'That's hardly Nick's fault, is it?' she flashed back. She removed her hand and sat back in the sofa. Sometimes there was no budging her mother from such entrenched attitudes. 'When I think that someone like that could come between you and John, I could cry.' She did, indeed, seem on the point of crying.

'That's not going to happen. I'm going out with John, aren't I?'

Vera drew a deep breath then said, 'Are you sure there's nothing going on between you and this...this Teddy boy?'

'Of course not. You worry too much.' As soon as the words were out of her mouth, she knew it had been the wrong thing to say.

'Of course I worry; it's what mothers do.' Vera rose from her chair. 'Well, we'll see what your father has to say about your behaviour when he comes home.'

In the event, Ron Armstrong said very little. He returned from work as Vera was bustling about in the kitchen in hurt silence. Kathy herself was reading that evening's Town Topics where she'd had another piece published. Her father looked tired and his face had a drawn look, causing a little niggle of worry in Kathy. Since he'd had flu, he'd been constantly tired and his bones ached, he said. She was sure, too, that his cough was getting worse.

When tackled after tea, all he said was, 'I'm sure our Kathy knows what she's doing.'

'I might have known you'd stick up for the girl.'

'I don't see what we can do, Vera love, short of locking her in her room and that sort of thing went out with the Victorians,' he reasoned in a tired voice.

'More's the pity.' She flounced out of the room and they could hear her filling the kettle for another cup of tea.

'I don't know, Dad, it seems the harder I try to please Mum, the less I succeed,' Kathy said.

'Don't be too hard on her, love,' her father said. 'You know her bark's worse than her bite.'

'I know, Dad,' Kathy sighed. She came behind her father where he sat in the armchair, put her arms round his neck, kissed

107

the top of his head, catching a faint whiff of Brylcreem as she did so. 'I love you, Dad.'

He patted her arm with a sturdy hand as if uncomfortable with such words. 'I know, love, I know.'

CHAPTER 13

One Saturday morning in early June, Nick, feeling pleasantly tired after a satisfactory morning at the garage, walked into the kitchen to find his mother sitting at the table with a cold, scummy-ringed mug of tea. He sat down opposite her at the table, took in her careworn face and tired smile and said, 'What's up, Mam?'

She glanced towards Lucy, playing 'house' with her doll in the corner behind one of the easy chairs and oblivious to them. 'I've had word from your Dad', she said quietly, 'telling me when he'll be home. Even though I was expecting it, it's shaken me a bit.'

'But you knew it would be soon, didn't you?'

She nodded, then, with a cautionary glance at Lucy, she said, 'I'm not sure I want him home anymore.' Her voice was so low Nick struggled to hear her.

He looked at her, stunned. 'Oh, Mam, I don't know what to say.'

She grasped his hand tightly with hers. 'We've managed all right, haven't we?'

'Probably better. There hasn't been the same atmosphere. And at least you know where you are with the money.'

'It's not as if the great lump is much use for owt else other than giving me babies. Well, there'll be no more of them,' she said, removing her hands and Nick had to smile at her ferocity.

'Have you tried talking to him?'

'It's difficult to talk in the visitor's room of a prison.' She gave a weary sigh. 'He says he's changed but can I believe him? It might simply be an act to get him through his time.'

'You could always tell him you don't want him home,' he pointed out.

She shook her head sadly. 'He's nowhere else to go. And he does love his children. I have to tell him every little detail when I visit him.'

'Bet he doesn't want to know about me,' he said grimly.

'He always asks about you,' Mary prevaricated.

109

'It's all right, Mam. I know Dad and I have a love-hate relationship.'

'Thanks, Nick. It's really helped talking to you like this.'

He reached out to touch her arm, giving it a squeeze. 'I'll always be here for you, Mam, if there's a problem. I'm older now and can handle meself – and him – better.'

'You're a good lad, Nick.'

He heard voices coming from the front room and seconds later, Joyce appeared in the doorway between the two rooms. 'I've brought a visitor,' she said and, to Nick's stunned surprise, ushered Kathy into the kitchen. 'Mam,' she said, with a mischievous glance at her brother, 'this is Kathy Armstrong, a friend of Nick's.'

He rose to suddenly unsteady feet. 'Kathy! What are you doing here?'

She glanced diffidently at Nick then at his mother. 'I had a slight argument with the pavement and Joyce rescued me.'

'What she should be telling you, Nick, is that it were my fault,' Joyce said. 'She were passing the Post Office as I were going out and I knocked her flying.'

'Clumsy clot!' Nick teased, ruffling Joyce's head.

'No, I was the one to blame,' Kathy said. 'My Mum's always telling me off for day-dreaming.'

'And I were putting the change in me purse and not looking where I was going.' Turning to her mother, Joyce continued. 'As she were in such a mess, I insisted she come here so we could clean her knee up.'

'Oh, you poor lass! Can you roll your stocking down?' Mary said.

With a blushing glance at Nick, Kathy turned her back on him and fumbled under her skirts. Though he looked away, he couldn't help fantasising about white thighs, stocking tops and a lacy suspender belt. Not surprisingly, he experienced a familiar tightening in his groin.

Mam indicated the chair she'd just vacated. 'Sit here, love, and I'll bathe it for you.' She prepared a bowl with hot water and a couple of drops of Dettol, then bathed the graze, causing

Kathy to wince. 'Sorry, lass, I should've warned you it'd sting a bit.'

Lucy peeped out from behind the armchair then sidled closer to Nick, resting her slight body against his knee.

Kathy, seeing her for the first time, smiled and said, 'Hello, what's your name?'

Nick put a loving arm round the child. 'This is Lucy, the baby of the family.'

'I'm not a baby,' protested Lucy. 'I'm six and a half.'

'Sorry, sweetheart, I know you're a big girl now.' He patted the little girl's head tenderly. 'Look, why don't you show Kathy your doll, take her mind off her sore knee.'

Mollified, Lucy brought the doll round to Kathy to be introduced and, while Mary finished cleaning and dressing Kathy's knee, she chattered away. 'You've made a friend there, Kathy,' Nick said.

'Is she your girlfriend, Nick?' Lucy asked, all innocence.

'Lucy!' Mam said, while Kathy blushed again and Joyce giggled with embarrassment.

'Mind your own business, young lady,' Nick said and turned to Kathy. 'You've not met the other two rebels, have you?'

'Your young brothers? No, not yet.'

'There's a treat in store for you.'

Mam turned to Kathy and said, 'You'll have a bit of dinner with us, lass?' It'll only be fish and chips but you're welcome.'

'That'd be lovely, if you're sure I won't be in the way.'

Mam laughed. 'Not likely. We're always a bit rough and ready on a Saturday, so much to do, you see, with us working during the week.'

'Thanks, but please let me contribute.' She made a move towards her bag on the table, wincing as she did so.'

'Wouldn't dream of it. What's a few penn'orth of chips, anyroad?' Mam stood and reached for her purse on the mantelpiece. 'Will you go to the chippie, Joyce, love? I'll brew some tea and butter the bread.'

While Mam and Joyce sorted out cash for the errand, Nick said, 'I think I'll call you Diddle-Diddle-Dumpling from now on.'

She gave him a quizzical look. 'The nursery rhyme – one stocking off, one stocking on.'

'You'll get a slap in a minute if you don't stop teasing the lass,' his mother said. 'Lucy, be a good girl and see if our Joyce has got a spare pair of stockings that Kathy can borrow.'

As the child scuttled up the stairs, Kathy tried to pull her skirt down over her bare bandaged leg. 'I must look a real mess,' she said.

'You look all right to me,' he said and, again, there was that momentary sense of connection between the two of them, even in the humdrum atmosphere of his own home. Then, squirming a little, he remembered that last time they'd met he'd so nearly compromised her. 'I'm sorry about what happened a couple of weeks ago. I hope what I said didn't give you any problems with John.'

'It caused me more problems with my mother. Our nosy neighbour, Mrs Westbury, had seen the whole thing and told my Mum.' She sighed. 'And she's one of these people who worries about what other people think.'

'I really am sorry. I don't know what came over me.' He had, though, seeing her with John at the pictures had caused a sudden spurt of jealousy that, combined with the memory of their kiss, caused him to open his mouth without thinking.

'If it wasn't that, it would have been something else.'

The tension between them was broken by the entry of the two boys through the back door. Brian, seeing Kathy, stopped abruptly and Derek, on his heels, crashed into him. 'Ow! What'd you do that for?' he yelled, rubbing his shoulder.

'Come in, you two, and wash your hands. Joyce'll be back soon with our dinner.' Mary grabbed each one by the arm and pushed them towards the sink. 'This is Kathy, a friend of Nick's, so think on you behave.'

'Lo, Kathy,' they chorused, as they washed their hands at the sink.

'The slightly larger one is Brian, the eldest...' Nick began.

'I'm twelve,' Brian interrupted.

'...And the other's Derek. He's ten.'

'Nearly eleven!'

'Yah, you'll never catch up with me!' jeered Brian. 'I'll always be the eldest.'

In reply, Derek launched himself at Brian and the two fell to the floor, water splashing everywhere from their still wet hands.

'Ignore them, Kathy, they're always like this,' Mary said, yanking them both upright by their collars and holding them apart.

Lucy appeared at the bottom of the stairs, puffing a little from her exertions. 'I couldn't find any stockings like Kathy's. Will these do?' What she held up was an old pair of thick lisle stockings that Mam wore when the weather was cold.

'Welcome to the madhouse, Kathy,' said Nick, laughing.

* * *

Walking home from the pub late on the following Friday evening, Nick's thoughts were full of Kathy when she had come to their house last Saturday. She'd looked stunning in a full-skirted summer dress and bolero, with her hair cascading round her face in waves. Over the course of a couple of hours they'd talked easily over the table, unaware of the time passing. It was only when Kathy glanced at her watch and jumped up saying her mother would be wondering where she'd got to, that the spell was broken.

The house in Winter Street, was in darkness at this hour of the night. Before going into the kitchen, he reached inside and flicked on the light switch, to see the figure of his younger brother sitting in an armchair, a cigarette in his hand. 'Bloody hell, Phil! I didn't know you were due home on leave.' Nick sank into the easy chair facing him, noting that Phil had filled out, seemed older somehow, and more closely resembled their mother, with his fair hair and blue-grey eyes. He and Nick had never been particularly close but Nick was pleased to see him now. Phil hadn't been home much since he'd started his National Service and Nick himself had been away much of the time before that.

Phil leaned back to look at Nick, the grin on his face softening an underlying seriousness. 'I've got a forty-eight hour pass and decided to come home.'

'Well, it's good to see you.' Nick leaned forward and shook his hand, the gesture a rare physical one. 'You were taking a chance sitting in the dark, weren't you?'

'What do you mean?'

'Had you forgotten the business with the cockroaches?'

'I remember us allus turning the light on before we went into a room but I can't remember why, I didn't take much notice at the time.' Phil reached for the ashtray on the table and knocked the ash off his cigarette into it.

'It were when our Joyce were a baby and Mam had come downstairs to get her a bottle,' Nick reminded him. 'As she switched on the light, she saw dozens of cockroaches scurrying for the darkness in all directions. Her screams woke us all up.'

'Hell, yes, I remember now. It was summat to do with Mrs Greenhalgh next door, wasn't it?'

'Ay, she'd put some stuff down to kill them off but it just made them seek new lodgings – our house. The Council came round to treat both houses and that seemed to cure the problem.' Nick reached for his own cigarettes. 'We're all still cautious, though, you never know with these old houses.'

Nick brewed them both some tea and, in all-too-rare companionship, the two sat down by the dying fire and reminisced about their shared childhood. An hour or so later, the fire now completely dead, and a full ashtray between them, Phil said, 'Do you remember the time Mam threw a mug of tea at Dad?'

'And she were left with the handle while the mug and the tea hit Dad,' said Nick. 'And what about when she threw the teapot at him and it smashed against the wall.' He leaned back and pointed to the wall behind him. 'The stain's still there.'

'No wonder she retaliated like that, he's such an aggravating sod,' Phil said, serious now. 'Isn't he due out soon?'

'Next week.' Nick, too, became serious. 'I tell you, Phil, I'm not looking forward to it.'

'Makes me glad I'm out of the way.'

'You'll be finished next year though, won't you?'

Phil was silent for moment, then said, 'That's one of the reasons I've come home. I want to sign on as a regular, make the RAF me career.'

Nick leaned forward in his chair, looking at his brother in a different light. 'That's a turn up for the book. What made you decide that?'

'There's nowt for me in Horwich,' Phil explained. 'I couldn't wait to get away, don't particularly like coming back.'

'We'd noticed,' Nick said.

'What's there for me here? Go into the Works like Dad, like most Horwich men? I want more than that, Nick.'

'You're not on your own, mate.'

'I know you wanted more, too, Nick. Do you never feel cheated?'

'Course I bloody do! Though it's better now I go to the garage on Saturdays.' He'd already explained to Phil about Mac and the garage. 'And I've started night school at the Mechanics Institute too.'

'Well done you,' Phil said. 'How do you think Mam'll react to me news?'

'She'll be disappointed, she were looking forward to having you home again.'

'But Dad'll have been home a good bit by then.'

'To be honest, Phil, I don't think she'll think he's much of a substitute. At least you used to bring in regular money, which is more than the old man ever did.'

'Whatever made her marry him in the first place?' Phil questioned. 'They've nowt in common.'

Thinking of his own wayward fancy for Kathy, Nick replied, 'Attraction of opposites, I suppose. Plus, me coming on the scene had summat to do with it.'

Phil gaped at him. 'Bloody hell, I never knew that!'

'Think about it, they married in June and I were born in the December.'

'So why has she stuck with him after all this time? Many another woman would have kicked him out.'

Recalling the conversation he'd had with his mother last Saturday, he said, 'I think she realises he'd really go downhill if she did that.'

'You have to wonder at his lack of common sense even if someone did come onto him in a public toilet,' Phil said. 'I know he knocked the bloke out but it still makes me smile when I think if it.'

They both laughed, remembering their Dad's telling of it. 'There I were at t'urinal, when this bloke next to me kept nudging me and nodding towards himself,' he'd said, with appropriate gestures. 'When I'd done, I fastened meself up, turned round, deliberate like, and whopped him one under t'chin. He hit t'wall behind and slid down slowly, his eyes glazing over.'

'The magistrate didn't think it was funny when he sent Dad down for GBH,' Phil said, still choking with laughter.

Nick was struggling to control his own laughter. 'Well, the fact that the bloke were unconscious and had a nasty gash on his head did influence his decision.'

'Do you think this stint inside will have changed him much?' Phil asked now.

'Time'll tell, I suppose,' Nick mused, 'but I think Mam's the one who's really changed. I don't think she'll put up with some of the stuff he used to get up to.' He stopped as something occurred to him. 'Does she know you're home yet?'

'No, I'd not been in long before you came.'

'So she doesn't know your plans?'

'I was hoping you'd help me out when I tell her.'

Nick leaned across the gap between them and grasped his brother's shoulder. 'You can count on it.'

* * *

Joyce woke with the light of a mid-June morning filtering through the threadbare curtains, a feeling of dread in her stomach. Her father was due home that day. She knew she oughtn't to feel like this but when he was at home there was always a heightened tension.

She turned on her back, feeling as she did so, the warm, curled-up body of her younger sister at her side. Mam had insisted that, now she was such a big girl, she would have to move into the three-quarter bed with Joyce. Lucy had always slept in a small bed in her parents' room but when Dad had been here before, she was little more than a toddler. At six, she would be that much more aware. Joyce's cheeks burned at the thought of what might take place between her parents that night. They were too old for that, surely. But then again, her father had been away for some time. Trying to block out such a disturbing thought, she burrowed closer to Lucy, putting a protective arm round the small body and drifted back to sleep.

The morning turned out to be more fraught than usual with Mam nagging the boys first to stay where she could keep an eye on them, then, because of the noise they were making indoors, shooing them out to play. Lucy, ever sensitive to atmosphere, was quieter than usual, clutching her doll close to her chest. Joyce felt frazzled trying to keep up with her mother's demands yet knowing it was Mam's own nervousness that was making her like this. The kettle had been almost constantly on the boil and Joyce had a metallic taste in her mouth from too many cups of tea. She was on her way to the stairs with a pile of clean clothes tucked under her chin, when the door between the front room and the kitchen opened and her father walked in.

His sudden appearance caused her load to slide and she had to grab it with her other arm to stop it falling to the floor. Mam, bending over the sink, heard Joyce's gasp and swivelled round.

'Is nobody going to give me a kiss, then?' asked Danny Roberts, smiling.

Joyce saw at once that the good-looking face was now drawn into deep lines around his eyes and though the hair was still thick, there were flecks of grey in it. She dropped the pile of clothes on to the table, all apprehension gone now that he was here. 'Hello, Dad.'

'What happened to my little girl? You're a young lady now, and a bonny one at that.'

'You've got another little girl, Danny,' Mam said and pointed to where Lucy sat on the pouffe by the fire.

'Hello, Lucy, love,' Danny bent down but did not try to force his attention on her. 'Remember me?' The child nodded shyly but still held the doll in a tight grasp. He rose and dropped a gentle kiss on the fair head before turning to his wife. 'What about you, Mary? You got a kiss for me?'

'I wondered when you'd get around to noticing me.' She slapped the tea towel down on the draining board, but only offered him a cheek.

'Come on, love, you know I've been longing to see the kids. You wouldn't let them come to see me.'

Joyce gawped at him. Mam had always said that children weren't allowed to visit the prison.

'I weren't having any of me children going to that place,' Mam said, her tongue tart, her lips set in a thin line.

'So you kept telling me,' Danny sighed. 'Where are the boys, anyroad?'

Mary turned back to where a few pots were still draining and began drying them vigorously. 'Out playing somewhere. Their stomachs'll bring them back soon enough.'

'What about Nick? Where's he?'

'I told you, he goes to that garage of a Saturday morning.' She hung the tea towel on its hook and picked up the kettle.

Danny lowered himself into one of the easy chairs. 'I'd have thought he might have taken the morning off to welcome his old Dad home.'

Setting the kettle on the stove, Mary turned back to him. 'Mac has a lot on with Horwich holidays coming up and Nick didn't want to let him down,' she said, hesitated, then continued, 'unlike some people.'

Joyce turned back to refold the clothes that had spilled over the table, hoping desperately that a row wouldn't develop this early on. To her surprise, Dad didn't take up the point Mam was trying to make. He would have done at one time, so perhaps he had changed.

Danny took a cigarette from Mary's packet, lit it and inhaled with obvious enjoyment. 'Any word from our Phil?'

Mary gave Joyce a warning look and she guessed it wasn't a good moment to reveal Phil's plans. There'd been enough of a hoo-ha last week when Phil had told her of his intentions. It had taken the combined persuasions of Phil and Nick to get Mam to accept his decision. Besides, Joyce knew, Mam would have to tread carefully as Phil would need his father's signature as he was still under twenty-one. 'You just missed him,' she said now, 'he were home last weekend on a forty-eight hour pass. First time he's been home in months.'

'Wouldn't surprise me if he didn't sign on as a regular.'

Mary seized the opportunity. 'Would you mind if he did?'

'If that's what the lad wants. He were allus a bit of a dark horse,' he conceded.

Mary let it lie there and passed him a cup of tea.

Danny turned to Joyce. 'Stop fiddling with that pile of washing, lass, and tell me what you've been doing. Enjoying working in the mill?'

She sat down at the table, surprised at the interest he'd never shown before. 'I suppose so. There's not much else, unless you want to work in a shop. If I'm going to be on me feet all day, I'd rather be earning good money in the mill.'

'That's the ticket, you earn the brass then your old Dad can retire.' He roared with laughter, making Joyce wince. This was more like the man she remembered, loud, raucous and full of his own importance.

The back gate banged and to her relief, Nick walked up the yard. He came in through the back door and started with surprise. 'Dad! You're back earlier than we expected.'

Danny looked as if he were about to hug Nick. Instead, he reached forward and grasped Nick's still grease-smeared hand. 'One of the lads were met by a mate in a car and they gave me a lift to Victoria station. From there I caught the train to Bolton.' He thumped Nick on the shoulders. 'By the heck, lad, you've filled out a bit. Being in the Army obviously suited you.'

'Being out suits me better.' Nick turned to the sink and reached for the tin of Swarfega prior to washing his hands.

'What's with all this garage nonsense, then? Does he pay you?'

Joyce saw Nick's back stiffen. It had always been like this between father and son, Dad needling Nick, he retaliating.

119

'No, but I'm getting a lot of experience,' Nick replied, wiping his hands on an old towel.

'Not much bloody use if you can't get a job in that line,' harrumphed Danny.

'You never know, there might be an opening somewhere. If there is, I'll be ready for it, won't I?'

Before Danny could reply, the back gate crashed open and two figures hurtled through the door Nick had left open. 'Someone told us they'd seen Dad coming up Curteis Street,' Brian said in a rush.

'I'm already here, lad.'

Brian looked as if he were about to launch himself at his father, then thought better of it. 'Hiya, Dad.' Derek was behind him and hung back as Brian had done.

Danny waved them forwards. 'Come on, then, let's have a look at you. See if you've grown as much as everyone else.' The boys lined up in front of him and he looked them over with a critical eye. 'A right pair of scruffy sods, aren't you?'

'They're lads, Danny; they've been playing out,' Mary sprang to their defence. 'You were young once, weren't you?'

'Never had much opportunity for fun in our family,' Danny said, his voice bleak.

Joyce recalled what her Dad had told her that, because his Dad was a heavy drinker and his mother unable to cope with a large family, he and his brothers and sisters had more or less brought themselves up. Although Grandma Roberts had died before she was born, she could just remember Granddad Roberts and that his loud ways and quick temper had frightened her. Thankfully, Mam did manage to keep some sort of check on Dad's wilder ways even if this led to rows. If Mam didn't stick up for herself, she'd be treated like a doormat.

Bringing herself back to the present, she saw that the two lads had drawn closer and were asking their father about life in prison. Lucy, too, was leaning against his leg, while Danny had laid his hand on her shoulder. Whatever else, there was no doubt that Dad loved his children, even if he didn't do all he should to support them.

'Are you going to stand there forever with that pile of clothes in your arms or are you going to take it upstairs?' Mary quizzed now.

'Sorry, Mam, I was daydreaming,' she said, juggling the load with one hand while opening the latch with the other.

'Will you go to the chippie when you come down?'

As she nodded her agreement and made to go up the stairs, she caught the satisfied look her Dad gave Mam and heard him say, 'This is what it's all about, Mary, love.'

'Think on you remember that, Danny.'

CHAPTER 14

For the second week of Bolton holidays, Kathy's parents had hired a caravan at Prestatyn in North Wales, leaving Kathy at home alone, the first time it had happened. Her mother would have preferred her to accompany them but she hadn't been able to get the time off. As the newspaper was still produced during the holidays, someone had to work.

She'd missed her parents, had been surprised at how quiet the house seemed. Tonight, though, Carole was coming to keep her company. She was still seeing Ian, whom she'd met that night at the Barn, and, with Kathy spending so much time with John, there hadn't been much opportunity for them to get together. Catching up with each other was long overdue. In the hall, the two girls hugged briefly and Carole took off her jacket, hanging it on the coat stand. 'It's on the chilly side for July,' she said.

'Not such good weather for the poor souls on holiday, is it?' Kathy said. 'I feel sorry for all those people who've worked and saved hard for their holiday at the seaside, only to have it spoiled by bad weather.'

'Have you heard from your parents?' Carole asked as she followed Kathy into the sitting room.

'Mum called from a phone box to see if I'm all right. I could hear her in the background, asking Dad if she should press button A or B.' She giggled and pointed to the postcard propped against a brass candlestick on the mantelpiece. 'Apparently, it's been a bit wet in Wales but they're in a caravan so they don't have to go out if they don't want to. Not like in a boarding house where you have to be out after breakfast and not go back till teatime.'

'There's nothing more miserable than mooching round, looking for something to do, when it's raining.' Carole sat down on the sofa, spreading her wide skirts about her. 'I remember a holiday we had in Morecambe, with the wind blowing across the promenade and the rain lashing our faces.'

'Morecambe can be a bit dire in bad weather,' Kathy agreed. 'Lovely when it's good weather, though, with the view across the Bay towards the Lake District.'

'Blackpool's better. At least there's the Tower to get out of the rain.' Carole said.

'Remember the Zoo with that strong animal smell?'

'And the Aquarium down in the depths with those small viewing tanks?'

'Not forgetting the annual visit to the circus with Charlie Carioli.'

'What about when our parents dragged us to the Ballroom to hear Reginald Dixon playing the Organ?' Carole sang a snatch of, 'Oh, I do like to be beside the seaside.'

'And which we thought was so boring.' She pulled a face at Carole. 'Listen to us, we sound like a couple of old fogeys, reminiscing about the good old days.'

In this easy-going mood, the two girls sat over cups of tea and chatted generally until Carole put her cup down and said, 'So tell me, how's it going with John?'

Kathy made a see-sawing movement with her hands. 'I know I'm being foolish. John's essentially a good man but I sometimes feel he's rushing things a bit.' She tried to put into words the uncertainty she'd been feeling recently. 'Was I carried away in the beginning that someone like him should find me attractive?'

'I don't know, never having been in that position,' Carole said. 'Ian and I are still in the initial stages, sort of feeling our way forward.'

'What makes it worse is that Mum keeps asking me if John has said anything,' she sighed. 'How crazy is it that you are considered 'on the shelf' if you aren't engaged or at least courting by the time you're 21?'

'That sounds like your Mum. Bless her, she is a bit old-fashioned, isn't she?'

'I think it's with them being older parents. Mum had several miscarriages before I came along when she was thirty. If she's a bit straight-laced, it's because I'm an only child and she worries about me.'

'I suppose you're right. My parents are a lot younger, but then they had to get married when Mam was eighteen and Dad was twenty. I'm lucky because they're pretty easy going, within certain limits. Plus I've got four younger brothers and sisters who keep them occupied.'

After a second cup of tea, the talk turned to Kathy's writing success with Town Topics. 'I've been reading it every night,' Carole said, 'but it never gives a name so I don't know which, if any, are yours. Have you done any more?'

Kathy shook her head. 'Not for a couple of weeks.' She hesitated then decided her news was too good not to share. 'There has been a development though.'

Carole put her cup down and sat up straighter. 'Oh, what?'

Drawing a deep breath, Kathy said, 'I've begun to wonder whether I could make a career out of it.'

Carole grasped immediately that Kathy was saying. 'On the newspaper, you mean?'

'Exactly. Today I went to see Mr Bleakley, the Features Editor, to ask what he thought my chances would be in transferring to Editorial.'

'Not be a secretary, you mean?'

She leaned forward to make a point. 'I want to become a reporter, Carole.'

'What did this chap, Mr…?'

'Bleakley.'

'Him. What did he have to say?'

She plucked a piece of paper from her pocket and flourished it. 'I wrote it down so I wouldn't forget it. He said my writing has a cadence and sense of climax many modern journalists lack.' Her excitement showed in her voice. 'And he's going to have a word with the Editor on my behalf.'

Carole stretched over and gave her a spontaneous hug. 'Oh, Kathy, that's brilliant. Have you told John yet?'

She grimaced. 'No, nor will I do until I know something more definite.'

Carole's eyebrows arched. 'You don't think he'll approve?'

'No, I don't.'

'What about your parents?'

'Same thing. Possibly when I've seen the Editor.' She sighed. 'I think Dad will be quietly pleased, Mum less so. She'll take John's part, I'm afraid.'

By the time Carole left shortly before 11 o'clock, Kathy was much more buoyed up about the future and looking forward to the weekend. As Carole's boyfriend was going on holiday with his mates and John would be away on his cricket weekend, the two girls had planned a day trip to Blackpool on Saturday. It would be the first day of Horwich holidays and the day her parents were returning home. She wouldn't even see them until the day after. Returning on the late train from Blackpool was not something her mother would approve of. Not for nothing was it known as the Passion Wagon.

* * *

Nick, Bragger, Ken and Ray strutted down Blackpool Promenade, conscious that people side-stepped to avoid them, many muttering under their breath, 'Bloody Teddy boys!' The attention gave them an added swagger, with shoulders thrown back and hands tucked into the tight waistband of their trousers.

'Should've got the tram,' grumbled Ray, who was breaking-in a new pair of brothel creepers.

'Do you ever do owt else than complain?' Nick wished it was only him and Bragger, or at a pinch, Ken. No matter how he tried, he could not like Ray.

'Ay, a right moaning Minnie, you are,' added Bragger.

As they approached the Pleasure Beach with the Big Dipper dominating the skyline, Nick could hear the sound of traditional fairground music clashing with the latest rock and roll hits. At the sound, he could feel a building sense of excitement, an injection of adrenaline pump through his body.

Moments later, they were through into the Pleasure Beach itself and surrounded by all the fun of the fair, with its flashing lights, the coaxing calls of the stallholders, the clanging of bells, and the wailing of sirens. Strolling, not being tempted for the moment by any of the attractions, Nick watched a little girl, perhaps about Lucy's age, being handed a froth of candy floss.

He was reminded of a time when, as a child, he'd clutched his mother's hand and watched the vendor swirl the spun sugar round a stick.

Bragger, nudged Nick's elbow. 'Fancy a go on the dodgems?' Ken and Ray were already hurtling round the dodgem track, laughing as they chased two screaming girls.

'Yeah, why not?'

From then on, the group shot from one attraction to another; a couple of rides on the Big Dipper; once on the Ghost Train; a go on the Waltzer, which Ken declined claiming it made him sick; various sideshows in an attempt to win cheap, tawdry knick-knacks, fit only for the dustbin. They finished up at the Fun House where they spent a couple of hours being thrown off cakewalks and similar bruise-inducing attractions.

As they came out of the Fun House and stood watching the 'Laughing Policeman,' responding to someone's sixpence, in the glass case outside, Bragger turned to Nick. 'Isn't that Kathy?'

Nick turned to look in the direction Bragger had indicated and saw Kathy, accompanied by the girl he'd seen her with that night at the Barn. The two girls were walking away from the Fun House as if they'd been heading in that direction then changed their mind. Even with simply her back view, he would have known her slender figure anywhere. His heart flipped at this unexpected sight of her and he wondered how the hell she'd managed to get away from the boyfriend again. She seemed to be making a habit of it.

'You going after her?' Bragger asked,

Nick thought briefly. 'Nah, I don't think so. No point, is there?'

A walk back along the Golden Mile, a bag of fish and chips and a couple of pints later, the quartet of Teddy boys found themselves on the periphery of the Tower Ballroom. Although it wasn't that late, the dance floor was already crowded with couples. With one accord, the quartet made for the bar where, they saw, customers were waiting four deep to be served.

'Bloody hell!' Ray said in disgust. 'No chance of being served here.'

'Then it's a good job we had a few pints before we came in,' Nick returned.

Muttering under his breath, Ray followed the others back to the ballroom. Fortunately, there were a fair few Teddy boys already there, so the four didn't stand out too much, yet they were surprised when several girls turned them down for dances. 'Bloody stuck-up bunch!' grumbled Ray, who'd had more than his fair share of refusals, more likely due to his attitude than his mode of dress.

'Can't say as I'd want to dance with any of them anyway,' Ken said.

Nick threw Bragger a quick grin of amusement. Ken's inability to attract girls was a standing joke with them. 'Now's your chance then, Ken.' He pointed to three girls standing close by, tight skirts emphasising neat bottoms, jumpers showing off Lana Turner-style bosoms, stockinged legs thrust into high heels.

Ray's eyes lit up. 'You up for this, Nick?'

'No thanks, but you go ahead. If we get separated, meet at Central Station for the last train, OK?'

'Ay, and if we're not there, you go without us.' Ray winked at Ken, then turned to Bragger. 'What about you?'

'Nope. I'll stay with Nick.'

'Hey-ey! More for us then, Ken.' Ray slapped his cousin on the back, the force of it causing the less well-built boy to stagger.

'Yeah, we can manage three between us, easy,' Ken said, an attempt at bravado in his voice.

'Rather them than me,' Bragger said, as the other two attempted to chat the three girls up. 'But then, beggars can't be choosers.'

The two lads were laughing about this when a voice from behind them broke in. 'Hello, Nick.'

Nick whirled round at the sound of Kathy's voice, knowing instinctively that he had been comparing all the girls he'd seen so far with her and found them wanting. Her full-skirted dress was made of some kind of green satiny material, its colour accentuating the green of her eyes. Under the shimmering lights of the ballroom, her hair cascaded to her shoulders and glinted with auburn highlights. 'This is my friend, Carole. I don't think you've met before.

Beside Kathy, Carole looked insignificant in a black taffeta skirt topped by a lime green velvet blouse with diamante buttons. 'Hullo, Carole. This here's me mate, Bragger – er, Dave – Yates.'

Carole gave Bragger a cool nod and said, 'I've heard about you.'

'All good, I hope. Fancy a dance?'

As Bragger spun on to the dance floor with Carole, Nick turned to Kathy. 'So, Kathy, how've you been?'

'Pretty good, and you?'

'Fair to middling, as they say.' To overcome the slight awkwardness between them, he said, 'I saw you earlier actually. At the Pleasure Beach, near the Fun House.'

'No, really? We couldn't make up our minds whether to go in then decided we weren't dressed for being thrown around.'

'I know what you mean. I'm still sore.' He rubbed his elbow, smarting where it had come into contact with the hard floor of the Fun House. 'Want to dance?'

She hesitated only briefly before saying, 'Why not?'

With her in his arms on the packed dance floor, the easy familiarity slipped into place as she relaxed against him. 'Where's the boyfriend this time, Kathy?'

Tall as she was, she had to tilt her head back to look at him. 'Having one of his weekends with his mates, cricket this time.'

'So while the cat's away, the mouse gets chance to play,' he said, hoping she was in a receptive mood for teasing. The tantalising thought that she was on her own this weekend was causing the familiar tightening of his groin.

She looked uncomfortable. 'Something like that.'

To help her out, he said, 'Did you know me Dad's home?'

'I bet that's been difficult for you all after so long.'

'A bit,' he said. 'Sometimes you can cut the atmosphere with a knife.'

'Are you having to play piggy in the middle?'

'I am,' he agreed. 'I have to bite me tongue when Dad wades in to the kids for what seems to me to be minor things.' Seeing the understanding in her eyes, he continued, 'Trouble is, I have a mind of me own now and keep wanting to disagree with him, not only about the way he treats the kids but how he tries to put Mam down. To be honest, I try to keep out of the way as much as possible, give them a chance to get on with it.'

'Your Mum especially will have got used to doing what she wants when she wants,' Kathy said, 'whereas for your Dad, time will have stood still. He'll have come home expecting everything to be the same.'

He looked down at her, surprised at the wisdom of her statement. 'I never thought of it like that.'

After some moments, she said, 'I saw your Joyce earlier.'

'Where?'

'Here. She and her friends were queuing to get in, just in front of us.'

'I hope she catches an earlier train. It can be a bit rough on the last one,' he said with genuine feeling.

'I'm sure she'll be all right.'

'I can't help worrying about her. I tend to forget she's growing up.'

'That's what big brothers do. Not that I would know, never having had a brother.'

Around them, other couples had come to a halt as the music stopped and were walking away. 'Have the next dance with me, Kathy?'

'I'd better get back to Carole.'

'Bragger will look after her,' he wheedled, wanting to prolong this time together.

'No, I can see her on her own. There's no sign of Bragger.'

Nor was there, he saw. Carole said he'd rushed off at the end of the dance, saying he'd seen someone he knew.

The two girls moved away, leaving Nick without a backward glance. He hung around for a while waiting for Bragger to reappear. When he did not, Nick, with no enthusiasm, was forced to join Ray, Ken and the three Teddy girls, to the girls' delight.

* * *

129

Nothing Kathy and Carole had heard previously prepared them for what was happening on the last train from Blackpool. Everywhere they looked, girls had paired up with boys. Where they had not paired off, shouting and swearing came from the boys, hysterical giggles from the girls. Thankfully, it was a corridor train so that when the antics of their fellow travellers had become too much, they'd been able to move on and search for an empty compartment. Even so, when they found one that seemed reasonable, three lads had walked in and one of them pulled down the blinds at the windows, while another tried to remove the bulb from the ceiling light. With one accord, Kathy and Carole had risen, leaving the girls who'd been in their compartment, shrieking with laughter and not seeming to mind when the lads moved in on them.

'Flippin' heck!' said Carole in the comparative freedom of the corridor, comparative only in that boys – and girls – pushed past them on the prowl. 'Do you suppose it's always like this?'

'Perhaps it's worse because we're still in the middle of the Wakes Weeks,' Kathy reasoned.

'I don't think we'll be doing this again in a hurry, do you?' Carole shrank back as a lad pushed past her, making exaggerated movements with his pelvis against her hip.

'Is it us, do you think?' Kathy was puzzled by the seemingly lewd behaviour of not only the lads but the girls.

Three lads came up behind them, their closeness threatening. 'What's two lovely lasses like you doing stuck out here? Come and have a bit of fun with us,' one of them said.

Kathy shuddered. 'No thanks, we prefer each other's company to yours.'

The three lads looked at one another knowingly and the lanky one said, 'Couple of dykes, are you? That should make it even more interesting,' and tried to move closer, only to find himself yanked backwards by a firm hand on his collar.

'They're with me.' Nick's voice was as strong as the hand holding the lad. Tall as the lad was, he was topped by Nick and no match for Nick in body. The other two looked as if they weren't going to argue either. 'Now bugger off, all of you.'

130

'Thanks, Nick,' Kathy whispered. His solid presence made her feel much safer.

'I thought you might be in need of a bit of assistance, so I came looking for you.'

'I'm glad you did,' Carole said. 'I didn't much like the look of them.'

'I saw you earlier making your way to the station so I knew you'd be on this train.' He grinned and indicated the corner of his mouth which was split. 'I'd have caught up with you sooner only we had a bit of trouble with the local Teds at the station.'

As some other lads pushed past, jeering at Nick having two girls to himself, he put an arm round both. 'Why don't you come to our compartment?' As wariness crept into Kathy's eyes, he laughed. 'No room for funny stuff, I promise. The rest of the lads are there, as well as our Joyce and her mates.'

'She missed the earlier train then?' Kathy asked as they manoeuvred their way down the corridor, past knots of both boys and girls preferring to stand rather than be trapped in a compartment.

'One of her mates met a lad and was late getting back to the station. The others waited rather than leave her on her own. Luckily, Bragger spotted them and ran on ahead to look after them. Then I came looking for you.'

They had, by now, reached the compartment where Bragger's long legs were stretched out over the doorway. Compared to the other compartments, it was a peaceful haven and the two girls squashed in gratefully, while Nick and Bragger stood to guard the doorway.

As she sat there, listening but not really contributing, she became aware of a pressing need. Damn! She should have paid a visit to the toilet before they left the Tower Ballroom. She stood and, swayed by the rhythm of the train, managed to whisper to Nick. 'I need the toilet, will you come with me?'

With his arm round her, they escaped once more into the corridor, to jeers from Ken and Ray. 'Course, you realise they'll all believe we're off to do a bit of necking,' he commented as they made their way to the toilet at the end of the carriage.

131

'I don't care what they think as long as I can get to the toilet.' She was glad to have him stand guard as she used it. There were still some comings and goings but things did seem to have settled down, probably as couples paired off. As she came out, Nick was standing by the open window at the end of the carriage.

'Mind if I finish this before we go back?' he asked, indicating the cigarette in his hand.

She shook her head then shivered as the night air rushed through the open window.

'You're cold. Come and stand by me.' He tugged the window up a little by its leather strap and pulled her towards him. Feeling the blessed nearness of him, the warmth through his shirt and, not stopping to think, she slid her arms round his waist. Tucked away in a corner between two carriages, they were virtually undisturbed.

'Bloody hell, Kathy!' he exclaimed and flicked the half-smoked cigarette out of the window where it glowed briefly before disappearing into the darkness. 'I'm not made of stone. Do you know what you are doing to me?'

She knew, of course, she could feel his hardness against her hips. Yet she did not pull back. As he lowered his lips to hers, a longing, never experienced before, surged through her and she responded eagerly to his kisses. His mouth moved to her neck and he feathered kisses there before returning to explore her mouth.

It was only when they pulled into Chorley station and people started getting off the train that the madness that had consumed them cooled a little to be replaced by a shaky tenderness. 'No one has ever made me feel this way,' he whispered, still holding her. 'We should be together. Bugger the boyfriend!'

'No!' The recklessness, like their kisses, had gone, and shame flooded through her. How could she have let herself be so carried away as to forget John? 'I'm going out with John, in case you've forgotten.'

'I never bloody well forget but for a short while I thought you had.'

CHAPTER 15

Kathy got off the bus at Trinity Street Station, outside the tiny transport café, closed at this time of night. During the day, it was always steamy, smoky and filled with bus drivers and she fancied she could still smell a whiff of cigarette smoke. As she stepped on to the footbridge over the railway, a train passed beneath her, enveloping her in a cloud of vapour, a hint of acridity tickling the back of her throat. The footbridge came out in Great Moor Street at the side of St Patrick's Catholic Church, where she was to meet John. As he'd had to work late tonight, they'd opted to meet in Bolton to save time.

As he reached her, he was breathing heavily as if he'd been running. 'Sorry I'm late. I got carried away with what I was doing and hadn't noticed the time.'

'Never mind, you're here now.' She leaned towards him for his usual kiss of greeting but he didn't acknowledge her gesture.

'Better hurry, love, if we're not to miss the start of the film.'

She was disappointed. After the episode with Nick on the train, she was eager to remind herself of her feelings for John.

As they reached the cinema, the show had started but luckily seats were still available towards the back. 'All right, sweetheart?' he whispered in her ear as they sat down, his attention already on the screen.

Conscious of the strict rule of not talking in the cinema, she nodded and concentrated on the short travelogue, a promotional film for £10 assisted passages to Australia, a scheme which had been in operation since just after the war. The Pathé News followed, with reports of some trouble in Suez with President Nasser threatening to take over the Suez Canal. There was a rumour, as yet unconfirmed, that National Servicemen might be recalled if hostilities broke out. Would Nick have to go, she wondered, then chastised herself. She should not be thinking about Nick when she was with John. The trouble was, she couldn't stop thinking about him and his kisses. She had never been so physically aroused, not even with John. Even recalling the feeling now gave her an unidentifiable ache in her private parts.

The last Newsreel item snapped her attention back to the screen. Marilyn Monroe had married an American playwright, Arthur Miller, a bespectacled studious looking man. 'She's wasted on someone like that,' hissed John, 'what the hell does she see in him?'

Kathy, more interested in the white fur trimmed jacket which showed off Marilyn's figure to perfection, could think of no reply, other than to agree with him.

The lights came up for the interval and John went off to queue for ice creams, Kathy following him with her eyes. Coming straight from work, he was wearing a dark business suit, crisp white shirt and sober tie. He looked so like the quintessential professional that she experienced a twinge of pride. His hair was a regimental back and sides, pristine in its neatness. Contrarily, she wished it wasn't quite so severe.

'Last two choc ices,' he said as he reached their seats.

'John, why don't you let your hair grow a little longer?' she said, stripping the wrapping off her ice-cream.

He gave her a horrified look. 'Why ever would I want to do that? I've worn my hair like this all my life and I'm not likely to change now.'

She could have kicked herself for voicing her thoughts aloud. 'No, of course not. I don't know what made me say that.'

'What did you think about Australia, by the way?' he asked, in between bites of his own choc ice.

The remark threw her. 'In what way?' She had finished her own ice-cream and wiped her lips with her handkerchief.

'I thought, maybe together, we could make a new start there.'

She stared at him in disbelief. 'Emigrate, you mean? The two of us?'

'Why not? It's the land of promise. And think of all that sunshine.'

Her immediate thought was one of panic. Were they to emigrate, she could not follow her desire to become a journalist. 'You've never said anything about this before.'

'Well, I've been thinking about it for a while, especially since we've been together. With seeing the film about the scheme, I thought it was about time I mentioned the idea to you.'

Her heart sank further as she thought of her parents. 'I…don't know what to say, John, springing the news on me like that. And what about leaving my family? I'm an only child, remember. I think it would destroy my parents.'

'Rubbish! They're stronger than you give them credit for. They came through the war, didn't they? Besides, they could always come out and visit us.'

'But it takes weeks to travel to Australia. Dad wouldn't be able to take that much holiday.'

'Calm down, love, I'm not talking tomorrow. We're talking a long time in the future. Even with the assisted passages, we'd have to save up for a few years. By that time, they might be able to fly there.'

A hard lump of resistance had, by now, built up in her chest but in all fairness to him, she said, 'You've taken me by surprise but I promise I'll consider it.'

'Kathy, if you loved me, you should be willing to follow me to the ends of the earth if necessary.' The hurt he was feeling at her reluctance showed in the curtness of his voice.

'That's what Australia feels like to me at the moment,' she said in a cold voice as the cinema began to darken for the main feature.

They sat in stony silence during the length of the film and for once, he did not hold her hand. Her own mind was too preoccupied in digesting the news of John's sudden suggestion to take in much of the film. But was it so sudden? He'd said he'd been thinking about it for some time. If that was so, why hadn't he mentioned it before? She wasn't happy about the idea at all. In fact, she was furious.

The cool distance between them lasted until they were parked in Travers Street. Finally, Kathy said, 'You mentioned that you'd been thinking about going to Australia for some time. If so, why didn't you tell me?'

135

'I'm sorry, I realise now I should have.' He had the grace to look sheepish. 'If I'm honest, it's what I've been working towards, getting qualified, so's I'll get a good job out there.'

'Weren't you also presuming we had a future together?'

He wriggled in his seat. 'I suppose I was but you know how I feel about you.'

In the dimness of the car, she turned to face him. 'Don't you think you might have asked my opinion when thinking about Australia?'

'The answer's simple, then, I won't go either, if it means losing you.'

'And probably resent me for the rest of your life,' she reminded him. 'It's not only that, John. It's the principle behind it. You're doing it again, expecting me to go along with you on everything.'

'I don't mean to. It's just the way I am,' he blustered.

She refrained from saying that he probably took after his mother for that. 'You don't seem able to help it. I'm simply asking you to think of me every now and then.'

He reached over and took her hand. 'That's the trouble, Kathy. I think of you, and a possible future, all the time. Since I met you, you've been part of any plans I have.' He reached over to pull her as close to him as the gear stick would allow, he said, 'Am I being unrealistic?'

In answer, she reached up to kiss him, trying to put as much feeling as she could into the kiss to make up for her wayward thoughts.

* * *

The crowd of young people stepped down from the bus on the outskirts of Wigan, Nick and the lads in one group, Sally Simcox and a couple of her mates in another, They were all on their way to Haigh Hall, as good a spot as any to visit on a warm July weekend, especially when it was the end of Horwich holidays.

The Hall was a good few minutes' walk from the bus stop, past the Leeds and Liverpool Canal, but it was pleasant enough walking along the dry, dusty track. Everyone straggled along at their own pace, the girls, with their tight skirts and high heel shoes, slightly behind the boys. Even so, it seemed the accepted thing that they should all team up.

'Do we have to have them tagging along?' whined Ray, giving the giggling girls a resentful look.

'It's not like you to grumble about the company of girls,' Nick said, determined not to let the other lad rile him today.

'But they'll cramp our style with other lasses,' Ray persisted.

'We couldn't do owt else, seeing as we all got on the Wigan bus together and we're all going to the same place,' Bragger reasoned.

'If you see anyone you fancy, you can always nip off,' said Nick. 'We won't stop you.'

By that time, they'd reached the entrance to the park, which spread over several acres, with the squat and square Hall looking benignly on. Blackened by the endemic soot and smoke even in this near-rural place, it had possibly once been beautiful. Strolling through the park, sometimes stopping by a bench for a cigarette, the time passed pleasantly enough. It was during such a break that Bragger spoke quietly to Nick. 'Don't look now but Kathy's coming.'

And, of course, Nick did look, cricking his neck in the process. She was walking towards their group, looking lovely in a full-skirted summer dress, in a kind of fabric that shimmered in the sun, sometimes blue, sometimes green, her face animated as she talked to her companion. With a surge of jealousy, he saw that it was the hated John Talbot, looking smooth in summer weight slacks and a light jumper. It was obvious she hadn't seen Nick but there was no way he could escape the imminent confrontation, their group being clustered around a bench next to the path. Nor was there anywhere to hide. The nearest trees and shrubs were a hundred yards away. In any case, why would he want to hide?

All this careered round his mind in the few seconds it took Kathy to register his presence and her face to become still and unreadable. 'Hello, Kathy,' he said.

Again, came that momentary sense of connection as if she and he were alone in the crowd, only vaguely aware of the others around them. She'd stopped as if to go back the way she had come but John had seen them too and carried on to stand in front of the bench. 'Well, if it isn't the Teddy boy! And surrounded by his acolytes, I see.'

'Posh bastard!' Ray rose to his feet, thrusting his body forwards and Nick had to put out a restraining arm.

John gave them a superior look. 'My apologies, you probably haven't a clue what an acolyte is. I'm referring, of course, to this sorry bunch you're surrounded by.' As he raked his eyes over them, the boys and girls rose with one accord and faced him. To give him his due, he did not flinch from the menace before him. He simply kept his eyes on Nick, challenging him. But to what?

'John, please don't cause any trouble,' Kathy said. Nick could tell she was afraid, by the tremble in her voice. That made him angrier still. He would dearly love to hit the bloke. Then, from where he did not know, came the realisation that turning away would be more of a defeat for John Talbot than tackling him.

'Come on, you lot, time to move on.' He made as if to go in the opposite direction but Ray grasped his arm to stop him.

'What? You intend to let him get away with it?'

'Yes, because he's a coward,' taunted John.

Nick shrugged Ray's hand off and turned to face John, noting with satisfaction the frustration on the other's face. 'If I stayed, I'd end up smashing your face in and Kathy doesn't deserve that.' Only then did he turn to Kathy, who had an unfathomable look in her eyes. Regret? Sorrow? He couldn't tell. 'I'm sorry, Kathy. This weren't of my choosing.'

He could hear the lads behind him muttering that John Talbot needed to be taught a lesson. He realised he didn't care. What really mattered was Kathy's opinion of him. Then he had to go and spoil it. 'What do you see in this – prick?' he asked. Behind her, John's face was livid with rage, his fists clenched angrily by his side.

Her face cold, she tucked her hand into John's arm. 'That's none of your business.'

The proprietary gesture maddened him. 'You're right, of course.' He turned away and jerked his head to the group waiting a little way up the path. 'Anyroad, I'm going out with Sally now,' he said but not loud enough for Sally to hear.

'There's no harm done then, is there?' she said, ice in her voice.

Nick walked away and up to Sally, standing a little apart from the others. 'Let's go, Sal.' He put his arm round her shoulder and she gave Kathy a quick look of triumph. His own feeling of sweet revenge was short-lived as he glanced backwards and saw Kathy's white face. He would have done anything then to have rushed back and told her that it wasn't true, that he hadn't meant to upset her.

He knew, in that moment, that he was in love with Kathy. All his confusion over the last few months coalesced into the glorious realisation. And what had he done? Alienated her even further. Whatever advantage he'd gained by being restrained in the confrontation with John had been lost by his loose tongue. In that moment, he could have kicked himself.

* * *

He woke the following morning with the same thought in his mind. The bedroom he was in belonged to one of Sally's friends and the girl in the bed beside him Sally herself. He looked at her now and saw, not the matted hair and smeared make-up, but a vulnerable young woman, tousled with sleep, whom he did not love. Aghast, he stared down at her. Bugger, what had he done? He knew only too well. Despite the heavy necking sessions he and Sally had indulged in, they had never gone all the way. Last night they had, more than once. In the dark and with the drink inside him, he'd been pretending the girl in his arms was Kathy. How could he have been so stupid? Jud would kill him if he knew. Fortunately, unless Sally was daft enough to say something, Jud would never know for he was at Butlin's Holiday Camp in Pwllheli with his mates. The only mitigating factor was that Sally had not been a virgin. She had been a willing and enthusiastic partner. Full of self-loathing, he knew he had to get out of here, if possible before Sally woke up.

He slid out of the bed, his bare feet flinching as they hit the cold linoleum, and reached for his clothes. Not daring to climb back on to the bed to pull his trousers on, he had to lie on the floor to do them up. With his worm's eye view, he could see dust balls and what looked like a pair of dirty knickers under the old-fashioned bed. A chipped mahogany-veneered wardrobe hugged the space opposite while an ancient chest of drawers squatted next to the bed, its top covered in make-up and spilled talcum powder. The curtains at the window were dirty and full of holes.

With a last shame-filled shake of his head as he glanced at the sleeping girl, he tiptoed out of the room, shoes and jacket in his hands. As he crept downstairs, he saw that the wallpaper on the stairs was peeling off in strips where it had been blackened by the insidious rising damp. Downstairs wasn't much better with shabby furniture and wallpaper that must have been there long before the war. Bottles, stained sticky glasses, and overfull ashtrays, evidence of the party last night, were everywhere.

Curled up uncomfortably on the threadbare sofa, his suit even more crumpled than usual, was Ken. On seeing Nick, he opened a bleary eye. 'Lo, Nick. What time is it?'

'Haven't a clue. Early, I think.' He shrugged himself into his jacket and sat down on a fireside chair, more springs than cushion, to put on his shoes. 'You go back to sleep.'

Ken stood up and stretched himself. 'Nah, I might as well get off home. I'll get it in the neck from me Mam when she finds I've been out all night. She's always up with the lark, holidays or not.' He gave a rueful laugh. 'And I'll get blamed for our Ray, as usual. She thinks the sun shines out of his backside.'

'Where is he, anyroad?' Come to think of it, where was Bragger? Then he remembered that Bragger had chosen not to come to the party. That puzzled him. It wasn't like Bragger at all.

'Upstairs with that mate of Sal's who lives here.' He waved his arm round the cluttered room. 'This is a right dump, isn't it?'

'It stinks too.' Nick wrinkled his nose at the smell of stale beer and cigarettes and not only from last night. Someone had been sick in the old stone sink and he was glad it hadn't been him. Despite all the booze he'd consumed, he had at least managed to keep it in his guts. 'Come on, Ken, let's get out of this midden. I thought our house were bad enough but this takes the biscuit.'

Outside the air was clean and clear with an early morning sun over towards Bolton. He took several deep breaths, something you couldn't do normally unless you wanted a lung-full of the fumes from the Works, closed now for the Wakes Weeks. He hadn't remembered where they'd ended up last night after a skinful of beer in the pub but saw now it was one of the streets that ran down from Chorley New Road to the very boundary of the Works. It didn't matter which one, they all looked the same, two-up, two-down terraced houses, thrown up to house the workers who flooded in to the town when the Locomotive Works opened.

'Wouldn't it be great if the air were always this fresh?' Ken said, echoing Nick's thoughts.

'Happen that'll be changing with this new Clean Air Act they're bringing in.'

'I read summat about that in the Bolton Evening News. Not afore time, if you ask me, with the terrible smogs we get in winter.'

Still chatting the pair dropped down into Horwich and separated at the Black Dog, Ken to go down Vale Avenue where he lived with his family and Nick up Winter Hey Lane towards Winter Street. He was nearly home when he changed his mind and decided to go to the garage instead. He'd have a bit of a swill there, change into his overalls and lose himself in the innards of a car that had been giving him problems yesterday morning.

He had been working on the car for some time, had in fact sorted the problem out, if not his personal demons, when he was interrupted by Mac's voice. 'Bloody hell, Nick! What're you doing here on a Sunday morning? I thought I'd got burglars.' Mac appeared in the doorway between the flat and garage, his thin hair wisping over his scalp and the shabby plaid dressing gown bunched around his middle.

'Sorry, Mac. Didn't mean to disturb you.' Nick straightened up, putting a grimy hand against the small of his back.

'I was awake anyway. When I heard a noise, I decided to get up and investigate.' Mac made an attempt to smooth his hair to his scalp.

Nick held up a hefty spanner in a rueful gesture. 'I dropped this beastie. Just missed me foot too.' He returned it to the toolbox by his feet. 'What time is it?'

Mac glanced at the well-worn and sweat-stained watch on his wrist. 'A few minutes after nine. How long have you been here?'

Nick shrugged his shoulders. 'Don't know. A couple of hours maybe.'

'You were up early, weren't you?'

'Haven't been to bed. At least...'

'No need to elaborate.' Mac grinned. 'Come up and have a brew. Kettle's on.'

'Thanks. Me mouth's like the bottom of a budgie's cage.' Nick followed Mac up the stairs, as dusty as ever. At least Mac's flat didn't smell the way that girl's house had. Even the thought of it turned his stomach. Or was that the remains of the beer? More likely to be self-disgust.

In the kitchen, Mac shifted a pile of newspapers from a chair. 'Could you manage a bit of toast, lad? You look a bit green.'

'A cup of tea is about as much as I can handle at the moment, thanks.'

'One of those nights, was it?'

Nick sat down in the chair Mac had cleared. 'One of those days and nights.'

'From the look of you, it wasn't a good one.' The flat being so small, his voice carried easily from the tiny kitchen.

'It started out OK. A gang of us went up to Haigh Hall. Nowt special but pleasant enough. Then I saw Kathy.'

'Surely that was good?' Mac turned to face Nick from the open doorway.

'Not really. She had the boyfriend with her and it made me angry.'

'You didn't start a fight?'

'No, I wanted to, but I managed to keep me temper.' Even after the events of the night, he was still proud that he hadn't risen to the challenge John Talbot had thrown his way.

'That's not all, though, is it? Mac poured boiling water from the kettle into the brown and heavily-tannined teapot.

'Me and me big gob! I told her I was seeing Sally.'

'Understandable. You wanted to show her you could get someone too,' he said.

'I suppose so, if you look at it like that.'

'So what happened next?'

'Nothing. That is…she went with John while I walked off with Sally.'

Mac gave him a shrewd look. 'And?'

'I wanted to forget the look I saw on Kathy's face and thought I could do it in drink. The upshot of it were that we all stayed together, first in the pub, then back to Sally's mate's house for a bit of a party. The lass's parents were away, things got a bit hazy and…well, one thing led to another.' Nick took a gulp from the mug of tea Mac had passed him. After the sour beer taste of his mouth, it tasted like nectar.

'And you slept with Sally.'

Nick hunched his shoulders deeper into the chair. 'I didn't mean to. I were hurting inside from seeing Kathy and Sally were there.'

'I hoped you used something.'

'I cadged a couple of French letters off Ray. He's always got some.'

'Bloody fool!'

'I know, Mac. I feel bad about it. She's simply a lass who's sweet on me and I took advantage of her. I couldn't even face her this morning, I sneaked out while she was asleep.'

'You're going to have to see her some time.'

'I don't know what I'm going to say to her.' Nick sighed and swilling the last of his tea down, he stood up. 'I'll get back to that car, if you don't mind, Mac. I've only to put it together again and it'll be as right as nine pence.'

'Don't be too hard on yourself, Nick.'

'Thanks, Mac, I appreciate that but I still feel a right bastard.' He stopped in the doorway and turned to face Mac. 'I can't remember much about the party except that somebody kept putting Dave King singing 'Memories Are Made of This' on the turntable. Every time I hear that bloody song from now on, it'll remind me of summat I'd rather forget.'

CHAPTER 16

Kathy was engrossed in typing a report when Mr. Mansfield called her over soon after receiving a phone call.

She stood in front of his desk. 'Yes, Mr Mansfield?'

'That was the editor's secretary. He wants to see you in his office as soon as possible.' He was looking at her with open curiosity. Linda was also giving her a speculative glance but no one else bothered to look up, for which Kathy was grateful.

She had been expecting this call since Mr Bleakley had mentioned that he'd have a word with the editor but now that it had come, her heart began to pound and her stomach to churn. 'Will it be all right to go now, Mr Mansfield?' she asked.

'As it appears to be in the nature of an imperial summons, I would say so,' he said.

In the cloakroom, she tidied herself up as best she could, wishing she'd thought to bring her handbag with her then she could have combed her hair and applied fresh lipstick. Gulping to swallow the dryness of her throat, she exited the cloakroom for the upper reaches of the Mealhouse Lane premises, where the editor had his office.

She was aware that the editor was like God to all departments. It was he who had the final say over the policies and production of the newspaper as well as writing certain lead articles. She knew him by sight, of course, as he strode about the building. His secretary, Mrs Pearson, was treated by lesser staff as some superior being but entering her office now, Kathy was greeted with a warm and friendly smile. 'Mr Coleman won't be long. He's had to take an urgent telephone call.'

Mrs Pearson's office was a lot less plush than Kathy would have expected for such a prestigious position. Indeed, it was as functional as the office in which she worked, containing a desk, two filing cabinets and a wilting plant. Perhaps she was too busy to water it. She directed Kathy to a chair and carried on typing, her fingers flying over the typewriter keys.

At that moment, the door to the editor's office opened and the man himself stood there. 'Miss Armstrong? Would you like to come through?'

His office, she saw now, was over the front entrance, its windows overlooking Mealhouse Lane. Every available surface, as far as she could see, was covered with files and old newspapers and she wondered how he could work in such chaos. Shoving a pile of papers to one side, he sat down behind the desk, and indicated the chair opposite. Ted Coleman was a large man, not particularly fat, but with a barrel chest and sturdy thighs. His ruddy face was topped by wispy white hair giving him an avuncular appearance at odds with his reputation. She mustn't allow herself to be overawed by him despite his god-like status. 'May I call you Katherine? Or do you prefer Kathy?' he asked now.

She gave a little cough to clear her throat of the dryness. 'Kathy, please.'

'Well, now,' he made a steeple of his fingers, rested his chin on them and his elbows on the desk. 'Mr Bleakley has told me that you'd like to become a reporter.' His thick fingers sorted through several loose pieces of paper on his desk and waved several cuttings at her which she saw were all the work she had done so far, some half-a-dozen pieces. 'Matthew – Mr Bleakley – has shown me what you've written and I would agree that you certainly show promise. But why did you not come into journalism when you first left school? Why now?'

'I didn't know it was a possibility. Had I known, I would certainly have applied sooner.' She smiled, feeling more at ease with this surprisingly genial man. 'I suppose I thought such opportunities were only offered to university graduates.'

He raised his eyebrows quizzically. 'Did you ever consider going to university?'

'Not really. It was always planned that I should go to commercial college to learn how to become a secretary. In the absence of certainty about what I wanted to do, I simply went along with it.'

'Your parents' influence, I suspect.'

She gave a rueful nod. 'Particularly my mother.'

146

'You were at college – for how long exactly?'
'Two years. I was 18 when I left.'
'So you're proficient in shorthand and typing. What else?'
'Book-keeping. Not one of my better subjects,' she admitted.
'But enough to keep a tab on expenses, that sort of thing?'
This was beginning to sound promising. 'More than adequate.'
'What's your English like?'
'My best – and favourite – subject at school and at college,' she enthused. 'My tutors seemed to think I have an instinctive feel for the grammar, a knack of knowing how words should fit together.'
'What made you come and work for the Evening News?' he asked now. 'Did you apply in the usual way, through an advertisement?'
'No, not really. Working for a newspaper appealed to me even then. I wrote a letter asking if I could be considered should any vacancies arise,' she said. 'Within a few days, a letter from the Advertising Manager arrived inviting me for an interview here.'
'That was enterprising of you.' He made a note on a pad before him. 'How long have you worked for us now?'
'Slightly over two years.'
'And do you like it here?'
'Very much so,' she said. 'I love the buzz about the place, even though I'm only a shorthand typist. I get a feeling of excitement when the presses start up.'
He gave her a smile which creased his face into furrows. 'I'm sorry to disillusion you but there is much that is mundane about reporting for a newspaper.'
'I know a lot of the work would involve ordinary everyday stuff, like attending the courts, flower shows, that sort of thing. Mr. Bleakley did warn me.'
'One more thing, Kathy. Do you have any immediate plans to marry?' He had the grace to look apologetic as he asked such a personal question but she'd been warned at College that bosses always asked that.

'Not in the foreseeable future.'

He leaned forward a little as if to make a point. 'Well, I don't know if you are aware of it but the Evening News has a training scheme for journalists. With your educational qualifications and enthusiasm, you would seem to be an ideal candidate. Of course, you'd be a year or two older than most of the others. Would that bother you?'

Her hopes rising with every statement he made, she said, 'Not at all. I see that as an advantage. I have more experience of working for the newspaper than someone coming straight from school or university.'

'I have to tell you, Kathy, that the decision isn't only mine to take. Matthew and I are part of a training panel and it's there that any decisions will be made. I've been told that there are some strong candidates.'

'Of course. I do understand,' she said, trying to swallow her disappointment that he couldn't be more positive.

'We will let you know before the next intake which is due to commence on…let me see…' he rummaged around on his desk eventually picking up what looked like a desk diary. 'Ah, yes, October. In the meantime, say nothing to anyone else. You'll find there are petty jealousies aplenty on a newspaper. I'll get my secretary to have a word with your immediate boss. Who is?'

'Mr Mansfield, the Office Manager.'

'Of course, Bob Mansfield. Only manners to keep him informed. Any further questions?'

'No, I don't think so. You've made everything very clear.'

Back in the office, she tried to pick up where she'd left off but she was too excited. She couldn't believe that it might be happening, that she could become a fledgling reporter. She yearned to be able to tell someone, anyone, but knew she couldn't, not yet. It was only with a supreme effort of concentration that she was able to finish off the work she had been doing.

* * *

'It looks like the lads have finally gone to sleep, thank goodness.' Mary heaved a sigh of relief as she sank into one of the fireside chairs. Joyce was in the other one, reading about the comings and goings of the film stars in her Picturegoer magazine.

'They were full of it tonight, weren't they, Mam?' Brian and Derek had been particularly argumentative and even in bed, had still been tormenting each other. Mam had been forced to go to the bottom of the stairs and shout up to them several times before they quietened down.

'Ay, they're hard work when they're like that.' She took the worn purse from her overall pocket, and shoved it deep down the side of the armchair. Joyce knew that with Dad home, he'd gone back to his old habit of taking a shilling or two if she left it lying around. 'For a pint and a ciggy,' he'd say, if tackled about it. 'A man's entitled to that at least.' To which Mam would retaliate, 'And your children are entitled to food in their bellies.' Joyce remembered the old argument from the days before Dad had gone to prison.

'Dad's late tonight, isn't he?' she said.

'Very late.' Mary emphasised it with a nod to the old clock on the mantelpiece. It was nearly nine o'clock and tea was long since over with, except for Dad's in the warming oven of the range. 'He's up to summat, no doubt of that.'

'Oh, no, Mam!' Joyce knew from the past what his lateness meant.

'That sounds like the back gate now. We'll see what he has to say for himself.' Mary rose from the chair and stood, her arms folded over her chest, facing the back door. 'Where the bloody hell have you been?' she asked, as Danny shambled in.

His movements were slow, his speech carefully pronounced and Joyce guessed that he was trying hard not to appear drunk. 'To the pub like all the other hardworking chaps. Now can I have me tea?'

'Not until you hand over your wages.' Mary went to stand in front of him, not cowed by his bulk and height.

'What bloody wages?'

'The wages you should have drawn today.'

He threw himself down on a chair by the table and bent to untie his shoelaces, nearly falling as he did so. 'They forgot to pay me.'

Mary yanked his head up by his hair. 'Don't lie to me, Danny. If you'd no wages, you'd no money to go drinking, especially the skinful you've had.'

He clamped his hand over hers and forced her fingers apart, easing his head out of her grasp but keeping hold of her hand, twisting it till she winced. 'I'm telling you they never bloody paid me.'

Mary managed to pull herself from his grasp. 'What have you done with it?' In the face of his silence, they both knew. 'You've lost it all on the horses, haven't you?' Mary yelled. 'Then drunk what little there was left? You bloody swine!'

She went to pummel his chest, a futile gesture, for he caught her wrists before she could make contact. 'I'm sorry, love. Someone gave me a sure thing on a late race so I had a bet. That came nowhere so I put some more on, hoping to get the money back but I lost that too.'

'Don't tell me anymore. I've heard it all before anyway.' Mary looked down in disgust at his bowed head. 'And what's me and the kids supposed to do for the rest of the week? You can starve for all I care.'

'You managed well enough when I were in prison.'

'Only because our Nick tipped his wages up.'

'Then you'll have to ask him again because you'll get nowt from me, woman.'

'No? But you'll get summat from me!' Mary pulled open the warming oven, grabbed a towel from the rail and took out the dried-up offering. 'You wanted your tea. Well, here it is.' With a quick movement, she upended the plate onto his head, from where it trickled down his face and onto his shoulders. The contents the plate had only been lukewarm and the gravy congealed but it was still moist enough to stick to his face, neck and shirt. 'Pity it wasn't boiling hot but then I'd have been had up for assault too,' she said, with a look of satisfaction on her face.

He roared and leapt to his feet as if to strike her, the remains of his tea scattering on the floor.

Mary dodged behind the armchair and grabbed the poker from the hearth. 'Don't you dare.'

In the face of her rebellion, he turned on Joyce and fetched her a stinging slap across her face. 'You can get this lot cleared up for a start.' Though her face burned, she did as she was told, shuddering as she tried to clean up the glutinous mess.

The latch on the door leading to the stairs clicked and Lucy's fearful face peeped through the crack. 'What's all the noise?' she whispered to Joyce.

'Mam and Dad are having a row. Go to bed, sweetheart.'

But Danny had caught their whispered exchange. 'Get back upstairs, you snivelling little brat.'

'Take Lucy back to bed, Joyce,' Mary commanded.

'But I want to stay with you, Mam.'

'Please, love, go with Lucy. I'll be all right.'

Joyce pointed to the brush and shovel. 'What about this?'

'Don't worry, I'll do that, just go to bed and try to sleep.'

In the bed they shared, Lucy clung to Joyce. 'It's not because Mam bought me those new shoes, is it?' Lucy whispered.

'No, love, it's because Dad's late home and he's drunk.' Joyce held the child until she drifted back to sleep, while she listened to the voices raised in anger downstairs. There'd be little sleep for her that night.

* * *

The Suez Crisis was on Nick's mind as he walked home from the bus stop the following Friday. He'd heard from a workmate who'd seen it in the Bolton Evening News that notices recalling reservists could possibly be sent out. So far, Nick had heard nothing but it was early days yet. He knew that Egypt's President Nasser had grabbed control of the Suez Canal Company in July, despite protestations from Anthony Eden, the Prime Minister. Talks were going on between the United States, Britain and

151

France but seemed as if it was a question of when, not if, troops would be sent in.

As he walked through the back gate, through the window he could see his parents confronting each other and he could tell from the hands on the hips, the wagging finger, and the working mouths, that they were exchanging harsh words. Bloody hell, another row! He hoped this one wouldn't go on as long as the one last week when Dad had gambled his wages away. That had spilled over into the weekend.

Danny pointed an accusing finger at his wife. 'Do you know what your bloody mother's done?' were his first words to Nick as he slipped out of his boots by the back door. 'Only shown me up in front of all me workmates.'

'How'd she do that?' Nick spoke quietly. He'd soon discovered it was the only way to defuse such situations though there didn't seem much chance of that here.

'Come to meet me at the Works gates and demanded I hand over me bloody wages, that's what!' His father's face was red, his fists clenched by his sides, his body tense as if poised for action.

'I weren't giving you opportunity to put it on the horses this time or to pee it up the wall,' she retaliated, probably not for the first time.

'You might've given me the chance, woman,' Danny yelled back. 'I hope you realise I'll never live this down.'

'Good, happen you'll not be the big 'I am' you think you are.'

'And you need a leathering.' Danny advanced towards her, his fists bunched.

'And you never think of anyone other than yourself.' Despite her inferior height and weight, Mam was standing up to him. 'You talk of your feelings, but what about mine every time I visited you in prison, what with being frisked and doors locked behind me, like I was the one being imprisoned.'

'Then you know what it was like for me.'

'You were the one convicted.' She drew in a deep breath. 'But it's always the same; it's the families who suffer.'

Danny reached forward and fetched a blow across Mary's face that knocked her to the floor.

Nick jumped forward. 'No, Dad.'

'Out of my way, this has nowt to do with you,'

Nick grabbed his father's arm. 'You'll not hit Mam again while I'm here.'

Danny yanked his arm from Nick's grasp. 'I can lick you any day.'

'I don't want to hit you, Dad,' Nick warned, squaring up to his father.

Danny laughed. 'I'd like to see you try.' He lunged at Nick who dodged out of reach.

His father came at him again but Nick parried the blow and knocked Danny's shoulder. As he staggered, he aimed for Nick's chin. Again Nick dodged but managed a punch to his Dad's stomach. Danny fell to the floor, gasping. Nick stood over him. 'You will never hit Mam again. Is that clear?'

Clutching his stomach, Danny nodded.

Bracing himself with his legs apart, Nick leaned down a hand to help his father up. Hesitantly, he took the proffered hand and with Nick's help, got to his feet. 'And another thing, Dad. You come straight home with your pay packet from now on. Any further slip-ups and I'll make sure I'm at the gates with Mam.' Only then did Nick turn to his mother, now sitting on a chair, dabbing her bleeding lip with a corner of a tea towel. 'You OK, Mam?'

'I'm fine, love, and thanks.'

With a wheezy 'Huh' in their direction, Danny reached into his back pocket and pulled out his wage packet. He removed a pound note which he pocketed and threw the opened packet on to the floor. 'There's me bloody wages! Satisfied now?'

'Pick it up, Dad, and put it on the table.'

'Pick it up yourself.'

'That money is for running your home, feeding your family. Now, pick it up,' Nick demanded.

'Bloody hell,' Danny wheezed, 'I never had this much bother in prison.' He picked the packet up, together with some coins that had fallen out, and put them on the table.

'I can always arrange for you to go back there. Or better still, I can throw you out. We managed all right without you before, we can again.' He looked for confirmation from his mother.

She shook her head. 'No, I'll give him another chance. Though if he does it again, he's out.'

'I'm off for a pint,' Danny said in disgust, 'that is, if no-one has any objections.'

'What about your tea?'

'I don't bloody want any.'

'Then make sure you're back at a reasonable time and not drunk.'

Danny made for the door, grabbing his work jacket. 'I'll come back when I'm good and ready. And I'll drink as much as I like.'

'Not on a pound, you won't. And that's to last you all week, there's no more where that came from.' Mary picked up the wage packet. 'This is all spoken for, with what I owe from last week.'

With a disgusted look in their direction, Danny stormed out.

CHAPTER 17

Kathy knew she'd have to say something soon but the mere thought of it caused her heart to flutter and her stomach to churn. She'd been like this for days now, knowing she needed to tell John about the possibility of her being accepted onto the journalism training course. Except that she knew instinctively he wouldn't like it.

They were driving once again to the Yew Tree in Anglezarke and she was reminded of that other evening in the middle of winter, when the fields and hedgerows were stripped bare. The scenery had all been so stark then, caught as it was in the beam of the headlights. Now, the fields were ripe for harvesting, the greenery on the hedgerows and trees tired and wilting. Then, she and John had been in the earliest days of their romance. Now they seemed to be established in a long term relationship. So, there was nothing to be afraid of, was there? Surely they could discuss the matter sensibly and John would see her point of view.

The pub was more crowded than usual, with people like themselves who had come out for a summer's evening drink. The fireplace was empty of logs; in their place was a huge vase filled with dried flowers and grasses. Their usual table by the fireplace was taken so they were forced to sit at a table near the window. At an adjoining table were a noisy group of young middle-class people, not exactly conducive to an important conversation. Should she wait until they were sitting in the car? No, that would only be putting off the moment. In the end, it was John himself who brought matters to a head.

'You're very quiet tonight, sweetheart,' he said. 'Is everything all right?'

Taking a deep breath, she said, 'Do you remember the first time I told you about writing for Town Topics?'

'Vaguely. I seem to remember I was a bit sniffy about it.'

'You said then that I shouldn't get any fancy ideas about becoming a reporter. Well, I have.'

For long seconds, he sat in silence. 'What…what the hell do you mean?' he said, his voice tight.

'That I have applied to become a trainee reporter at the Bolton Evening News.'

'What's brought this on?'

The anger in his voice made her waver but she ploughed on. 'Maybe it's something that's been at the back of my mind since I first went to work there. And you put the idea in my mind yourself. I hadn't given it a thought before then.'

'What makes you think you'll be accepted?' His fingers were wrapped tightly round the glass he was holding.

'I don't yet but I've been to see the editor and my application is to go before the rest of the training panel,' she explained.

'So it's all up in the air?'

She was feeling more deflated by the minute. 'I suppose so.'

'Well, I'm glad you've told me now, before it's too late. Presumably, you can still withdraw your application.'

'What?' she said, sitting upright and banging her glass down.

'That there's still time to change your mind.'

'I've no intention of doing that.'

'Come on, Kathy,' he said, more reasonably, 'you know it's only a silly girlish dream.'

'It's no more a silly dream than going to Australia.'

'It's not the same thing at all,' he reasoned,

'So it's all right for men to have aspirations and goals but not women?' Despite this being their first quarrel, she was determined not to back down.

'We all know women are destined to marry, have children and run the home.'

She wanted to slap him. 'Well, this young woman wants more than that. I want a career.'

He actually laughed then. 'A career? Writing about flower shows and galas? That's all the work you'll be allocated. The men will see to that.'

'May I remind you that during two world wars, the women practically ran this country, doing all the jobs men did and more?'

156

'And got shoved out of their jobs when the men came home,' he jeered.

'Because men couldn't stand seeing how well women could do the work.'

From the patchy red blotches on his face and neck, she could tell he was livid. He stood abruptly. 'Get your jacket, I'm taking you home. Perhaps you'll come to your senses when you've slept on it.'

She picked up her jacket from the adjacent chair. 'I shan't change my mind.'

Usually, on the way home, John would stop somewhere quiet where they could kiss and cuddle. She knew there would be none of that tonight for the silence in the car was icy. He sat rigidly, his hands tight on the steering wheel, a look of fierce concentration on his face. She didn't know how to break the barrier between them. It seemed as if their thoughts were poles apart. He finally pulled up outside her house and turned to face her.

'Do you know, I was going to ask you to marry me at Christmas?'

She stared at him. 'Marry you?'

'Not immediately, of course, we'd have to save up for a couple of years first.'

She drew in a shaky breath, knowing he was using this as bait to get her to change her mind. 'It might not be what I want.'

He drew in a deep breath. 'Kathy, if you persist in this…foolish whim, then we're through.'

His words were like cold water in her face. 'You can't mean that,' she gasped.

He leaned across her to open the door, making it obvious that he wasn't coming round to do it for her. 'I do. If you insist on going ahead, I can see no point in carrying on.'

'Then there's no more to be said.' As she climbed out of the car, he slammed it shut and drove off at speed. She stared after him, feeling empty and drained but knew she had not finished yet. She still had to break the news to her parents and she was dreading that, knowing her mother would side with John and tell her she was crazy. Maybe she was. Yet she knew, with absolute certainty, that she was doing the right thing.

* * *

Kathy was surprised to find her legs shaking and her hands trembling as she fitted her key into the front door. Breathing deeply in an attempt to calm herself, she opened the door to the sitting room. Both her parents looked up. 'You're back early, love,' her father said, a look of concern on his face. 'Nothing wrong, is there?'

The last thing she wanted to do was to talk about what had happened but knew that her mother, at least, would not be content to be fobbed off with some excuse or other. 'John and I have finished,' she said.

Her mother's knitting dropped mid-row into her lap. 'Oh, no, love! Why? What's brought that on?' As always, there was a note of censure in her voice as if she immediately thought the fault was Kathy's. Which in a way, it was. She might as well face this hurdle now as later. At least this way her parents would be aware of what was going on. 'It's because I might be leaving my job in Advertising.'

'You've not been sacked, have you?'

Trust her mother to think the worst. 'No, of course not. I've applied to become a trainee reporter.' She held her breath as she waited for the reaction.

'A reporter? But surely...' Vera stopped. Such a career choice was clearly beyond her comprehension.

'How's that come about, love?' Ron asked.

'You know the pieces I've written for Town Topics?' Her mother, in particular, had been showing friends and neighbours the cuttings she'd saved. 'That, and what someone said to me, made me think that I'd like to do that instead of secretarial work.'

'But what about all that training, your two years at college, your shorthand and typing?' Vera asked now, picking up her knitting again.

'It won't be wasted, Mum. I'd need shorthand for taking notes quickly and I'd be able to type up my own reports.'

She told them about Mr Bleakley complimenting her on her writing and how that had made her think. That she'd discussed the possibility with him and he'd said he would have a word with the editor, Mr Coleman, and that she'd been to see him. 'He said the decision isn't only up to him; he would have to consult others.'

'What's this got to do with you and John finishing though?' Ron asked.

'John doesn't approve,' Vera guessed.

'That about sums it up, Mum.'

'Are you sure this is what you want, love?' her father said. 'We'd both hoped things were getting serious between the two of you.'

'They were, Dad, but John doesn't want me to do it. If we were to get married, he'd want me to be a stay-at-home wife.'

'And what's wrong with that, I'd like to know? It's what I've done all my married life and I've no complaints,' Vera huffed.

'Despite what you think, Mum, I believe there's more to life than being a housewife.' She glanced at her mother who had the grace to look away. 'I've never wanted anything as much as I want this. Of course, a lot of what I'd have to write would be boring stuff but if I work hard at it, I should progress to better things.'

'Would they want you to give it all up if you did marry?' Ron asked. 'After all, training someone is considered an investment, an investment they wouldn't want to lose out on.'

Her heart lurched as she realised that the fact that she was a woman might be against her. 'I'm not sure about that, Dad. Though Mr Coleman did ask me if I had any plans to marry in the near future.'

'I understand it's a standard remark these days,' Ron added.

'Well, it's most unfair.' Kathy hadn't realised quite how strongly she felt about it until the question had arisen with John.

'But most women are glad to give up working when they marry, not to have the responsibility of a job,' her mother pointed out. 'It's the natural order of things.'

'I'm not most women, Mum,' she said quietly. 'I want more than that.'

'But John's such a nice stable young man, in a steady job with good prospects. You're mad to miss this opportunity.' Her mother wasn't willing to give up on John as the ideal husband for Kathy, even if she was.

'Don't forget, Mum, it was John who finished with me,' Kathy said.

'Because you're persisting in this foolish notion of becoming a reporter,' her mother flashed back. 'I'm sure John would take you back if you dropped the idea.'

Ron took off his spectacles and put them on the arm of the chair. 'Your mother has a point. I suggest you think some more about whether it's really what you want to do.'

She drew herself up to her full height. 'I shan't change my mind,' she said.

* * *

Kathy's heart was thudding and her mouth tight with anger when she left the house one Saturday morning. She was sick of hearing how wonderful John was, how foolish she was to pursue what was at best a dream. Finally, this morning, she'd snapped at her mother. 'If you're so keen on him, you marry him,' she'd yelled and stormed out of the house.

By the time she reached Chorley New Road moments later, she was regretting her words. Her mother was under a great deal of strain because of her father was still far from well and she would probably be in tears by now. She was about to go back and apologise when she heard her name being called and the person doing the calling was Nick Roberts.

She wasn't sure if she had conjured him up, yet knowing from the dryness in her mouth, the trembling in her knees, that she had not. She turned and spotted him on the other side of Chorley New Road.

He waited for a gap in the traffic then bounded across to her, looking nothing like his usual smart self. Gone was the immaculate Teddy boy suit; instead he wore a crumpled pair of old trousers, a threadbare, slightly-too-small shirt open at the neck and with his sleeves rolled up. His usually pristine hair flopped over his brow and there were smudges of dirt on his face. He looked so much like he had as a youth, her heart skipped a beat. She wanted to reach out to stroke the hair back off his face.

'Guess what? We've finally got a council house up Brazeley,' he gasped as he reached her.

'And you're moving in today.' His face had a faint sheen of sweat and there was what looked like part of a cobweb on his forehead.

'How did you know?'

With gentle fingers, she wiped the remains of the cobweb from his face with her fingers and showed him. Their eyes met and held until she looked away in confusion.

He laughed. 'The house is a bit mucky. So's our furniture, come to that. Where you off to?'

She didn't want to tell him about the argument with her mother. That would involve explanations about the cause. 'Nowhere particular. I thought I might go and see if Carole is in.'

'Have you got a minute to sit down and chat?' He indicated the seat opposite the Greenwood where the old men usually sat to watch the world pass by.

Once seated, she said, 'I'll bet your Mam is thrilled about the new house, isn't she?'

'Over the moon. In the end, it were so unexpected that it took us all by surprise.'

'What's it like, then?'

'It's got three bedrooms, which means the girls can finally have a room of their own,' he enthused. 'And a bathroom! Much to the lads' disgust.'

'Whereabouts is it?'

'Lancaster Avenue. There's a bit of a garden at the front and a biggish one at the back. Dad's full of enthusiasm, says he's going to grow some vegetables. I'll believe that when I see it,' Nick snorted.

'How've things been with him recently?'

His eyes clouded over. 'Not easy. We had a bit of bother with him for the first few weeks after he'd started work but he seems to have settled down again. How's your Dad?'

'Much the same. In fact, he's been to the Infirmary this week for some tests. We should know something soon.'

'I'm sorry to hear that.' He went quiet and shifted uncomfortably on the seat. 'I'm sorry, too, about what happened at Haigh Hall.'

The way he was looking at her, it was as if Haigh Hall had never happened. 'It was more John's fault than yours. You made every effort to avoid the confrontation.'

'The trouble is, when I see you with him, I'm wishing it was me.'

Over the past couple of weeks, she'd deliberated on how she should tell him when she did see him. In the end, she said quietly, 'You won't be seeing me with him again.'

'Does that mean what I think it means?'

'That I'm no longer with John? Yes.'

'Bugger me! I feel as if I've had the stuffing knocked out of me.' He threw himself back against the form. 'Was it owt to do with that Saturday at Haigh Hall?'

She hesitated before answering. 'Not really. I've applied to transfer to Editorial to train as a journalist. He didn't like it, said it was a silly whim. Yet only days before he'd told me he'd been thinking about Australia. To my mind, that amounts to the same thing.'

'Australia? Emigrating there, you mean?'

She nodded. 'He told me he'd been thinking about it for ages but he'd never said anything to me.'

He raised a quizzical eyebrow. 'And had you told him of your plans?'

'Not until after I'd seen the editor,' she admitted.

There was a slight pause then he said, in such a light-hearted way she wasn't sure if he was serious, 'Will you come out with me then?'

'What about Sally?' she asked mischievously.

'Sally?'

'You said you were going out with Sally.' When he still looked mystified, she reminded him. 'Haigh Hall.'

He looked uncomfortable. 'I were trying to make you jealous.'

She laughed. 'I sort of guessed that.' Then her face turned serious. 'I'm sorry, Nick. It's way too soon.'

He was silent for a long moment. 'Since that night on the Passion Wagon, I can't stop thinking about you, Kathy. Wherever I am, whoever I'm with, you're always on me mind.'

Again there was that spark arcing between them, that momentary sense of connection. Firmly, she said, 'Friendship's all I can offer at the moment.'

'I'll settle for that.' He gave a rueful grin. 'Look, I have to get back to help with the unloading and sorting out. I'd only slipped out for some tea. Mam didn't want to send the boys with them not knowing the area. She probably thinks I've got lost too.' He paused for a moment then continued, 'Why don't you come back with me?'

She shook her head. 'I'd be in the way.'

'No, you wouldn't. You'd be a much-needed extra pair of hands.'

'Well, if you're sure,' she said, thankful that she was wearing an old pair of slacks and a blouse tied round her midriff.

As if reading her thoughts, he said, 'Are you OK in those togs? Only it's chaotic up there.'

When she arrived home at teatime, tired and dusty, she was greeted with, 'And where do you think you've been, young lady?'

She went to stand in the doorway of the kitchen, where her mother was preparing tea. Time to be truthful, she thought. 'I've been helping Nick Roberts and his family move into their new house up Brazeley.'

Vera poured boiling water from the kettle into the warmed teapot. 'What you bother with the likes of him for when you could have a lovely young man like John, I don't know.'

Kathy sighed. 'We've had all this out before, Mum.'

'I only want what's best for you, love. To see you settled and happy.'

'I know you mean well, Mum, but you can't live my life for me.' Vera sniffed and busied herself with the tea things. 'I'm sorry for yelling at you before I went out.'

'That's all right, love. I'm sorry too.' She turned and quietly closed the door between the kitchen and the lounge, where Ron dozed in the armchair. 'I've been that worried about your Dad, it's made me a bit snappy.'

Kathy put her arms round her mother and gave her a hug. 'I know, Mum. I'm worried too.'

Vera returned the hug then detached herself. 'Best get yourself cleaned up, you look a bit mucky. Happen the Roberts's deserve a break after all they've been through,' she said, leaving Kathy gaping at the conciliatory tone in the remark.

CHAPTER 18

'Kettle's on, Nick.' Mac called as Nick unlocked the garage. 'Come up for a brew.' It was a habit they'd fallen into, lingering over their tea as they set the world to rights.

Nick climbed the stairs to the flat. Mac was dressed this morning, though often he wasn't. 'What's it like out, Nick? Feels as if there's a bit of a nip in the air.'

'There is but I think it will warm up later.' Nick moved the ubiquitous stack of newspapers and motoring magazines from one of the chairs and, sitting down, took the mug of tea Mac had brewed.

'I can't believe it's nearly the end of August already. I don't know where the year has gone.' Nick gave Mac an amused grin, knowing the remark to be one of Mac's most well used ones. 'You seen the paper this morning?'

'Apart from the News of the World on a Sunday, we don't bother. Dad buys the racing paper and an Evening News occasionally.'

'Our troops, along with the Frogs, are massing somewhere in the Mediterranean with a view to invading Egypt.'

'Will they do that, do you think?'

Mac was not one of those who believed that it was right for Britain to go in and uphold the might of the Empire. 'The Empire! A 19th century anachronism! We're half way through the 20th century, for heaven's sake! This little island has all on staying afloat after the massive debts we ran up in the war,' was his opinion.

Nick didn't mind the rhetoric. Mac had opened his eyes to what was going on in the world and he enjoyed debating the issues with him. 'Bloody Anthony Eden!' he said now, 'thinks he's made in the same mould as Churchill. Well, this Suez business will be his downfall, you mark my words.'

Nick had been marking Mac's words for weeks now about the Suez Crisis. 'I still haven't heard owt about being recalled. I'd have gone willingly if I'd been called up.'

'Course you would, lad, wouldn't have expected anything less from you. Any word about your brother? The one that's in the RAF?'

'Only that he's on standby,' Nick said, 'but then he's a regular now. Has to expect moves like this at critical times.'

'Happy enough, is he?'

'I think so, from the last letter Mam had. Being at Kirkham, it's easy enough to nip into Blackpool when he does get any time off.'

'And what about that young lady, Kathy? Seen anything of her?'

Nick grinned. He couldn't wait to tell Mac. 'She's broken off with her boyfriend. She told me last Saturday.'

Mac's face registered surprise. 'Did she say why?'

'Apparently, he didn't like it when she told him she wanted to become a reporter.'

'A reporter, eh? What's brought that on?'

'She's been writing pieces for Town Topics in the Evening News and found she'd a talent for it.'

'Do you think she'll go back with him?' Mac cocked his head to one side, pipe halfway to his mouth.

'I don't think so, she seems pretty determined. It didn't help that he'd like to emigrate to Australia. With her, if possible. She didn't fancy that.' He rose and made as if to take their mugs into the kitchen. 'Better be making a start.'

'There's no rush. Sit down again, I have a proposition for you.' Intrigued, he did as he was told. 'Are you going back to night school?

'The new term starts in a couple of weeks and I've already enrolled,' he replied.

'Do you intend carrying on with it?'

Nick nodded. 'I'm determined now I've got this far.'

'It's like this, Nick. It isn't getting any easier crawling about under cars and my eyes aren't what they were.'

'You're not thinking of selling up, are you?' Nick asked in swift concern.

'Nay, I can't afford to pack it in yet. Nor,' he said, using his now cold pipe as a punctuation mark, 'do I want to. You've given me a new lease of life and business has picked up since you've been here. It could do a lot more if you worked here full-time, especially if you were a qualified mechanic.'

The impact of Mac's words registered only slowly with Nick. 'You're offering me a job?'

'If you want it, yes.'

He slumped back in the chair, humbled by the offer. 'I don't know what to say, Mac,' he managed in the end. 'But I have to ask, what about pay?'

Mac named a figure well below what he was earning on the building site, qualifying it with, 'It's not much but until we can expand, it's all I can afford.'

He would love to jump at the chance but was aware that he needed to take time to make a decision. 'Can I sleep on it, Mac, give it a coat of looking-at?'

Mac laughed. 'You take as much time as you want. It's a big decision – for both of us.'

* * *

The following evening, Nick walked off the dance floor of the Fling to be faced with a belligerent Sally. She stood, hands on hips, breasts thrust forward, making a statement of her mood. 'Well, Nick, I haven't seen you in a good while.'

'Not now, Sal, there's a good girl.' The girl he'd been bopping with gave him a sympathetic look and walked off towards the toilets.

'I'm no girl, I'm nearly 21. As for being good, well, you should know about that.' He shifted uncomfortably, still suffering from a guilty conscience about the way he'd treated Sally. 'Nowt to say for yourself, Nick?'

'What's there to say?'

'The last time I saw you we spent the night together,' she hissed, 'making me think we were finally getting it together. Since then I've seen nowt of you. It's like you've been avoiding me.'

'I know I behaved badly that night and I've regretted it ever since.'

167

'And that's supposed to make me feel better?' All belligerence gone now, she seemed to droop. 'You used me, didn't you? Only I was too blind to see.'

'I'm sorry, Sally, truly I am.'

'You will be, Nick Roberts, you will be!' Sally turned quickly and thrust her way into a group of people standing nearby.

Bragger appeared at his side. 'What was all that about?'

Nick shook his head. 'You don't want to know.'

'As bad as that, eh?' He proffered Nick a cigarette. 'Have you seen who's here, by the way?'

Still uncomfortable after the exchange with Sally, Nick said, 'Who?'

'Kathy Armstrong.'

His heart started hammering as he scanned the shabby mediocrity of the Fling. 'Where?'

'She and that Carole have just come in. They're over by the cloakroom.'

He looked over to where Bragger had indicated. She was looking round, a little uncertainly, her head tilted as if listening to something Carole was saying. The gold and green skirt she was wearing seemed to shimmer in the subdued lighting. With an apologetic word to Bragger, he went over to the two girls. 'Kathy, I didn't expect to see you here.'

Her green eyes were sparkling and she gave him a warm smile. 'I'm full of surprises.'

With the insistent beat of Bill Haley and the Comets penetrating every corner of the room, he pulled her towards the dance floor. 'Let's dance.' They gave themselves up to the rhythm, her full skirt and starched petticoats flying as he twirled her round, their feet performing the intricate manoeuvres automatically, his hands catching hers in a sure grasp as she swung free of him then came back.

As they walked off the dance floor, someone said, 'If it isn't the King and Queen of rock and roll.' The voice belonged to Jud, arms crossed, a leering grin on his face. By his side was Sally, annoyance plain to see on her face. 'So they'd like to think,' she said. 'Come on, Jud, let's show 'em how it should be done.'

Nick groped for Kathy's hand. 'Ignore them,' he said in a low voice as Sally pulled her brother on to the dance floor and they began bopping.

'I'm trying to pretend they're not here,' she whispered back.

That was difficult to do when they were momentarily hemmed in by a group who'd gathered to watch for brother and sister were undeniably good. And they were bopping right in front of Nick and Kathy, Sally was dressed in the ubiquitous tight black skirt and black sweater hugging her breasts, her hips thrusting provocatively in Nick's direction. As Bill Haley's 'Razzle Dazzle' drew to a close, the pair walked off the dance floor. 'That's how it should be done,' Jud said, standing directly in front of them.

Nick tried to pull Kathy sideways out of the group surrounding them but they, perhaps sensing trouble, had drawn even closer.

Jud saw the manoeuvre. 'It's not like you to back down, Nick.'

'Call yourself a Teddy boy!' jeered Sally.

'Bet you don't know what your kid sister is up to,' Jud said.

As if against his will, Nick let go of Kathy's hand and faced up to Jud. 'What did you say about me sister?' His voice was steely.

'You should ask her where she is when she's supposed to be with her mates.' Jud didn't sound so sure of himself now.

Sally thumped her brother's arm. 'Big mouth.'

'You can say what you want about me but you'll say nowt against me sister. She's nobbut a kid. Happen you should look to your own sister before slagging mine off,' Nick said. Around them, people had fallen silent although the music was still playing in the background.

'You bastard!' yelled Jud and lunged at Nick, fists flailing. The suddenness of Jud's move and the force of his body behind it, carried both of them to the floor as each tried to get a punch in.

Suddenly, all the lights came on and a voice rapped, 'What's going on here?' The music ground to a halt abruptly and people parted to let the manager of the club through. 'Pack it in, now!'

Nick and Jud struggled to their feet, both dusty from the floor and stood before the man. 'Bloody Teddy boys! What's your names?'

Nick was the first to speak, with some difficulty from a split lip. 'Nick Roberts.'

Jud had to wipe blood away from his nose before giving his name 'Jud Simcox.'

Nick glanced in Kathy's direction, saw that her face was pale and distressed, but she wouldn't look at him. Instead, she was looking at Carole who was handing Kathy her jacket. Now they were leaving and he couldn't stop her.

He turned his attention back to the manager who was saying, 'Well, you're both banned from now on. Get out, the pair of you.' As he and Jud made a move towards the exit, the man grabbed Jud's arm and said, 'No, not together, one at a time.'

A few minutes later, Nick caught up with the girls at the Black Dog. He'd run all the way from the Fling and he had to lean against the bus stop to catch his breath. 'Kathy, I'm sorry. I didn't mean for that to happen.'

'You never do,' she sighed.

'Don't catch the bus, Kathy. Let's talk some more,' he pleaded.

As the bus slowed to a stop, she shook her head. 'There's no point, Nick.'

'Please, Kathy.' He tried to detain her with his hand but she shrugged him off.

'You catching this bus, love?' asked the conductor from the platform, tapping his fingers against his ticket holder.

'Goodbye, Nick,' she said, as she climbed aboard and there was a finality in the words. As the bus pulled away, she did not turn round.

CHAPTER 19

The bus home from Bolton was running late and Kathy looked at her watch with an impatient sigh. It would happen today of all days when she was anxious to get home. The conductor on the bus had announced there'd been an accident on Chorley New Road and it was taking some time to clear the traffic. Sympathetic though she was, she couldn't help feeling resentful about the delay. For it was today that her parents had been due at the hospital for the results of her father's tests. The possible outcome was making her stomach churn.

Alighting from the bus opposite the Greenwood, she noticed a group of people standing around, serious looks on their faces. The accident, then, must have happened close by. A police car was parked in front of the Greenwood and a policeman was talking to a woman, her hair done up in a turban and wearing the ubiquitous weaver's overall. Kathy turned away from the scene. Someone would tell her soon enough. They always did in a place like Horwich.

When she opened the back door, the house was unusually quiet with no sign of any preparation for tea. Normally, the kitchen would be steamy with vegetables simmering on the stove and an appetising smell coming from whatever main dish Mum was cooking. She knew instinctively that something was wrong and her heart dropped. 'Mum?' she called, aware of the slight panic in her voice.

'In here, love,' came her mother's voice from the sitting room.

Vera sat in front of the empty fireplace, her hands cupped round a mug of tea, as if drawing strength from holding on to it. The fact that she was sitting in Ron's chair rather than the one she usually occupied, alerted Kathy that the situation was serious. Confirmation was in her mother's blotchy face, puffy eyelids and persistent sniffs as if she had only recently stopped crying.

'Where's Dad?' whispered Kathy.

Her mother drew in a ragged breath. 'Having a lie down. The journey really took it out of him.'

'You didn't go in the car?'

She shook her head. 'He didn't feel up to driving though in my opinion he wouldn't have been as tired if he had.'

Shrugging her coat off and draping it over the arm of the sofa, Kathy sat down and reached out to touch the hand nearest to her. 'What did the doctors say?'

Vera bent down and put the mug on the hearth, something she usually discouraged. 'It's not good news, love.' Her red-rimmed eyes spilled over again.

Kathy was by her side in an instant, kneeling on the floor to put her arms round her mother who was sobbing now. 'Is it cancer?' she asked softly.

Vera nodded. 'They reckon it's too far advanced to do anything,' she said in a voice breaking with emotion.

'How...long has he got?' Kathy stumbled over the words, almost too stunned to take in the immediate implications.

'A few months at the most,' Vera croaked.

'Does he know?'

'Yes, he insisted. He's not said much. Went straight to bed. I've been sitting here ever since.' She clutched hold of Kathy's arms. 'Oh, love, what are we going to do?'

It was the helplessness in her usually-so-capable mother's voice that started her own tears. 'I don't know, Mum.' They clung to each other for some moments and Kathy couldn't have said who was comforting whom.

Eventually Vera spoke, in her usual no-nonsense way. 'This won't do, won't do at all.' She pulled away from Kathy so that she could look down at her upturned face. 'Your Dad will be down soon and we don't want him to know how upset we are. We have to be strong for him, do our grieving in private.' She pushed herself upright, straightening her skirt as she did so. 'Time to think about some tea.'

Kathy knelt back on her heels and pulled herself up with the arms of the chair and the sofa. 'You won't want to start cooking at this time. What about having fish and chips tonight?'

'Good idea. Your Dad won't mind for once, I'm sure.'

'He hasn't been eating much anyway.'

'You've noticed?'

172

'The way he picks and pokes at his food? Yes, I've noticed.' She reached for her jacket and slipped it back on. 'I'll go to the chippie.'

'And I'll warm the plates and brew the tea.' The familiar creak of her parents' bed came from the bedroom above. 'Sounds as if he's stirring. Best get a move on.'

As Kathy walked up Travers Street, she couldn't rid herself of the feeling of unreality. It seemed odd that people were going about their business as usual while her Dad was…dying. A sob rose in her throat and she drew in a ragged breath to stop it forming. She couldn't, mustn't cry in the street.

The chip shop, adjacent to the Greenwood, was doing good business as usual. The fuggy warmth, the acrid smell of salt and vinegar as they were liberally sprinkled on someone's order, the crackling of fish frying in the huge fryers, enveloped Kathy in a comforting embrace. Crowded with good-natured weavers on their way home from work, the shop was alive and bustling. The talk was all of the accident earlier that evening. Some kiddie had been knocked down while chasing after a ball. Kathy's heart went out to the parents of the child, to the child itself, if it had survived.

Back at home, her father appeared to be in a quiet, but resigned, mood while her mother was determined to be cheerful. Yet Kathy sensed that tears were never far away, much the same as her. They did not discuss her father's illness. Instead they talked of more mundane matters.

Their cosiness was disturbed as they were finishing off a second cup of tea, what her father called 'a chatting cup,' by a knock at the door. It was Mrs Westbury from across the road, ostensibly come to see how Ron had fared at the hospital. Sitting her down at the table with a cup of tea, Vera hedged enough to infer that the tests had been inconclusive. Ron, meanwhile, had taken himself into the sitting room to read the Bolton Evening News.

Kathy stayed in the kitchen but was lost in her own thoughts until she noticed that Mrs Westbury had now moved on to the accident. 'Poor mite,' she said, 'I don't think he stood a chance.'

'Was he dead, then?' Vera asked.

'I think he was still alive – barely – when they took him to hospital.'

'What was his mother thinking of, letting a little one run around on his own on Chorley New Road?' said Vera.

'He wasn't that little. Someone said he was about 11 or 12,' Mrs Westbury sniffed. 'Old enough to know better than chasing after a ball on a main road.'

'Do we know who it was?' asked Vera.

'Somebody said it were one of the Roberts' boys, just moved up Brazeley.'

The shock of the woman's words hit Kathy like a blow to the stomach. Flashing into her mind came the memory of Brian and Derek playing football in the back garden of their new home when she'd gone up there. The news that one of them had been seriously injured, coming as it did on the heels of the news about her father, made her feel sick. Drawing a deep breath to stop the sudden nausea, she rose to her feet, her chair scraping on the linoleum. 'I must go up there, Mum, see what's happening.'

'They'll be at the hospital.' Vera's voice was cold with disapproval. 'You won't be able to help.'

'I don't care. Nick's my friend and I have to go.' All thoughts of the words they'd exchanged when last they'd seen each other had gone.

* * *

Enveloped in the strong antiseptic smell of the hospital, Nick wondered how his parents were faring at Brian's bedside. If his guts were churning with fear, what must they be feeling? His mother would be heart-broken. Although she always claimed the two boys were the bane of her life, she loved them both equally and dearly. Who didn't, he reflected; they were such engaging, if exasperating, lads. And so close, too.

Derek had seen the accident and had been brought in too, to be treated for shock. He was sleeping now, his face white against the pristine pillow, his hair stuck up in its usual tufts, his hands, for once spotlessly clean, lying still on top of the bed cover. He'd lain like this for a couple of hours now, not moving, not speaking. The increased activity in the children's ward by nurses told him that any moment now a bell would signal the end of visiting time. Nick was heartsick. How could he leave this poor lad alone with his own personal horror? Yet he knew they would not let him stay. Would his parents be allowed to stay with the desperately injured Brian? He doubted it.

The clanging bell signalling the end of visiting time rang, seeming louder than usual, lost as he was in thought. The noise roused Derek with a start. 'Nick?'

'Hello, soldier,' Nick replied.

'What are you doing here?' Derek asked drowsily.

Nick pulled his chair closer to the bed. 'Keeping you company. Any objections?'

'No, but where's our Brian?' Derek peered at the neighbouring beds. 'Why isn't he here?'

'He's in a different part of the hospital.' Nick hesitated, wondering how far he dared to go. 'Do you remember what happened?'

Pain flickered in Derek's eyes. 'There were an accident,' he replied falteringly. 'Brian ran out into the road and got hit by a bus.'

A staff nurse came up to Derek's bed. 'I'm sorry, Sir, but you'll have to leave.'

He gave her what he hoped was a winning smile. 'Please, a few more minutes. It looks like me brother's coming round a bit.'

She glanced at the watch lying on the bosom of the starched uniform. 'Five more minutes but that's only because Sister's been called to an emergency.' She turned, her heels squeaking on the pristine floor.

'Now, about the accident. What else do you remember?'

Derek gripped Nick's hand tighter, pain etched on his small face. 'Brian flying up in the air, the bus stopping and the driver getting out and bending over him. I tried to get to Brian but a lady grabbed hold of me and wouldn't let me go, even when I kicked her.'

'It was as well you didn't look,' Nick said in a low voice.

'Is he...badly hurt?' Derek said.

'I'm afraid so.'

Derek started crying and Nick didn't hesitate. Matron or no Matron, he sat on the bed and pulled Derek into his arms.

'It were my fault, Nick, I shouldn't have kicked the ball so high.'

'Don't blame yourself,' he soothed. 'Brian shouldn't have taken his football down to the main road, or run after it. He knew the rules.'

'But I could have stopped him,' Derek wailed.

'No-on could have stopped Brian if he were that way out.'

'Then I wish it had been me,' he sobbed, clinging to Nick.

A moment later, with his sobs subsiding a little, Derek pulled away from Nick and looked up at him. 'Is Brian going to get better?'

'That I don't know. I don't think anyone does at this stage.' Not knowing what to say next, Nick watched the staff nurse approach Derek's bed.

'Mr Roberts?'

Nick grimaced. He didn't think her respect would have been as great if he'd been dressed in his Teddy boy suit instead of his work clothes. 'That's me,' he said finally.

'Sister would like to see you in her office.' At his querying look, she continued, 'I'll stay with this young man for a little while.'

As he stood up, she slipped into the place on the bed he'd vacated and took hold of Derek's hand. And, with a sick feeling in his stomach, Nick knew that Brian had died. Stumbling a little, his throat suddenly thick with unshed tears, he made his way past the ranks of beds occupied by children.

Sister's office was tucked away at the end of the ward and his parents were already there. His mother was sitting in a chair, sobbing into a handkerchief as his father, beside her, made clumsy attempts to console her, silent tears tracking down the suddenly more noticeable lines on his face.

Sister, a vision of starched efficiency yet with a kindly face, stood as he entered. 'It's Nicholas, isn't it?'

'Nick,' he said. 'I prefer Nick.'

She made an apologetic gesture with her hands but cut straight to the point. 'I'm sorry to have to tell you, Nick, that your brother died a short time ago.'

'I'd guessed.' He indicated the huddle of his parents. 'Was it quick and…painless?'

'He wouldn't have felt anything. Your parents were with him at the end.'

Unable to bear the sound of his mother's grief, he stood over her, a hand on the shoulder of each of his parents, trusting that the pressure of his hand alone would convey his presence. 'What happens now?'

She picked up a piece of paper from her desk and handed it to him. 'Confirmation of Brian's death from the doctor. You'll need to take that with you to register the death.'

Nick stared at the piece of paper in his hand, unable to read the words for his wet eyes. 'What about an undertaker?' He couldn't believe he was actually saying those words, indeed that there was a need to say them.

'I've already notified Livesey's Funeral Service at your parents' request and they're on their way now.' At his silence, she continued, 'The best thing you can do now is to take your parents home.'

Checking in his back pocket that he had enough money on him, he said, 'In that case, can you ring for a taxi to take us home, please?'

* * *

Joyce sat on the battered sofa and wished they'd never moved to Lancaster Avenue. If they'd stayed in Winter Street, where the only risk in kicking a football was to someone's window, Brian would never have been knocked down. Surrounded by the silence of an empty house, broken only by the soft breathing from a sleeping Lucy, Joyce sat stunned silence. Why had this thing happened to them? Surely they deserved better? It wasn't as if they were evil people, deserving of punishment. Her parents, particularly her mother, had tried so hard to better the family, thought they'd succeeded with this council house. And now this.

She could see the scene. The two boys laughing, perhaps giddy with the thought of the September holidays ahead, as they kicked the football – forbidden on main roads – from one to the other as they ran an errand for Mam. Then a wide kick that sent the football soaring into Chorley New Road. Forgetting the warning not to dash out into the road, Brian would have gone straight into the path of a bus on its way to Bolton. The sickening thud, the squeal of brakes, a boy tossed into the air. Unable to rid her mind of the horrific images, Joyce turned her thoughts to earlier this afternoon.

She'd been talking to Sally, or as close to talking as one could get in a noisy weaving shed, a combination of hand signals and words mouthed with exaggeration – mee-mawing the older weavers called it – when her tackler approached. There'd been a phone call, an accident, he said. One of her brothers had been knocked down and was in hospital and would Joyce go home to look after Lucy while her parents went to the hospital. Feeling sick, she'd sat down quickly on the stool Sally had pulled out for her. Her mind reeling from the shock, she'd been grateful for the other girl's steady hand on her shoulder.

She'd been home in ten minutes, brought here by one of the managers from the mill office in his car, to find the house in chaos especially as Dad had dashed in at the same time. He was adding to the chaos, shouting at the top of his voice, demanding answers to unspoken questions. Mam, meanwhile, had tight control of her emotions, her face pale and set but Joyce knew it was only willpower on her mother's part. Her only thought would have been to get to the Infirmary as quickly as possible. Lucy had looked fearfully from one to the other and clutched her doll tight to her chest. Joyce went to her first, pulling the child close. In the confusion, no one had thought to explain properly to Lucy and it fell to Joyce to do so.

Lucy had wept then, especially when Joyce had to explain the seriousness of the situation to her. They'd both cried, holding on to each other, until Lucy had fallen asleep. It seemed that hours had passed since then but that was unlikely. The

178

accident had happened in the late afternoon and the clock on the tiled mantelpiece showed it was still only seven o'clock.

Her thoughts were interrupted by a knocking on the front door. Easing herself away from the sleeping child, Joyce went to answer it. It was Kathy, her own face drawn and pale. 'I heard about the accident and wanted to see if there was anything I could do,' she said, her voice faltering, 'but please tell me if I'm in the way.'

'I'd be glad of a bit of company. There's only me and Lucy here at the moment.' Joyce opened the door wide and Kathy followed her in.

'Was it Brian or Derek?' Kathy asked in the dimness of the hall.

'Brian. He's in a bad way too,' Joyce whispered.

'Oh, I am sorry, Joyce. How's Derek taking it?'

'In shock, I expect. Nick's with him at the hospital.'

Kathy shivered at the implication in Joyce's words. 'Derek was there?'

She nodded. 'He saw it all.'

'How dreadful for him,' Kathy said.

In the front room, Lucy had woken up and was staring wide-eyed at the visitor, her doll still in her arms. 'Poor Lucy, she doesn't properly understand what's going on,' Joyce said.

'Have either of you had anything to eat?' Kathy said.

'I'm not hungry but I suppose Lucy had better eat summat.'

Kathy bent down to speak to Lucy. 'Can you manage a buttie or something, sweetheart?'

Lucy shyly nodded. 'Come on then, we'll see what we can rustle up.' Kathy held her hand out to Lucy but she shook her head and clung to Joyce instead.

In the kitchen, with the kettle on the stove, things seemed a little more normal except that Lucy wouldn't leave her side and Kathy had to do all the work. 'Don't worry,' she said, pulling some mugs out of the cupboard. 'I know roughly where everything is with helping out when you moved.'

'I think there's some boiled ham in the larder. I seem to remember Mam saying it needed eating up before she...' Joyce filled up again and was comforted by Kathy's quick squeeze of her arm.

'I know how you must feel, love,' she said, 'I've had some bad news myself today. My Dad has…is very ill.'

'Oh, I am sorry! And you've trailed all this way to comfort us.'

'There's nothing I can do about Dad for the moment.' She looked at the uncut loaf on the bread board and said, 'I hope you don't mind doorsteps only I'm not very good at cutting bread.'

Even Lucy managed a giggle at the end product which was the thickness of a wedge at one end tapering to paper thinness at the other. The remainder of the loaf was lopsided too, which Kathy ruefully held up to show Lucy. 'See what I mean? If your Mam says who's been at the bread, you'll have to tell her it was me.' Despite the size of the sandwiches, Lucy ate hers eagerly and even Joyce felt better for eating.

In a rare burst of assertiveness, Lucy declared that she would not go to bed until her Mam came in. Joyce gave in but insisted that Lucy change into her nightdress so that at least she was ready for bed. Now, as the evening drew in, she lay asleep again next to Kathy, her earlier reticence overcome, while the two girls talked. At first, it had all been of the accident and its possible outcome; more latterly, as they discovered a personal affinity, of themselves. Then, as they heard footsteps in the alleyway between the houses, they looked at each other and fell silent. Joyce reached over the sleeping child and grasped Kathy's hand.

Moments later, the door to the front room opened and Nick entered, his face set in grim lines.

Joyce jumped up. 'Nick! How's Brian?'

Nick shook his head. 'He died, love.'

'Oh, no!' Joyce gasped, falling back on to the sofa.

Nick rubbed a hand across tired eyes and nodded. 'He didn't know a thing.'

Joyce's eyes filled with tears and, aware of Lucy between her and Kathy, bit her lip to stop the sobs she could feel gathering. 'Where's Mam?' she croaked.

'In the kitchen, weeping. Dad's making a brew.'

'I must go to her.' Joyce rose to her feet and was surprised at how shaky her legs were.

The last thing Joyce heard as she dashed through to the kitchen was Kathy saying to Nick, 'I should go.'

CHAPTER 20

There was an age-old chill about the parish church on the afternoon of Brian's funeral. The sound of Kathy's footsteps echoed as she walked down the central aisle and took her place with the other mourners. There were some two dozen or so, she reckoned, huddled together in the first few pews of Holy Trinity Church.

People spoke in hushed whispers, accentuating the solemnity of the occasion, in marked contrast to the nervous giggles of a wedding or a christening. She slid into a pew and bent her head for a minute or so in silent prayer. As she sat upright, the woman sitting in the pew beside her gave a brief nod. She was about the same age as Mary Roberts with a careworn face and greying hair with a perm towards the end of its life. The woman said in a low voice, 'It's a rotten do, isn't it?'

'It certainly is.'

'I've known him since he were a babby,' the woman confided. 'My Bernard and him used to play together afore they moved.'

'You were a neighbour of the Roberts, then?'

'Ay, that's right. We live in Autumn Street.' After few seconds silence, the woman leaned towards Kathy, as if inviting confidences. 'You a relative, then?'

'I'm a friend of Nick's.' At that point, the funeral party appeared in the doorway. Those in the church rose to their feet as the pallbearers, Nick wearing his Teddy boy suit among them, carried the achingly small coffin down the aisle to where a wooden stand waited. One of the other pallbearers was a tall young man wearing RAF uniform, whom she guessed to be Nick's brother, Phil. The family came next, Mr and Mrs Roberts in front, Joyce following holding the hands of Derek and Lucy. An elderly gentleman, leaning on a stick, followed. And the people now filling up the two front pews must be various brothers and sisters.

Kathy was acutely aware that, in only a short time, it would be she and her mother following another coffin down this aisle.

With eyes blurring and emotion clogging her throat, she couldn't join in the introductory hymn. The voices of the mourners sounded thin in the vast emptiness of the large church, as if they too were struggling with emotion. Or perhaps it was the non-churchgoers' unfamiliarity with the words of the hymn. After that, the service passed in a fog, as she supposed it must be doing for the family.

It was a miserable sort of a day to be standing around a yawning graveside in Ridgmont Cemetery. The newly turned earth was wet with recent rain and she noticed a puddle at the bottom of the hole. How dreadful that Brian's body had to be lowered into a cold, unwelcoming hole.

Cringing from such thoughts, she looked instead at Nick, standing solemn and upright at the side of his parents and holding on to Lucy's hand. The child was crying quietly but Derek, between his mother and Joyce, was sobbing. Mrs Roberts pulled him close in a protective gesture and he buried his head in the folds of her shabby coat. Joyce stood next to Kathy, biting her lip as if to trying to stop crying. Impulsively, Kathy reached for her hand and Joyce flashed her a grateful look. Phil stood on the other side of Joyce, his eyes not visible beneath his cap. She could see that he was good-looking in a blond, fair-skinned sort of way, more like his mother in looks than any of the others.

Finally, it was all over and everyone wound their way over ground made uneven by sinking graves and sloping headstones. There was a little light talk as if in relief that the worst was over. Kathy found Nick, still holding Lucy's hand, by her side. 'You'll come back to the house with us, won't you, Kathy?'

'Are you sure I won't be in the way?' she asked uncertainly.

Despite looking pale and drawn, he gave her a smile. 'Course not.'

'How are your Mum and Dad?'

He grimaced. 'Just about holding themselves together. Having to organise this has given us all summat to think about.'

'It'll be hard on everyone afterwards, especially your Mum,' Kathy said.

'I can't believe he's gone. The house is so bloody quiet now.'

On the way back to the Roberts' house, she recalled that bleak night when she'd waited with Joyce for Nick and his parents to return. She'd wanted to leave them to their grief but Nick had said, 'I'll walk you home. It's getting dark out there.'

She'd been glad of his company as they walked down the unlit path from Gloucester Avenue to Mount Street though he didn't say much. He'd taken her hand and it seemed the most natural thing in the world. She hoped he gained as much comfort from the touch as she did.

'Thanks for coming to the house and keeping Joyce company,' he said. 'It meant a lot to me.'

'I'm so sorry about Brian.'

'I can't believe he won't be around anymore.' His voice was bleak in the darkness and Kathy squeezed his hand in unspoken comfort.

She didn't mean to say anything, to intrude on his grief, but suddenly she couldn't hold back any longer. 'I found out today, my Dad's dying too. He has…cancer.'

'Oh, no! Love, I'm so sorry.' He pulled her into his arms and they'd stood together, arms round each other for some moments and it would have been difficult to say who was comforting who.

After the funeral, the house on Lancaster Avenue was crowded and Kathy stood awkwardly to one side, feeling very much an outsider no matter what Nick had said.

'You must be Kathy. Nick mentioned you were coming,' a quiet voice said at the side of her.

She turned to face Nick's brother and noted the red mark on his forehead, the ridge in the short fair hair, where his cap had rested. 'That's right. And you're Philip.'

'Phil, please.' He held out his hand. 'Pleased to meet you, Kathy.'

'And you, Phil.' She returned the assertive handshake and decided she liked this young man.

'It's a pity we had to meet under such circumstances,' he said.

'You're on compassionate leave?' Someone laughed then quickly stopped as if aware of the solemnity of the occasion.

'Yes. I go back tomorrow. To be honest,' he said, leaning closer as if in confidence,' I shan't be sorry.'

Detecting a certain wistfulness in his voice, she asked, 'But you're happy in the RAF?'

His face lit up. 'Love it. I really feel I belong.'

'Nick said you'd signed up to become a regular.'

He edged closer to her as someone pushed past him on their way to the kitchen. 'Yes, I'm in for the long haul.'

'Does the possibility that you might be in action in the Middle East bother you?'

'I'd be lying if I didn't admit to being scared.' His eyes were troubled. 'But I knew what I was letting myself in for when I signed up.'

'You've met me brother then,' came Nick's voice from behind her.

She moved aside to make room for him. 'We've been discussing the Suez Crisis.'

Nick pulled a rueful face. 'That's serious stuff.'

'Has to be faced, Nick,' Phil said.

'No denying that. It's been at the back of my mind for a couple of months now. As a reservist, I might get recalled.'

'I think they'll send in the regulars like me first,' Phil said.

'Good to know me kid brother's protecting the country.' Nick laid a hand on his brother's shoulder.

'How's Mam now?' Phil nodded over to where their mother was talking to her father.

'In a strange way, I think, a bit relieved,' he added. 'She was dreading the funeral. I do worry how she'll cope once everything settles down to normality.'

'They say that you never get over the shock of losing a child,' said Kathy. 'Mum miscarried several times before she had me and she's always wondered what they would have been like had she been able to give birth.'

'If you two will excuse me, I think I'd better show willing and have a word with Granddad,' Phil said and left them.

'How'd you get on with our Phil?' Nick asked.

'Fine, I liked him.'

'Aye, he's a good bloke.'

'Not at all like you.'

He raised his eyebrows in a quizzical gesture. 'Are you saying I can't be good?'

'I mean he doesn't look anything like you.'

Nick looked over to where Phil was leaning forward to talk to his grandfather. 'No, he's more like Mam in looks and temperament. I take after Dad a bit too much for my liking.' He nodded in the direction of Danny who was laughing boisterously at some remark, slopping beer out of his glass, his gut straining over his trousers. 'It's almost as if now our Brian's been buried, it's back to things as they were.'

'I'm sure he's feeling it too. People have different ways of dealing with grief.'

Nick shuffled his feet. 'I'm sorry for what happened at the Fling the other Sunday.'

She reached for his hand and squeezed it. 'In the light of recent events, it doesn't seem important.'

* * *

A few days after the funeral, Joyce came home after work to find her mother sitting in the kitchen, fidgeting with a cold mug of tea, a faraway look in her eyes.

'Mam?' Joyce was almost afraid of disturbing her mother.

Mary looked up, startled. 'Oh, hello, love. Is it that time already?'

'Are you all right, Mam?'

She patted the chair at the side of her. 'Yes, I'm just thinking.'

Guessing that her mother wanted to talk, Joyce did as she was bid. 'What is it, Mam?

'Life goes on as normal, doesn't it? None of us says owt about the gap in our lives that can't be filled.'

Mary looked at Joyce, her eyes red-rimmed from a recent bout of crying. 'I only need to come across an old sock of Brian's, or a tattered comic under the bed, for the tears to flow again.' A new sob caught in her throat. 'Oh, Joyce, I regret every angry word I said to him, every slap I gave him.'

Mary's back was to the open kitchen door and she didn't see or hear Danny come in. Joyce gave him a warning look, an almost imperceptible shake of the head. For once, he took the hint and stood quietly at the back of the kitchen.

'How could he die? It's not like the old days when death among children was a way of life. It all goes to show,' she said, her voice harsh now with the anger she felt, 'that we're never more than a hair's breadth away from tragedy. I don't think I'll ever take life for granted again.' Shakily, she took a sip from the mug in her hands, grimaced, and pushed it away from her. 'On the face of it, your Dad seems to have shrugged off Brian's death but, after living with him for more than twenty years, I know better.'

Joyce shot her father another look but his whole face had sagged and she saw the old man he would become.

'I know it's a cover-up though. He's a man and men don't give owt away, do they?' Mary continued, still oblivious to Danny's presence.

A sob broke from her father then and he stumbled towards Mary. Hearing him, she rose to greet him and the two stood, sobbing in each other's arms. Joyce left them to it.

In the front room, Lucy was reading a book while Derek listlessly looked out of the window, as if he expected to see Brian running up the path. She knew she wasn't the only one to miss Brian's cheery, noisy, "'Lo, Mam. We're starving. Can we have a jam butty?" Within minutes the two boys would have been wrapping their mouths round bread doorsteps, a crust if there were any available, smeared with their favourite strawberry jam.

Lucy, who seemed to have left her babyhood behind, looked up when Joyce entered the room. 'Hello, love. School all right?'

'It's ok, I suppose. Don't like doing tables though.' Lucy screwed her face up in a comical gesture.

'Nobody does, love, but you'll be glad of them when you're older.' Joyce turned to Derek, aimlessly kicking his legs back and forth. 'Hello, Derek. How come you're not out playing?'

'I've no-one to play with round here.' Which was, of course, true. With the move to Lancaster Avenue, Brian and Derek had left behind the mates they'd had since they were toddlers and had not yet had chance to make new ones before Brian was killed.

'What about playing football in the garden then?' Joyce asked, aware that it would probably be therapeutic for him to kick a ball again. A bit like getting back on a bike when you'd fallen off, she thought.

'Don't feel like it,' Derek muttered. 'It's no fun kicking a ball on your own.' His voice was thick and Joyce guessed tears weren't far away.

'I'll play with you, if you like,' volunteered Lucy.

'Don't be daft! Girls don't play football,' Derek scoffed.

The normally reticent Lucy stood, squared up to Derek, small hands bunched into fists on her hips. 'Who says?'

'You don't know how to play.'

'You can show me, can't you?' Lucy demanded. 'That's what big brothers are for.'

'Well, I suppose we could have a kick around,' he conceded, 'but you've got to do exactly what I say, no messing.'

'I understand,' Lucy said sweetly and shot Joyce a look of triumph.

'Come on then, Lucy.' Derek beckoned with his hand impatiently.

Back in the kitchen, Joyce watched the children from the window. Derek was showing Lucy how to kick the ball then laughing at her attempts to emulate him. It was the first time she'd heard him laugh since the accident. The sound brought a lump to her own throat and she had to gulp it down before facing Mam and Dad who were watching with her.

CHAPTER 21

The Long Pull on Friday night was the usual mixture of lads and lasses of Nick's own age, or regulars like Mac who either stood at the bar or sat at tables playing dominoes. He wasn't sure he should be here; it didn't feel right somehow. It was, after all, only a matter of days since Brian's funeral but when Bragger had called on his way home from work to suggest a drink, his mother had insisted. 'Nay, lad,' she'd said, 'you've been cooped up long enough. Get yourself off out, it'll do you good.'

'Is there anybody there?' Ray snapped his fingers in front of Nick's face, bringing him back to the noisy reality of the Long Pull.

'Sorry, mate, what did you say?'

'I asked if you were up for Wigan Emp tomorrow night.'

Nick shook his head. 'No, I don't think so. I'm not in the mood.'

Ray turned away with a gesture of disgust. 'You're no bloody fun anymore, Nick.'

'Howd on a bit, Ray!' Bragger retorted. 'He's just buried his brother.'

Nick had to clench his fists at his side to stop him punching Ray. Then the tension left him and he knew he was tired of all this. Maybe it was time to move on. Ignoring Ray, he said to Bragger, 'I'm off to the bog,' and walked away from the group.

When he came out of the toilets, he found Sally, her hand on the door handle of the Ladies' as if she was about to go in. He hadn't seen her since that night at the Fling when he'd fought with Jud.

'Hiya, Nick. Sorry about your brother.' Her manner was hesitant but he had learned this last couple of weeks that people didn't know what to say in such circumstances.

'Thanks.' He made to push past her.

Instead, she stepped sideways to block his exit. 'Nick, I need to speak to you.'

'What about?'

She looked round furtively. 'Not here, it's too public. Someone might come.'

A suspicion so terrible in its implications popped into his mind that he jerked back involuntarily. 'Let's go outside.'

The night air was cool on the suddenly heated skin of his face and neck as he faced her. He leaned against a wall, arms folded, his mouth dry, his legs shaky. 'Well?'

'There's no easy way to say this, Nick, but….'

The suspicion hardened into a knot of dark dread inside his stomach. 'You're pregnant, aren't you?'

She looked up at him and he saw her eyes glistening with wetness. 'Yes.'

He managed to stop himself from querying whether the baby was his, knowing that wasn't fair. Despite her flirtatious ways, Sally was no slag. OK, she hadn't been a virgin when they'd spent the night together but he'd heard no rumours of anyone else she'd been with. And, knowing Horwich, there would have been had she been putting herself about. 'How far gone are you?'

'I've missed me second period.'

He reeled a little with the starkness of her words. 'Bloody hell, Sally! Why didn't you let me know sooner?'

'Because I wouldn't let meself believe it. Then there was your brother's accident.' She was crying openly now.

Despite the tumult going on in his brain and the dread in his stomach upping a couple of gears, his heart went out to her and he pulled her into his arms. 'Let's go and find somewhere to talk.'

The two of them went out of the Long Pull yard, aware of the need to avoid anybody, heading with unspoken agreement towards the back streets, deserted at this time of night. They walked aimlessly for some distance, a yard apart, until he realised they were heading towards Coffin Alley and he was reminded of Kathy. Not now, he told himself. Glancing at the girl by his side, his heart plummeted. Hell, what had he got himself into?

He stopped and pulled Sally into the shadow of a large gateway. 'Now, tell me all about it.'

190

'What's there to tell? I'm late, I'm pregnant, and I'm bloody scared.' There was more than a hint of defiance in her attitude.

'But how? When I wasn't using a rubber johnny, I was careful – withdrew in time.' It was something that had been niggling at the back of his mind since she'd broken the news.

'That's what I thought, why I didn't want to believe it,' she sniffed, 'but after I'd missed a second time, I went to the doctor's. He told me that the method you used…,' she hesitated as if searching for the right words 'weren't infallible, that providing it was the right time, even a leak can do it.'

'Bugger me, I never knew that! Was he able to confirm it?'

'He did after he examined me, said it would be due mid-April next year.' She drew in a deep breath. 'I've thought about trying to get rid of it but I couldn't try the gin and hot bath method in our house. It's like living in Piccadilly Station.' She hesitated. 'I suppose somebody in the mill would know of someone, somewhere.'

He grabbed hold of her arms. 'No, Sally! Not some back street job! It's too dangerous.'

'But what am I going to do?'

'We'll have to get married.' The words were out before he could stop them or grasp the import of them.

She gave him a tremulous smile. 'Would you really do that, Nick? Marry me?'

'I'll stand by you, Sal.'

She threw her arms round him, clearly thrilled at the thought of getting married. 'Thanks, Nick. I'd sort of hoped…but I didn't take it for granted.'

'We should get things sorted over the next week or two.'

'The worst for me will be telling me family. You know what Jud's like.'

'We'll do it together. It's only fair.' And Kathy, he thought, how was he to tell Kathy? Just when he'd thought there was a possibility for him, with no boyfriend on the scene, through his own stupidity, it had been blown away. His thoughts were bleak and close to despair especially when, as he'd walked Sally home, she held up her face expecting to be kissed.

It was only as he began walking towards Brazeley that he realised that there would now be no chance of taking the job with Mac either. He wouldn't be able to afford to do that with a wife and a kid. And it was all his own fault.

* * *

When Joyce came downstairs on Saturday morning, she was taken aback to see her brother sitting at the kitchen table, a cigarette in his hand, his good-looking face etched in misery. 'Not at the garage this morning, Nick?' she asked as she checked that the kettle had enough water in to brew some tea.

'Not today. Summat I need to get sorted. I went out earlier to ring Mac, let him know.'

Alerted by the deadness of his voice, Joyce looked at him, 'Is summat up, Nick?'

'You could say that.' He stubbed out his cigarette in the already full ashtray.

'Want to talk about it?'

'When Dad comes down, I'll tell you all then.' He nodded to where Mary was clattering at the kitchen sink. Through the window, open because of the unseasonably warm weather for September, Joyce could hear Lucy and Derek, now the best of friends, playing in the garden.

Danny appeared in the doorway, yawning and rubbing his belly, covered only by a grubby vest, his trousers crumpled from where they'd lain all night on the floor. 'Any chance of a brew?' he asked and gave a loud belch.

'Kettle's on, Dad,' Joyce replied, avoiding looking at Nick, knowing there'd be a look of disgust on his face.

'Good lass.' Danny sat at the table opposite Nick. 'Can you spare me a cig, Nick? Forgot to pick mine up from the side of the bed.'

More like he'd deliberately left them there, Joyce thought, as Nick reached for the pack on the table, offered it to his father and pulled another one out for himself.

She busied herself brewing the tea in the old brown teapot that had served them for years. 'You having another, Mam?'

'Go on, then, love,' Mary said, wiping her hands on her pinny. Her mother still looked tired and peaky, her face etched with lines that had not been there before.

Danny called Derek from the back door. 'Fetch us a paper from Pickles', there's a good lad.'

'Aw, Dad, do I have to?' Derek groaned as he dribbled the ball to Lucy, who nimbly caught it with her own foot.

'You do an' all and take the little lass with you.'

Derek came reluctantly to the door and held his hand out for the money. 'Can I have some money for sweets, then?'

'All right, then, six penn'orth between you. And be careful near that main road.' Danny handed over the money and Derek and Lucy disappeared down the alleyway between their house and their next-door neighbour, their footsteps echoing off the narrow walls.

'Now then, Nick, what's all this about?' asked Mary as she sat down at the table.

Nick drew in a deep breath. 'I've got summat serious to tell you.'

'You haven't got that lass who came to the funeral in the family way, have you?' Danny joked.

'Not Kathy, no.' A look of pain flickered across her brother's face.

'If not her, then who?' Judging by the leering grin on Dad's face, this was a big joke to him. Joyce could have kicked him.

'Sally Simcox.' In the shocked silence that followed Nick's admission, Joyce was intensely aware of the ticking of the clock on the sideboard, the whirr of someone's lawn mower and her father's heavy breathing.

'That little tart!' Mary leaned back in her chair as if stunned.

'She's not a tart, Mam,' Joyce piped up. 'She's a nice lass when you get to know her.' Sally's frequent visits to the toilets, claiming a recurring bilious attack, now made sense.

'Keep out of this, Joyce, it's nowt to do with you,' said Mary. 'In fact, you can go through to the front room.'

Nick reached out to take Joyce's hand. 'No, Mam, with her working with Sally, it'd be hard to keep owt from her.'

Mary sniffed but said nothing further. 'I only found out meself last night.' A bleak look came into his eyes. 'What happened with Sally was a mistake and one I'm going to have to pay dearly for.'

'And what are you going to do about this lass?' asked Danny.

'I'm going to marry her.'

'No, Nick,' gasped Mary, a catch in her voice. 'You'd be throwing your life away.'

'I've no choice, Mam. The baby's mine and I have to take the consequences.'

'Stupid bugger!' Danny said. 'Didn't you take precautions?'

'Danny!' Mary flashed a warning glance in Joyce's direction.

'Mam, I'm sure Joyce knows the facts of life,' Nick said. 'To answer your question, I was careful but obviously not careful enough.'

'How far along is she?' asked Mary.

'About two months.'

'You'll have to get a move on, then, or people will be talking.'

'They'll talk anyroad, Mam,' he sighed. 'When the baby's born, everyone will be counting backwards.'

'Has Sally told Jud yet then?' Joyce asked.

'I told her not to. It'll be better if I'm there. I'm going to her house later to tell her Mam and Jud.' Nick pulled a face. 'Not looking forward to that, I can tell you.'

'Serves you right if he gave you a good hiding,' Mary said.

'No more than I deserve.'

'When's all this going to happen?' asked Danny.

'As soon as we can arrange a special licence, I reckon.'

Mary reached over and laid her hand on Nick's arm. 'Where will you live? We haven't the room here.'

'It'll have to be the Simcox's front room until such time as we can get a council house. Bloody hell, what a way to start married life!'

Danny reached for another of Nick's cigarettes without asking. 'Well, you've made your bed...'

Nick shoved his chair away and stood, his hands on the table, his face furious. 'You've no need to be so bloody smug about it, Dad. I know that Mam was three months gone with me when you married her. A bit reluctant, were you? At least I'm willing to face up to me responsibilities.'

'Your grandfather were being difficult about it,' Danny blustered.

Joyce sat in stunned silence, never having bothered to add up the discrepancy before and looking at her parents with new eyes. Somehow you never thought of them being carried away with youthful passions.

'If I know Granddad, he'd have wanted to marry Mam off as soon as possible to avoid the scandal.'

'That's enough, the pair of you,' said Mary. 'The past's over and done with. It's the present we've to deal with.'

'It's time I were going to Sally's anyway. She must be on pins by now and I promised I wouldn't be late.' He reached for his leather jacket on the back of the chair and shrugged his shoulders into it, then, with a regretful look in their direction, headed towards the back door, leaving them all in stunned silence.

CHAPTER 22

Nick's heart dropped like a stone to see Sally waiting for him at the front room window of the house in Mary Street West. He realised that he hadn't given a thought as to what he was going to say. Sally pulled open the front door and stretched up to plant a kiss on his lips. 'I've got butterflies in me stomach, Nick,' she whispered.

'Are you sure it's not the baby moving?' he said. Though he was trying to be supportive, the baby seemed more of a threat than something to look forward to.

'Don't be daft! You can't feel the baby move until about the fourth month.'

The kitchen was similar in size to the one they'd had in Winter Street but there the similarity ended. Shabby old furniture filled the room and it was cluttered with the paraphernalia of life. The only occupants were Sally's mother, a blowsy woman with frizzy blonde hair, lounging in a fireside chair, and Jud, wearing only a vest and trousers, sitting at the table. Above all was the unpleasant odour of stale cigarette smoke and sweaty socks. Jud's face dropped when he saw Nick. 'What's he doing here?'

'We've summat to tell you,' Sally said. Nick realised that she was as nervous as he was. Poor girl, she hadn't asked for this any more than he had.

'You're not pregnant, are you?' Sally's mother said.

With a quick glance at Nick, Sally said, 'Yes, I am. Two months gone.'

Her mother's mouth fell open. 'Bloody hell! I didn't think you'd been going out with anyone.'

Jud rose to his feet and pushed his face close to Nick's. 'It's yours, isn't it? You bastard!'

Nick took a step back. 'I've already said I'll marry her.'

'What makes you think I'd let you,' Jud sneered.

'He's got to, Jud. Think of the disgrace.' Mrs Simcox broke into loud gasping sobs.

Jud said, 'Sally, take Mam into the front room and try to calm her down.'

'But I want to be here.'

'Do as I say, Sal. Leave this to me and Nick to sort out.'

With a regretful glance at Nick, Sally heaved her mother out of the chair and left the room.

'So, what have you got to say for yourself?' Jud said, once they were alone.

Nick shrugged. 'What else is there to say, Jud? I've admitted it's my baby and that I'll marry her.'

'When did this happen?'

'What's that got to do with it?'

'Just tell me.'

'Last week of Horwich holidays.'

'You took your time, didn't you?'

'Sally only told me last night. I said I'd marry her straight away.'

'You wouldn't under normal circumstances, would you?'

'Probably not but the fact is, I've admitted responsibility for Sally's baby and I'm willing to stand by her. What more can I do?'

'How soon do you reckon on getting married?'

'As soon as it can be arranged.'

'Have you thought about where you'll live?'

'We'll have to find lodgings somewhere until we can get a council house.'

Jud took a cigarette from a packet but didn't offer Nick one. 'I suppose you could lodge in our front room for a while.'

Nick's heart sank. Just what he'd be dreading. But what alternative was there? 'Would your Mam be OK with that?'

'As long as you pay her, she'll agree.'

He left soon after, agreeing to meet Sally the following night and made his way to Mac's. He badly needed to talk to someone. Mac wasn't in the garage so he pushed open the door to his flat and called up the stairs. 'You there, Mac?'

The older man appeared on the landing, a look of surprise on his face. He took the pipe from his mouth and said, 'I'd just knocked off for a brew. Come on up.'

In the sitting room, Mac inspected Nick's face. 'Something on your mind, Nick? You look worried.'

197

Nick nodded. 'Mind if I make meself a brew? I've been through the mill a bit this morning and I could do with a cuppa.'

'I'll do it.' Mac put a firm hand on Nick's shoulder and shoved him into an armchair. He must have only recently vacated it for it was warm and the battered cushions still bore the imprint of his body. Nick sank into its depths with a grateful sigh, shaking his head in an attempt to clear it of some of the thoughts jostling for attention in his brain. 'I knew there was something up when you rang to say you weren't coming this morning.' Mac plonked a mug on the table, some of its contents splashing over the side. 'Do you want to talk about it?'

Nick reached for a cigarette. 'If you don't mind.' Pulling an ashtray towards him, Nick said, 'Do you remember me telling you about that party where I slept with Sally?'

'Don't tell me, Sally's now pregnant.'

'Two months gone. I've said I'll marry her, accept my responsibilities.'

'I wouldn't expect anything else from you.'

'Then this morning, I went with her to tell her mother and brother. Her Dad died a couple of years ago.'

'Am I right in thinking that her brother is Jud Simcox?'

'Yes, and you can be sure he made the most of it.'

'I can imagine. How did her mother react?' Having finished his tea, Mac pulled his tobacco pouch towards him.

'She was almost hysterical and Sally had to take her out of the room.'

Mac raised a quizzical eyebrow. 'Leaving you and Jud on your own?'

Nick grimaced. 'That was the funny part, he seemed to run out of steam. We ended up talking about where me and Sally would live.'

'What did you decide?' Mac was feeding threads of tobacco into his pipe,

'There's the offer of the Simcox's front room but I don't fancy that. The house is a bloody mess and it would be purgatory living in close proximity with Jud. For him too.' Nick shuffled uncomfortably in his chair. 'The thing is, Mac, I won't be able to take the job you offered me, with a wife and baby to look after, much as I'd like to.'

'I can see that, lad,' he said, trying to get his pipe to draw. 'Happen you'll still give me a hand from time to time.'

'That's really good of you, Mac.' Nick leaned across and held his hand out which Mac shook.

'Least I can do for you,' he said gruffly.

They were silent for a moment or two, then Mac said, 'Have you told Kathy yet?'

A deep gloom settled on Nick. 'No, but I'll have to before she hears the news from someone else.'

'What will you say to her?'

'The truth, that Sally's in the family way.' He groaned and hung his head in his hands. 'How the hell am I going to tell her, Mac? That'll be even harder than the session with the Simcoxs this morning.'

'You'll think of a way, I'm sure,' Mac said gruffly.

Nick wished he felt as confident. His stomach churned at the thought of telling Kathy.

* * *

Hanging her jacket on the old-fashioned coat stand in the hall, Kathy pushed open the door to the sitting room. Her father was reading the Bolton Evening News football final but her mother had put her knitting to one side and seemed to be waiting for her, that familiar disapproving look on her face. Kathy sighed. 'Is there something wrong, Mum?'

'There might be,' she said, her voice tight.

Ron put his paper down and took his glasses off. 'That Nick Roberts called.'

Her heart thumping, she said, 'Here? He's been here?'

'Yes, he's left a note for you.' Vera thrust a battered looking envelope in her direction. 'He was hoping you'd be here but had written a note just in case.'

Fingers trembling, Kathy ripped open the envelope and took out the single sheet of paper. 'Dear Kathy,' the note read, 'Please will you meet me at the Crown tonight about 7 o'clock?

It's really important that I see you. If you've already made arrangements, I'll understand but I'll wait half an hour in case you can come.'

'Well, what does he want?' her mother demanded.

'He wants me to meet him tonight.' Kathy folded the note and put it back in the envelope. There was a smudge of what could be an oily fingerprint in one corner and she guessed he'd written it at the garage and called here on his way home.

'And are you going?' Ron asked.

'Of course. Whatever it is, it's important enough to call here.'

'More fool you,' Vera harrumphed. 'Going running when he calls you.'

'Mum, he's only a friend. There's nothing to worry about.' Despite the effort to appease her mother, Kathy was filled with a nervous anticipation, one minute excited at the thought of seeing him, the next worrying about why he wanted to see her. The hours until 7 o'clock seemed endless, especially with her mother stiff with disapproval.

Nick was waiting for her as she got off the bus at the Crown and he gave her a hesitant smile. 'Not late, am I?' she said.

'No, I've only been here a few minutes meself.'

She gave him a direct look. 'What's on your mind, Nick?'

He nodded to the people who'd got off the bus with her. 'Not here. Too many people around.'

'You're worried they'll have us married off before we know where we are.' At her teasing remark, his face set in a scowl. 'Hey, I'm only joking, Nick.'

'Sorry. I'm a bit on edge tonight.'

'Family problems?'

'Summat like that. Look, do you mind if we go for a walk up Rivi?'

Puzzled, she said, 'OK, if you like.'

They started along the road to Rivington in silence. Once they'd got clear of the houses on Lever Park Avenue, she turned to him and said, 'Nick, you haven't had your recall papers, have you?' He shook his head.

She stopped and turned to face him. 'I'm not going another step until you tell me what's going on.'

'You'd better sit down.' He indicated a bench she'd never noticed before, so ancient that the wood was crumbling away at the ends.

Her heart racing, she sat down gingerly, waiting for him to speak.

'I wanted you to hear it from me rather than from anyone else.' He paused and drew in a ragged breath. 'Sally's pregnant and we're getting married.'

She sat in stunned silence, unable to take in what he was telling her, then, as realisation hit her, she started shivering. Nick took off his jacket and swung it over her shoulders. Clutching it close to her neck, she drank in the scent of him to store in her memory. For she knew, in that moment of pain and anguish, that she loved him. What she'd thought was a continuation of her girlish crush had become a deep and abiding love.

He reached out as if to hold her but she recoiled. 'Don't you dare touch me!'

'I'm sorry, Kathy, if my news has hurt you.'

'I'll get over it. It's not as if we ever really got started.' The shivering was easing now. 'When did this happen?'

'After Haigh Hall.' His face was a mask of wretchedness but she was unable to feel pity for him. 'I couldn't get you out of my mind and I took advantage of her. I don't feel proud of that.'

'You know, I almost feel sorry for Sally.'

'It won't be a good start to married life.' He looked at her then and she saw the anguish in his eyes. 'But I have to try and make the best of it for the baby's sake.'

She struggled to her feet and yanked his jacket off her shoulders, thrusting it at him. 'I don't want to hear this. I'm going home.'

They walked back to Horwich in silence. She knew that if she said anything, she would burst into tears and she couldn't, wouldn't let him see how much he'd hurt her. And she did hurt. A pain was growing in the region of her heart threatening to overwhelm her. Somehow she managed to hold on to her tears while she sat on the bus though the effort made her throat hurt.

At home, she pleaded a headache and vanished to the haven of her room. There, the storm of tears broke while outside a thunderstorm wreaked its worst on Horwich. It seemed fitting somehow. The rain lashed against Kathy's bedroom window as she lay sleepless, her head aching for real, her nose blocked, her eyes gritty and swollen.

Finally, by the early hours, she was drained and empty. For the moment there were no more tears though she knew there would come a moment when a special memory, or a particular tune, would bring them on again. It seemed like the end of the world to her.

CHAPTER 23

Nick trudged up the hill from Chorley New Road, the heaviness he'd had in his heart since last Friday still lodged there. Getting up of a morning, going to work, doing what he had to do there, coming home again, were all tasks that now seemed burdensome. The grey and dismal weather today matched his mood. Was it really only a matter of days since Sally had broken the news to him? It seemed much longer.

Today he'd called in at the Register Office in Bolton to apply for a special licence and booked a date for the wedding three weeks from Saturday. He hadn't had chance to tell Sally yet but didn't doubt for a minute that she'd flap her hands and say it was too soon. He'd had a battle on his hands getting her to agree to a register office wedding. She'd been set on marrying in church. He'd stuck to it though; no way was he going through this farce of a marriage in a house of God even though he was not particularly religious.

Sally, full of the wedding, seemed determined that they should spend every spare minute together now that they were 'engaged'. He knew he would have to spend more time with her but he still needed space to come to terms with all that had happened. The arrangements he'd made today only served to remind him that the special world he'd once aspired to, a relationship with Kathy, working for and with Mac, were now out of his reach. Giving up on night school wasn't an option, though. He was determined on that.

As he walked down the alleyway between their house and the one next door, he became aware of shouting coming from the house. Bloody hell, not another row between his parents! But no, he could hear Joyce shouting too. Alarmed, he thrust open the kitchen door to be met by Joyce, her hair awry, a red mark on her face that looked suspiciously like a hand print, throwing herself into his arms. 'What's wrong, love?' he asked.

'You won't be soft-soaping her when you hear what she's been up to.' Mam stood in the kitchen, arms folded over her overall-covered chest, her face set in grim lines.

Joyce detached herself from his arms and looked up at him with beseeching eyes. 'Please don't be mad at me, Nick.'

'What could you have done that would make me do that?' Nick was puzzled. Whatever it was, it was serious enough to cause a major – and rare – row between Joyce and their parents.

For the first time, he noticed his father lounging in the doorway, a smug look on his face, which made Nick instinctively wary. 'She's only been going out with your mate, Bragger Yates,' Danny gloated.

'What?' The shock surged through Nick and he thrust Joyce away from him so that he could look into her face. 'Is this true?' He saw from the imploring look she gave him that it was. 'How long?'

'A few months,' she whispered.

'Are you completely mad? I know he's me mate but he's not called Bragger for nothing.'

'That's what I said,' jeered Danny. 'Bragger by name, Bragger by nature.'

Nick tightened his hold on her arms. 'Has he…touched you?' Even as he said it, he realised how hypocritical he sounded. What right had he to judge when he'd been a complete bastard with Sally. But, hell, this was his kid sister!

Her chin came up in defiance. 'No, he hasn't. He's been a perfect gentleman, which is more than I can say for some round here,' she said, casting a venomous look at her father.

'I only asked if they'd gone all the way.'

'And I'm telling Nick the same as I told you, no, we haven't.' She pulled herself out of Nick's grasp and, collapsing on to one of the kitchen chairs, started to cry.

'I'll bloody kill him,' Danny said.

'No, you won't, Dad. He's my mate and I'll be the one to sort him out.' He was heartsick.

'Nick, don't! He hasn't done owt,' cried Joyce.

He turned to his mother. 'How did you find out?'

'Mrs Yates came up this afternoon. Apparently her sister saw them together,' she answered.

'When? Doing what?'

'Her brother-in-law's recently got a car and they'd been out for a run up Rivi. They passed Bragger and Joyce holding hands and laughing together.'

'I bet Mrs Yates wasn't laughing.' Nick knew Bragger's mother had struggled to cope with her grief. She didn't need this, neither did they so soon after Brian's death.

'She were screaming and shouting, saying our Joyce was no better than she should be and had egged him on.' Nick knew that whatever Mam thought of Joyce in private, she'd defend her to all comers. Come to that, so would he. 'But I were more than a match for her and I got rid of her in the end by promising they wouldn't meet again.'

'Oh, Mam, no!' Joyce cried.

'That's not only me, Joyce, Mrs Yates was adamant too.'

'I notice the lad himself hasn't appeared,' Danny smirked.

Mary shot her husband a look that spoke volumes. 'To be fair, he won't know yet. Mrs Yates had been to the hospital this morning and didn't see her sister till this afternoon.'

'He'll come up once he finds out,' Joyce said, through her tears, 'I know he will.'

'I hope he does. I've a few things I want to say to him,' Nick said, his lips tight.

'But I love him,' Joyce said in a broken voice.

'Huh!' his father harrumphed. 'What does a kid like you know about love?'

Nick put a hand on Joyce's bowed head. 'Happen more than you've ever done in your whole life, Dad.'

'Why, you arrogant sod! You've no room to talk, the mess you're in!' his father moved as if to go for Nick, his fists bunched.

Mary stopped him by laying a firm hand on his arm. 'No, Danny. There's been recriminations enough today.'

He grunted in disgust. 'Then how about getting us some tea, woman. I'm off out tonight.'

'What, again? You went out last night.'

'Had a bit of a win on the horses, didn't I?' He shot her a triumphant look and patted his back pocket.

Bragger did appear as Joyce had predicted, still wearing his work clothes, his blue eyes mournful and his mouth set in grim lines. 'I had to...come up and face you,' he said to Nick who'd opened the door to him.

'Not to see Joyce, then?' Nick stood in the doorway, one hand against the jamb, barring Bragger's entrance.

'That too, if you'll let me.'

'You'd better come in.' Nick stood back.

'Is there anyone else about?' Bragger asked, looking around.

'Dad's gone to the pub, the kids are out playing somewhere and Mam's in the front room.'

'And Joyce?'

'Up in her room, crying her eyes out.'

'Oh, hell!' Bragger sank down into the chair Joyce had vacated, head in hands. 'I never meant for it to be like this.'

'How many of your mates at work have you been bragging to?'

Bragger shook his head in emphatic denial. 'I haven't. Didn't you realise most of that was talk?'

Nick managed a grim smile. 'I did wonder if it was possible for one lad to be so versatile.'

'Thanks, Nick, I appreciate that.' He went to shake Nick's hand but Nick backed away.

'I haven't finished with you yet,' he said. 'What about all the girls you've boasted about when you were supposedly seeing Joyce?'

A flush filled Bragger's face and he had the grace to look uncomfortable. 'All made up as a cover for seeing Joyce.'

'So now your sins have found you out.'

He gave a rueful lift of his shoulders. 'Joyce said it would backfire on me.'

'What did you think you were playing at, getting involved with her in the first place?'

'I'd fancied her for a year or so but I did wait until she'd turned 16 to ask her out. It was only then did I realise she liked me too.'

'Why the secrecy? You could have mentioned it to me.'

'Joyce seemed to think you wouldn't be so keen on the idea.'

Nick nodded in agreement. 'She had a point there.'

'Then there were me Mam, you've heard by now that she's totally against Joyce.'

'Any particular reason?'

'You know we're Roman Catholic?' When Nick nodded, he continued, 'Well, since me Dad died, she's gone all religious, reading her missal daily, going on at me about going back to church.'

'What's all this got to do with our Joyce?' Nick was becoming impatient.

'I'm coming to that. Mam now has this crazy idea that eventually I'll take Holy Orders.'

Nick couldn't help it, he laughed. 'That's priceless! You a priest?'

'That's what I keep telling her but it's how she's been since Dad died.'

'But now she's put her foot down, told you you're not to see Joyce again.'

Bragger hung his head. 'That's about the way of it.'

'Far better to finish it now. That way our Joyce has a chance to recover.'

'Can I...?' He faltered, before drawing a deep breath, '...have a word with her?'

'Better not, I think.'

'I don't want her to think I've deserted her,' Bragger pleaded.

'I'll tell her, explain that I wouldn't let you see her.'

'I suppose that's the best I can expect.'

Nick folded his arms over his chest. 'It's me final word.'

After he'd gone, Nick slumped in the chair and reached for his cigarettes. He was emotionally buffeted with the events of the past few weeks, Brian dying and the funeral, Sally's pregnancy, breaking the news to Kathy, and now this row over Bragger. He leaned forward and laid his head on his arms, as close to despair as he had ever been.

* * *

A week later, Kathy's pain had dulled to a raw ache in the region of her heart. The days since then had been a trial as she'd refused to tell her parents why Nick had wanted to see her. She still thought of Nick constantly, alternately yearning for him or raging in anger. Yet why should she feel betrayed? He had made her no promises, had no idea that she loved him. She knew she had to accept the inevitable, that he was lost to her, but the thought of him with Sally still festered in her heart.

She was reflecting on these things while pretending to watch television on Sunday evening, when the phone in the hall rang.

'Is that Kathy?' asked an unknown voice with a Scottish accent.

'Yes,' she said diffidently. 'Who's that?'

'You don't know me. My name's Mac, Nick Roberts works for me sometimes at my garage.'

At the mention of Nick's name, fear rose and tightened her throat. 'Is there something wrong?'

'Yes and no. He's been beaten up but it looks worse than it is,' the disembodied voice came down the line.

The news turned her knees to jelly and she had to sit on the bottom step of the stairs. 'No need to ask who. Jud Simcox. Have you told the police?'

'He's adamant he doesn't want to, says it will make things worse. The thing is,' Mac pleaded, 'he's in a bit of a mess but I've no first aid kit.'

She tried to harden her voice. 'But why are you ringing me?'

'Because he specifically asked for you when he first rang my bell. He was a bit confused but it was as if you'd been on his mind.'

Her heart raced in alarm. 'How badly is he injured?'

'Mostly superficial cuts and bruises from the look of it. Are you able to come?'

She knew then that nothing would stop her going. 'Where are you?'

She put the phone down, her mind racing. Before going up to the bathroom to collect what she'd need, she poked her head into the sitting room.

Her mother looked up from her knitting. 'Who was it, love?'

'Someone called Mac. Nick works for him at his garage. He's been beaten up and has been asking for me.'

'If he's hurt why doesn't he go to hospital?' her father asked.

'He doesn't want the authorities involved.'

Vera harrumphed. 'Probably deserved it.'

'No matter what you say, I'm going,' she said, in a firm voice.

Ron sighed. 'If you're that determined, I'll take you in the car.'

'Dad, I can't put you to that trouble,' she said.

'Don't worry, love, I wouldn't offer if I didn't feel up to it. And I don't like the idea of you walking around, not so much now, but later on.' He turned to his wife. 'Where did you put the leaflet that came through the door about that private hire chap, Vera?'

She rose and went to the bureau from which she extracted a piece of paper. 'Here it is, Says he's recently started up so he'll be glad of the business.'

Ron passed the leaflet to Kathy and some money from his pocket. 'I want you to give him a ring when you're ready to come home.'

She leaned forward and kissed her father. 'Thanks, Dad, you're a star.'

He dropped her off outside the garage and she walked up to the side door, as Mac had told her to do, carrying a bag of bits and pieces she'd collected. In answer to her knock, came the call. 'Come up, the door's open.'

Her heart was pounding as she climbed the stairs, wondering what she'd find. Although she'd her Girl Guide first aid badge, would she be capable of doing what was needed? What if he was so bad, he needed stitches? He'd have to go to hospital then.

Nick was awake and raised his head from Mac's bed as she entered the bedroom. 'Kathy! You came!' At first sight, he did indeed look a mess. His face and hands were bloodied and bruised and his Teddy boy suit was in ribbons.

She looked at him, her head on one side. 'Did you think I wouldn't?'

'I wouldn't have blamed you if you'd chosen not to.'

She looked at him critically. 'Where does it hurt most?'

'Where doesn't it hurt would be a better answer,' he managed with a rueful grin.

She turned to Mac who was hovering in the doorway. 'Can you help me take his jacket and shirt off?'

Between them, they removed his jacket which had been deliberately slashed, probably with a razor. Some of the cuts were deep enough to penetrate through his shirt and into his skin. With fierce determination, she set about bathing the cuts, a slow and messy business, but he did look much better at the end of it, his face, torso and arms cleaned of blood but with a variety of plasters adorning him.

After she'd finished, she looked critically at the bed, now stained with blood and damp with the dettoled-water. 'I'm sorry, Mac, we seem to have made a bit of a mess of your sheets.'

The older man shrugged. 'They'll soon wash.'

For the first time, she took a good look at Nick's friend. Short and stocky, with thinning hair and bushy eyebrows, she saw the kindly concern in his eyes as he looked at Nick.

'I think you'd better stay where you are at least for tonight,' Mac said. 'I can kip down on the sofa in the other room.'

'You sure you don't mind, Mac?' Nick asked

'I can keep an eye on you,' he said, giving Nick a knowing grin. 'Return the favour, so to speak.'

'What about your parents?' Kathy asked. 'Will we need to let them know?'

'No, they're used to me staying out for the odd night.'

'If you like, I can pop up there tomorrow, bring you some clothes back,' Kathy said.

'I can't ask you to do that.'

'It's probably the last thing I'll be able to do for you,' she said. 'I take it this was about Sally. Does she know?'

'About the beating? I shouldn't think even Jud would have been daft enough to tell her what he was planning.'

'How did it happen? Where were Bragger and your other mates?'

A look of pain passed across his face. 'Bragger and I have had a bust up so I went to the pub on me own.'

'Where did it happen?' Kathy asked now.

'I'd gone to the toilet in the Long Pull and Jud, Bill Murphy and another of their mates, Jim Stevens, were waiting for me when I came out. They dragged me into the back alley and gave me what for.'

'It's a good job I didn't go for my usual drink or I wouldn't have been in when you banged on my door,' Mac said from where he lounged in the doorway, 'but I fell asleep over the Sunday papers then couldn't be bothered getting washed and changed.'

'Thanks, Mac. I couldn't think where else to go.'

'What happened with your suit?' she held up the remnants of his jacket.

'They took razor blades to that.'

'They could have sliced an artery and you might have died,' she pointed out.

'Believe it or not, they were careful about that,' he sighed. 'And I can't retaliate because of Sally.'

Kathy stood up abruptly. 'I think I'd better go. May I use your phone, Mac, to ring for a taxi?'

'I'd offer to take you but I had a wee dram or two earlier,' he apologised. 'Give me the number and I'll phone for you.'

As soon as he'd left the bedroom with the leaflet her father had given her, Nick reached up to grab her hand. 'Thanks, Kathy, for coming.'

At the touch of his hand on hers, the heat of her outrage suddenly spilled over. 'Next time send for your future wife!'

* * *

When Kathy arrived at Mac's flat with the promised change of clothes the following evening, Mac was in the garage, his head under the bonnet of a car. 'Hello, Kathy,' he said, in reply to her greeting. He indicated the engine of the old Wolsley. 'Sorry about this. Got an urgent job I need to finish.'

She paused by the open garage door. 'How's Nick?'

211

'Much better but very stiff and sore. He's up though, looking bonny in my dressing gown. He says he's going in to work tomorrow, though.'

'Is he fit enough for that?'

'Probably not, but he's determined to do so.' He hefted a spanner from one hand to the other.

'I'll go up then, shall I?' she indicated the entrance to the flat.

'Aye, lass, help yourself to tea or coffee. Nick knows where everything is.'

'Thanks, Mac.'

She called out as she entered the flat door and Nick answered her. 'I'm up here.'

'You'd hardly be anywhere else,' she said as she entered the cluttered sitting room, 'the state you're in.'

He was sitting in one of the dilapidated armchairs, a newspaper on his lap. She had to laugh; he looked so incongruous, Mac's too short dressing gown exposing a bruised but shapely leg. 'I know I must look a sight but there's no need to laugh about it,' he said, with a grin. Her breath caught in her throat because the ease and warmth between them was back bringing with it feelings it wasn't wise to dwell on. Nick seemed to sense it too for he shifted uncomfortably in the chair and said, 'Did you see Mam and Dad?'

'I did, and I got you some clothes.' She held up the tattered brown paper carrier bag Mary Roberts had given her.

'What did they say?'

'Your Dad laughed, your Mam tutted and said she wasn't surprised, given what had happened with Sally.'

He indicated his bruised face with one eye all but closed. 'Mam said this would happen when I told her about Sally.'

She sat down on the sofa opposite him. 'Does she know yet, by the way?'

'As far as I know no-one's told her.'

'I'm not offering to do that job for you,' she retorted.

'I wouldn't ask you to,' he said quietly.

'How are you feeling, by the way?'

'It hurts me to move, I ache all over, but apart from all that, I'm fine.' He folded up the newspaper and added it to the pile at the side of him.

'Mac says you're going into work tomorrow.'

'I shall have to. I'm going to need the money with the wedding coming up and setting up home.'

His words brought on the now familiar combination of hurt and anger and reinforced the fact that he now belonged to someone else.

'I'm sorry, Kathy, I shouldn't have said that,' he said, in the face of her stricken silence.

'Why not? It's a fact of life.' She tried to stop the tears gathering but failed.

'What a bloody mess! And I've no-one to blame but meself.' He buried his battered face in his hands. 'How in hell am I going to get through this, Kathy?'

His anguish was plain to see and unable to resist, she dropped to her knees before him, taking his hands in her own. 'You've no other choice, Nick.'

'Seeing you like this has brought it all back. I should never have asked you to come. 'He pulled one of his hands out from hers and gently stroked her face. 'I'm sorry for all the pain I've caused you. If I could take it back, I would.' He drew her into his arms and kissed her, murmuring, 'I love you...I love you...' against her mouth in between kisses.

Touched by his intensity and thrilled by his words, she whispered, 'And I love you, Nick.'

He groaned and pulled away from her, 'I'm sorry, Kathy, I shouldn't have...'

'Oh, very touching!' came a voice at the door. 'Now you can get away from him, Kathy Armstrong.'

Kathy struggled to her feet, unable to take in for a moment, because of the mistiness in her eyes, who the visitor was.

'Sally, what are you doing here?' Nick said, swiping at his own eyes.

'I did call out but you were both so carried away, you mustn't have heard me.' Sally's own face was puce with rage.

213

Mac puffed his way into the room, having mounted the stairs in record time. 'I'm sorry, Nick, I was under the car and couldn't get out quick enough.'

'It's all right, I suppose she has a right to be here,' Nick said, his voice dull.

'No, it's not all right! What's she doing here?' Sally asked, jabbing a finger in Kathy's direction. So threatening was her attitude that Kathy backed up against the wall.

'She came to bring me some clothes, me own were cut to ribbons last night,' Nick said.

Sally put her hands on her hips. 'How come she knew about this yet I had to find out from our Jud? It isn't fair, it should have been me.'

'By the time Jud and his mates had finished knocking hell out of me, I wasn't thinking straight.'

'You bastard!' Sally yelled. 'We're getting married in two weeks' time.'

'I'm sorry, Sally.' Nick looked uncomfortable and Kathy's heart went out to him.

'I should think so! But that's it now, no more,' Sally said, pointing a finger at Kathy. 'She's out of your life from now on. You have a child on the way and you said you'd stand by me.'

'And I will, I promise.'

The scene between Nick and Sally was an agony for Kathy and she pushed herself away from the wall. 'Goodbye, Nick.'

'Kathy, please…,' Nick called but she stormed out and ran down the stairs.

CHAPTER 24

Despite still feeling sore and with aches and pains in places he didn't know existed, Wednesday night found Nick queuing with Ken and Ray outside the cinema showing the Bill Haley film, 'Rock Around The Clock.' After much deliberation and despite near riots in neighbouring Burnley when the film had been shown, Bolton Corporation had hesitatingly allowed the film to be shown in Bolton. Once inside the cinema, a tense anticipation seemed to vibrate among the audience. By the time the main feature started, the noise reached overpowering proportions, with concerted yells and much stamping of feet in which Nick found himself joining in. As the title music began, there was a roar that threatened to bring the ceiling down and Nick accepted there would be no chance of following the plot of the film. Like him, everyone was here for the music which pulsated through the auditorium and already boys and girls were dancing in the aisles. In vain did the manager and usherettes try to make people sit down. Any attempt to do so brought threats of violence and in the end, they stood helplessly to one side. Then Nick was out in the aisle himself, bopping with a girl dressed in regulation tight skirt and even tighter jumper. When he got back to his seat, Ken and Ray were missing.

About half way through the film, he realised that he needed a pee and during one of the speechy bits, he slipped out in the direction of the Gents'. He was in the act of fastening his fly up when, from one of the cubicles, came a soft moan. His senses alert in case it was a trick, Nick pushed warily at the door, feeling the weight of a body behind it. Slumped on the floor was Jud Simcox, bleeding from what looked like a stab wound to his stomach. 'Bloody hell, Jud! What's happened?' Heart thumping, he knelt down, not knowing whether to move Jud or leave him where he was. He went to pull the knife out then thought that might be more dangerous for Jud. 'Who did this to you?'

Whatever Jud said was indecipherable; it seemed as if he might be slipping into unconsciousness. Nick rose to his feet. 'I'm off to find help. I'll be back as soon as I can.'

In the auditorium, he struggled to make first an usherette, then the manager, understand the seriousness of the situation. Only when the manager followed him to the Gents' toilet, did he take action, telling Nick to stay with Jud while he phoned for an ambulance. From the moment the ambulance arrived, quickly followed by the police, Nick was whirled into a situation over which he had no control. As the ambulance men lifted the now unconscious Jud onto a stretcher, Nick made to go back into the cinema, only to find a restraining hand on his arm.

'Oh, no, you don't laddie, we need a statement from you,' the copper said.

'But I've told you everything I know. I only found Jud by chance.'

'Just get in the car, will you?'

They escorted him to the police station where he was interviewed by two coppers. It was clear from the way the interview was progressing that they thought it was he who'd stabbed Jud. His suspicions were proved right when he found himself banged up in a prison cell, wondering how the hell he'd ended up there. Maybe half a dozen times in his life, he'd come close to being in trouble with the law but never this close. He'd been in this green-painted, part-tiled cell from which disinfectant had failed to eliminate the faint smell of urine for what seemed like hours.

It was on the chilly side too and he was glad of his leather jacket. Had Jud's family been informed? What would Sally think about him being banged up in here? Come to that, what would Kathy have to say about this? No, mustn't think of her. That way lay anguish and heartache. Yet his mind went back to their final moments together, wondering what would have happened if Sally hadn't burst in on them. His love for Kathy then had been all-consuming and he'd yearned to keep her in his arms forever.

A key grated in the lock and the door opened to reveal another copper. 'Come on, lad. You're wanted.'

216

'What time is it?' Nick asked. They'd taken his watch from him when they arrested him, along with his belt, his bootlace tie and the laces from his shoes.

'Two o'clock and the gaffer wants to see you.'

He ushered Nick into the same interview room as previously, to find one of the policemen who'd attended with the ambulance men and another, he guessed, more senior policeman in plain clothes. He sat down at the table indicated and the older man sat opposite him while the constable stood in the background.

The senior copper seemed friendlier than the constable. 'You're Nick Roberts, right?' At Nick's agreement, he reached into his own pocket and offered Nick a cigarette, lighting it for him. He pulled on the cigarette gratefully. 'Now, Nick, tell me again about finding the young lad, George Simcox.'

For a moment, he was flummoxed by the unfamiliarity of the name. 'Oh, you mean Jud. I went for a pee and found him slumped on the floor. End of story.'

'Don't get clever with me, sonny,' the copper warned, his previous friendly manner gone. 'I want every detail, how long you were there, whether anyone saw you, what you said to this Jud.'

Slowly, painstakingly, the copper took him through every minute, almost every second, from the time Nick left his seat to go to the toilet. He struggled with impatience. It all seemed so pedantic to him. 'Who saw you leave? Were any of your mates with you?'

With a sinking feeling, he said, 'No, they'd disappeared some time before.'

'And who were they?' The copper was hunched over the table between them and never took his eyes from Nick's face.

'Ken Johnson and Ray Brown,' Nick replied. The copper made a note of the names and passed a slip of paper to the constable who left the room with it.

'How come they weren't with you?'

'I don't know. It was pretty chaotic in there, with people dancing in the aisles. We must have got separated.'

'So no-one saw you go to the toilets?'

217

'I guess not.'

'Was there anyone in the toilets at the same time as you?'

'I've told you, only Jud.'

'Did you see anyone coming away from the toilets as you approached?'

'No, everyone was concentrating on the film.'

The copper smirked. 'If you can call jigging about to a bloody racket concentrating!'

Nick kept his patience. 'We happen to like the music.'

The copper snorted. 'Then heaven help us if there's ever another war and you lot have to protect us.'

'I've done my time in the Army,' Nick retorted swiftly.

Once again, the copper took him through the moments when he'd found Jud. 'And you say you didn't touch him?'

'No, I was afraid to make matters worse. I just went for help.'

The copper once more offered Nick a cigarette but this time he refused. 'Is Jud a friend of yours?'

'No, we don't get on.'

'And why is that?'

'Jud likes to think he's top dog. Then there's his sister, Sally.'

'She your girl-friend?'

Nick sighed. 'Sort of. Fact is, she's pregnant and we're getting married soon.'

'And Jud didn't like that?'

'No.'

The copper's next question caught him off guard. 'How did you get that bruise on your face?'

'I were beaten up last week.'

'Wouldn't happen to have been Jud Simcox, would it? Perhaps for getting his sister pregnant?'

'Ay, it were,' Nick admitted, 'and a couple of his mates. Jud couldn't have done it by himself.'

'And you retaliated by stabbing him in the toilets of the cinema.' It was a statement, not a question and Nick gasped.

'No, I've told you. I only found him.'

218

'I reckon, Nick, that finding Simcox alone in the toilets, you argued some more then pulled out a knife with which you stabbed him.'

'You've got it wrong! I don't even have a knife.'

'Well, if you're right, your fingerprints won't be on the knife, will they?'

With a sinking feeling, Nick recalled putting his hand on the knife to pull it out then changing his mind. In the face of his silence, the copper stood up. 'I think we can safely say you are guilty of this crime and will be charged accordingly.'

'But I didn't do it! I'm innocent!'

The copper snorted again. 'Half the prison population is innocent. According to them, that is. The courts say differently.' He rose and indicated to the constable who'd just come back in the room. 'Take him back to his cell.'

Back in the cell, his heart filled with dark despair. How the hell was he going to get out of this one? His only hope was that Jud would be able identify his attacker. But what would happen if he died? He tried to push the thought out of his mind but it kept coming back to haunt him. Sitting down on the bench lining one wall of the cell, he tried to think of some plan of action, some way of proving he'd not been the one to stab Jud. It seemed that only Jud — and the attacker, of course — knew that. Who could it have been? But then, emotions had been considerably heightened by the film, so Jud could perhaps have provoked someone. He was good at that.

Finally he fell asleep on the wooden bench, curled up in a foetal position to keep warm. Worn out by the pressures and sheer physical exhaustion, he slept soundly and woke only when someone came in with some breakfast. Needing a pee, he hated having to ask to go to the toilet, but knew better than to do it in the cell where he'd be forced to scrub it out on his hands and knees.

He felt a little better after the lukewarm and too-milky mug of tea and thick doorsteps of bread ladled with butter. Sitting on the wooden bench, he wondered what would happen next. Presumably he'd be formally charged and taken to the adjoining Magistrate's Court sometime today. After that, he had no idea.

Locked up on remand as his father had been? Or let out on bail? As he was pondering these matters, the door opened, this time by the senior policeman who'd interviewed him during the night.

'Morning, Nick. Manage to sleep, did you?'

'A bit,' Nick replied.

'Well, you're free to go for the time being.'

It took a second or two for the news to sink in. 'Last night you were going to charge me.'

'Let's just say we're following other lines of enquiry.' He held the cell door open wide. 'Now take yourself to the front desk and sign for your belongings.'

When Nick stood on the steps leading down to the pavement in Le Mans Crescent, he stopped and breathed in the clear and cold air of a late September morning, thinking that fresh air had never felt so good. What did it matter if he would be a married man in a matter of days, with a child on the way, that he couldn't take the job with Mac and that he'd lost Kathy irrevocably? At least he could walk away from here a free man. He'd reached rock bottom during the night, the only way from now on was up.

* * *

Kathy had a sense of *déjà vu* when Mr Mansfield looked up after receiving a phone call. 'Miss Armstrong?' Was she imagining the disapproving look on his normally bland face?

Wondering what she could possibly have done wrong, she stood. 'Yes, Mr Mansfield?'

'You're to go up to Mrs Pearson's office immediately.' Not just Linda's head shot up this time. So did everyone else's.

She walked to the office door with her head held high and colour flooding her cheeks. Her heart was pounding with excitement. This was the moment of truth. Today she would know if she was going to become a reporter or not.

Mrs Pearson was on the telephone when Kathy first entered and she waved Kathy to the same chair she'd occupied before. After a moment, she replaced the receiver and turned to Kathy. 'Sorry to keep you, Kathy. Mr Coleman has asked me to hand you this letter personally.' With friendly smile, she held out a slim white envelope to Kathy. 'You can open it here, if you like.'

Kathy took it from her, knowing that her future was in its contents. With trembling fingers, she pulled out the single sheet of paper and read that she had been awarded the place on the training scheme starting on Monday 15th October. 'That's only a week away,' she gasped, looking up.

'That's why Mr Coleman wanted you to have it right away,' Mrs Pearson said.

'But will Mr Mansfield let me go with such short notice?'

'He has no choice. Editorial always comes first.'

'Then he already knows,' she said, understanding now the disapproval on his face when the summons came.

'Yes, Mr Coleman told him on Friday.' Mrs Pearson took off the functional spectacles, revealing a softer side to her features. 'Have you got a minute?'

'Oughtn't I to be getting back?'

'It hardly matters if you're a few minutes longer, does it?' She settled back into her chair and rubbed the back of her neck. 'First of all, I wish you all the best for your future career.'

'Thank you.'

'I wanted to become a reporter too, you know.' She looked wistful. 'Like you, I was working here as a shorthand typist. My widowed mother wouldn't hear of it. It wasn't the thing when I was a young girl to be mixing with unsavoury male reporters. My only career option was to become a secretary until such time as I married, when I would retire to become a full-time housewife and mother. Which I did for a while.' A fleeting look of sadness passed across her face. 'Then my husband was killed by a machine gun bullet on the beaches at Dunkirk and I returned to work as my contribution to the war effort.'

'Did you have any children, Mrs Pearson?'

'Sadly, no. We somehow never got around to it. Then, of course, it was too late.'

'I'm sorry.'

'Don't be. I have a good job which I love. My only regret is that I didn't get the chance to do what you are doing. Make the most of it, Kathy.' She used her spectacles to emphasise the point.

'I intend to.'

It was only back in her own office that full realisation hit her and she sat down with a thump. She couldn't believe it was actually going to happen, that was going to become a reporter.

'You ok, Kathy?' Linda asked in concern.

'I'm fine,' she whispered back. 'Tell you at lunchtime.' But it was only with a supreme effort of concentration that she was able to finish off the work she had been doing.

By lunchtime, it appeared the news had travelled fast throughout the newspaper offices for, when she walked into the canteen with Linda, conversation died a little then started up with renewed vigour. She'd already told her friend on the way to the canteen and Linda was thrilled for her, though sad they wouldn't be working together any more. The two news typists, Pauline and Rita, were whispering, staring at her pointedly, and she guessed she was the subject of their conversation. As she and Linda walked past their table, carrying laden trays, Pauline said, 'Who does she think she is? Becoming a reporter, indeed.'

Kathy stopped. 'What is it with you two? Jealousy? Or plain nastiness?'

'I'm sure I don't know what you mean,' huffed Pauline.

'Oh, yes, you do. You've been getting at me ever since New Year's Eve,' she said. 'I've not forgotten that you left me on my own at that party without a clue as to where I was or how I was going to get home. Had it not been for John rescuing me, I'd have been stranded.'

'It wasn't intentional. We'd been invited on to another party by two lads,' Rita said, looking uncomfortable.

'If that was the case, how come you knew about me and John?'

'Someone told us,' Pauline said, but without conviction.

'Come on, Kathy. They not worth bothering with,' Linda said. As she passed the other two girls, she let her tray slip a little so that her glass tipped sideways and some water splashed onto Pauline's head. 'Oops, sorry about that, girls.'

She and Kathy sat at a table as far away from Pauline and Rita as they could. When they'd settled themselves, Linda said, 'I hope you're not going to have trouble with those two.'

Kathy knew what she meant. She wouldn't put it past either of the two girls to insert a deliberate mistake if she needed to file a report quickly but the news of her success had given her a new confidence. 'I can handle them,' she said.

* * *

Joyce had been struggling to get through each day. At work, she deliberately kept her head down, concentrating on keeping her looms going. Her dedication mustn't have fooled Sally, for, when she came back from brewing up she mouthed to Joyce, 'What's up, Joyce? You've got a face like a wet Sunday in Wales.'

'It's nowt,' she mouthed back.

Sally shrugged her shoulders but later, in the canteen at dinnertime, she approached Joyce. 'You can't fool me, Joyce, I know there's summat's up.'

Trying to check the tears that always seemed to be at the back of her eyes, she mumbled back, 'I don't want to talk about it.'

Sally put her head to one side in a questioning gesture. 'It wouldn't have owt to do with Bragger Yates, would it?'

Joyce gaped at her. 'How did you know?'

Sally grinned. 'Joyce, love, half of Horwich knows!'

'Yet you never said owt to our Nick?'

'I knew he wouldn't be too keen on the idea with Bragger's reputation. And I thought it were quite sweet, you being so young and all.'

'How long have you known?'

'Quite a while. I was coming out of Ferretti's once and saw you both sneaking round the back of St Mary's School,' she said, with a pert grin. 'It weren't too hard to imagine what you were doing there.'

'There were no hanky-panky, if that's what you thought!' Joyce snapped.

'I meant nowt by the remark, honest. We all like a bit of a kiss and a cuddle, after all.'

'Sorry, I'm a bit touchy. Now that it's come out, they've all been on at me.' She gulped to hold back the threatening tears. 'I haven't seen Dave – Bragger – since. I'd just like to talk to him one last time.'

'Is there no way you can see each other?'

'No.' She hesitated. 'One of the things I feel bad about is that he and Nick are no longer mates. They were such good friends.'

'I shouldn't worry about your Nick,' Sally said. 'He'll soon have other things on his mind than his mates.'

'I wouldn't be too certain,' Joyce flashed, stung by the smirk on Sally's face. 'He's always been very loyal, not only to his family but to his mates.'

'But it'll be different when we're married, his first loyalty will be to me.' Then, as if realising that Joyce might misinterpret her remark, she blustered, 'Of course, his family will always be welcome.'

Sally seemed so full of herself that Joyce thought a timely warning was necessary. 'Look, Sally, I know this marriage means a lot to you, but Nick needs some breathing space.'

'Because of Kathy Armstrong, you mean?'

Joyce gaped at her. 'You knew about her?'

'I saw them together. After Nick was beaten up,' Sally said, her voice bleak.

For the rest of the afternoon, it was Sally who was subdued, so much so that Joyce had to say something. 'Hope I didn't upset you with what I said,' she shouted in Sally's ear.

Sally shook her head. 'You've given me summat to think on, that's all.'

At going home time, Sally usually went off with her own mates but that afternoon, she chose to walk out of the mill with Joyce. She seemed about to say something to Joyce but then stopped and put a hand on her arm. 'Looks like you've got your wish.' She nodded in the direction of a figure waiting by the gable end of the terraced houses that backed on to the Beehive Mill.

224

Joyce followed her nod and gasped. 'Dave!' She felt her heart lift and a smile light up her face. 'Thanks, Sally. You won't say owt, will you?'

'I haven't before, have I? Now go on with you.' She gave Joyce a shove in the direction of Bragger, whose own face was wreathed in a smile. 'If I were you, I'd keep to the back street.'

Bragger didn't need telling, he automatically pulled Joyce into the doorway of a back gate and put his arms round her. 'Oh, Joyce, I'm sorry, love, I never thought it would get so nasty.' There was a catch in his voice and she knew that he too was on the verge of tears.

She clung to him as if she could never let go, her own tears falling down her cheeks. 'I don't know if I can bear it, not seeing you again.'

'What can I say?'

'Just hold me for the moment.' She tried to pull herself closer to him and he responded by tightening his arms around her. They kissed, their tears mingling and tasting salty on their lips.

'I couldn't let it go like that. Has it been very bad for you at home?' he asked finally.

'It were when it all came out. Mam and Dad were especially hard on me but Nick wasn't so bad.' She looked up at his face, inches from her own. 'What about you and your Mam?'

'After the initial screaming match, she's maintaining a hurt silence. I've tried talking to her but she refuses to discuss it anymore.'

'I'm sorry about that. I wouldn't have upset her for owt.'

He held her away from him to look down at her. 'We need to show them all that we're mature enough to handle all that they're throwing at us and bide our time. Times and attitudes change, they always do and in another 18 months I'll be 21.'

'But what do we do in the meantime?'

'We wait. And we promise each other we'll be together, some time, some place. I'm willing to do that if you are.'

'Oh, yes, as long as there's a chance for us to be together at the end of it.'

'A couple of years is nothing in a lifetime, Joyce. It'll soon pass.' He took both of her hands and, holding them up to his chest, looked deep into her eyes, his face serious. 'I swear to you, Joyce Roberts, that I will wait for you, forever if needs be.'

'And I swear to you, Dave Yates, that I will wait for you, forever if needs be.' They sealed their pact with a long lingering kiss.

They'd been oblivious of people passing on their way home until a group of youths jeered and shouted at them, one of them making a rude gesture that made Joyce blush. 'I'd better get going or Mam'll wonder why I'm late.' But she didn't want to leave, not knowing when she'd see him again, at least alone.

'You go first, I'll hang back ten minutes so that we're not seen together.'

'We've been seen already.' She nodded to the last of the stragglers leaving the mill. 'But you know what? If anyone says owt, I shall tell them we've been saying goodbye and pretend I'm reconciled to the idea.'

'That's my girl! And remember you always will be.'

CHAPTER 25

Kathy burst into the sitting room, the letter of acceptance in her hand. 'I've got it! I've got a place on the training scheme.'

Ron had been asleep, a newspaper half on, half off his lap, his spectacles sitting lopsidedly on his face. 'Whas…what…?' he said, grabbing at the paper to stop it sliding off his lap and straightening his spectacles. 'Oh, it's our Kathy.'

Vera appeared in the kitchen doorway, wiping her hands on a towel. 'What did you say, love?'

She waved the envelope in front of them. 'I've got the job. I'm going to be a reporter.'

Her father gave up the struggle with the newspaper and stood to give her a bear-like hug. 'Eh, I'm that pleased, Kathy, love. We both are, aren't we, Vera?'

Her mother put the towel down on the back of the sofa and came across to hug her too. 'Of course we are but it'll take a bit of getting used to.' She picked up the towel, folded it neatly, and said, 'But tea's ready now. Don't want it to get cold.'

They were still seated at the table, finishing off a second cup of tea when the doorbell rang. 'Who can that be?' her mother asked, of no-one in particular. 'Are you expecting anyone, Kathy?'

She put her cup down on the saucer with a clatter. 'No, but I'll go and see.'

John was standing on the doorstep, an apologetic look on his face. 'I'm sorry to call without warning, Kathy, but I had to do it on the spur of the moment or I wouldn't have come at all.'

It was an odd feeling to see him standing there when she hadn't seen him for two months. 'I don't think we have anything else to say to each other. You voiced your opinion quite clearly when we broke up.'

'Hear me out, please,' he begged. 'May I come in? I'll only keep you a few moments.'

She held the door open and indicated that he should go through to the sitting room. 'I'd rather not, if you don't mind.

What I have to say can be said easier in here,' he said, waving his hand round the hall.

She popped her head round the sitting room door to tell her parents it was John then turned back to him. 'Well?'

He looked uncomfortable, as if what he had to say wasn't going to be easy. 'I've been doing some soul-searching, Kathy, and I'm sorry I was so harsh with you last time we saw each other. Of course you have the right to a career, if that's what you want.'

'It is and, in fact, I've just heard today, I start next Monday.'

'Congratulations. I wish you lots of luck with it.' She knew from the tone of his voice that he really meant it. 'I underestimated you, Kathy. I should have remembered the saying, 'Still waters run deep'.' He glanced down at his feet as if for inspiration. 'The thing is, I've realised how much I love you. These last few weeks have been hell. So I've come to ask you if you'll give me another chance.'

Sensing it had cost him dearly to say what he had, she reached out to touch his face with gentle fingers. 'No, John. I'm sorry.'

'Is there no way I can persuade you to come back to me?'

'Believe me, my life would be much easier if I could but I don't love you as you deserve to be loved.'

'But couldn't we work on that, get to know each other all over again?'

'There's no point, John.'

'I have to ask, have you…is there someone else?'

Telling John she loved Nick would only cause unnecessary hurt. 'No, there's no-one else.'

'Then this is goodbye, Kathy,' he said, his voice bleak. 'I've decided I'm going to Australia as soon as it can be arranged.'

'Oh, John, what can I say, except to wish you good luck?'

'Perhaps a hug for old times' sake?' He gave a rueful grin and her heart went out to him, as did her arms. They stood together for perhaps a moment then he pulled back. She saw that there were tears in his eyes, as there were in her own. 'Goodbye, sweetheart,' he whispered, a catch in his voice. 'Say goodbye to your parents for me, will you?' With a last glance at her, he walked down the short path to the gate.

She nodded, too overcome by the finality of the moment, to say anything. After she'd closed the door, she sat on the bottom step of the stairs and let the tears come. She'd thrown away the love of John, a perfectly suitable young man, because she loved Nick, who was lost to her. How pointless it all seemed! Eventually, she drew a deep breath and dashed away the last of her tears before going back into the sitting room.

Her father looked up expectantly as she entered. 'John not coming in, love?'

She gulped to swallow the lump still in her throat. 'No, but he said to say goodbye to you.'

'What did he want then?' her mother asked.

'He asked if I would take him back.'

'And you refused?'

'My feelings for him have changed, Mum. I wish it could have been different, for your sakes, but I can't help how I feel. Or don't feel in John's case.'

'Oh, that's a shame,' her mother said, then, as she heard Kathy sigh. 'No, I'm not going to say anything else on the subject. I realise it's closed. But I liked John, he was a nice young man.'

'He told me he's going to Australia to make a new start.'

'Probably be the making of him,' her father said. 'It's definitely an up and coming country.'

She sat down, emotionally wrung out from John's final goodbye.

Her father took off his spectacles, a sure sign that he had something to say. 'Your mother and I have had a serious talk about this reporter business.'

Her heart sank, wondering if they were going to persuade her to change her mind.

'Your Mum has been worried about you having to work all sorts of weird hours. Have you given any thought as to how you would get home in the middle of the night, say if you've been reporting on a big fire?'

Thinking how unlikely it would be that she'd be sent to cover such a major event, she said, 'There's such a thing as taxis, Dad, and Mr Coleman did say I could claim expenses.'

'How about you learning to drive instead, then you could use the car?'

It wasn't something she'd given any thought to but it was an excellent notion. 'That would be wonderful, Dad, Mum. But can you afford the driving lessons?'

'We wouldn't suggest it if we couldn't.'

Her father went to bed soon after, as he often did these days, and Kathy and her mother sat on in companionable silence. Kathy broke it by saying, 'Mum, you are pleased about my new job, aren't you?'

Vera looked at her in some surprise. 'What makes you say that?'

She wriggled a little in her chair, wanting to use the right words. 'It's just that you didn't seem very keen at first.'

'Well, the news did come as a bit of a surprise, but I'm getting used to it now. And if it's what you want to do.'

'It is, Mum. I'm looking forward to it.'

'I suppose…' Vera hesitated, 'I always thought you'd stick to office work until you got married, like I did.'

'Did you never want to do anything else?'

'All I ever wanted was to get married and have a family. As an only child, I'd longed for a brother or a sister.' Kathy looked at her mother in amazement. She couldn't remember her mother talking like this before. 'When your Dad and I were courting, having a large family was one of the things we both wanted.'

'It didn't happen though, did it, Mum?'

Vera shook her head, a suspicion of tears in her eyes. 'We were bitterly disappointed though your Dad tried not to show it. I've always felt a failure because of that.'

Kathy reached out and squeezed one of her mother's hands where it lay in her lap. 'I never guessed, Mum.'

Vera looked up at Kathy. 'That's why you're so precious to us, why we only want the best for you.'

Kathy dropped down to her knees and put her head on Vera's lap. 'I know that, Mum.'

Vera lifted her hand and stroked Kathy's hair tenderly. 'I know you think we're a bit over-protective with you but you see now why.'

'Thanks for telling me all this, Mum.' She was feeling choked up herself.

When she stood finally, yawning on her way to bed, she looked at her mother and saw that she wasn't infallible, she made mistakes as much as everyone else. By showing her vulnerability tonight, Kathy had never loved her more.

* * *

Nick knew that Sally expected him to take her hand, as they started down the slope leading to Bolton Royal Infirmary. Somehow he couldn't bring himself to do that yet. He hoped it would come – it was, after all, only ten days or so to their wedding.

'Are you nervous about seeing Jud?' Sally asked.

He reflected on her question. It wouldn't be easy, facing Jud, after all that had passed between them in the last few months but he comforted himself with the thought that Jud had requested this meeting. 'Not really,' he said finally, 'it will be good to settle things with Jud especially as we'll all be living under the same roof.'

When they entered the portal of the grim old building, the ever-present antiseptic smell assailed his nostrils. He was painfully aware that the last time he'd been here was after Brian's accident. Was it really as long ago as four weeks? In many respects, it still seemed like yesterday.

When they reached the pristine men's ward, Jud was sitting up in bed, but with no welcoming smile on his pale face. Nick acknowledged that this was probably as hard for Jud as it was for him. Despite the seriousness of his attitude, Jud did reach out to shake Nick's hand. 'Thanks for coming, Nick.'

'Glad you're on the road to recovery.' The handshake was brief on both sides.

Jud grinned and rubbed his hands together. 'I'm getting there but I'll be glad when I can tackle a plate of fish and chips again.'

His remark broke the ice a little and Nick and Sally settled themselves on to a chair on either side of Jud's bed. 'Still on the slops then?' Sally asked.

Jud grimaced. 'Aye, and I'm dying for a fag.'

'Thanks for getting me off the hook, Jud.' Nick had learned from Sally that Jud had told the police it was Ray Brown who'd stabbed him.

'Least I could do. If you hadn't gone for help, I might have bled to death.' Jud shifted a little in the bed.

'What happened with you and Ray, by the way? I know he's a cocky little sod, but I never knew he carried a knife.'

'I were having a pee when he came in, full of it. He started taunting me about...about Sally.' Jud looked at his sister, but she had her head down, a faint blush on her cheeks. Nick remembered the way Ray had inferred there was something suspicious about Jud's possessive attitude towards his sister and guessed something similar had passed between him and Jud in the cinema toilets. 'I retaliated and we ended up scrapping, mainly on the floor. I were doing OK but I were distracted by Ken coming in to see where Ray was. Next thing I knew, he had a flick knife in his hand and shoved it into me.'

'How long had you been lying there when I found you?'

Jud shook his head. 'I don't know, a few minutes perhaps. I remember Ray looking down at me, then Ken trying to pull him away. Then I passed out.'

'I wondered where they'd got to. They must have left the cinema.'

A gleeful grin appeared on Jud's face. 'With a bit of luck, Ray'd have been covered in blood as well.'

'Serves him right. Pity neither of us saw the end of the film, eh?' Nick said.

Sally was subdued on the bus going home. Finally, walking with her through dark streets damp from an earlier rainfall, he said to her, 'Is summat up, Sally?'

She didn't answer straight away but stopped and said, 'Nick, why are we getting married?'

In the light of a nearby street lamp, he saw that she looked troubled. 'Because you're pregnant.'

'But you don't love me,' she said, a catch in her voice.

'I've never claimed I did but I'll stand by you and any vows we make,' he said.

'That's not good enough for me, Nick. I want someone who'll love me for who I am.' When he tried to say something, she continued, 'I know you're in love with Kathy Armstrong.' He saw the glisten of tears in her eyes as she looked up at him. 'This is probably the hardest thing I'll ever have to do but I don't want to marry you under those circumstances.'

Her words hit him like a hammer blow and he actually took a step back. 'But...what about the baby?'

She made no attempt to stem the tears now sliding down her cheeks. 'There is no baby. I had a miscarriage a couple of weeks ago.'

'Hell, Sally, I'm sorry. Why didn't you tell me before?'

'Because I thought once we were married I could make you love me.' The words tumbled out of her now. 'I've been tussling with me conscience ever since.'

He pulled her into his arms, feeling more genuine affection for her now than he ever had before. 'Oh, Sally, I'm sorry it's turned out like this.' He meant it too. 'What will you tell Jud and your Mam?'

'The truth. That there's no longer a baby. In a way, I shall be glad. It'll be a chance of a fresh start for me.' Her tears had dried and her face held a look of fierce determination. 'I shall go and work in Blackpool. It's summat I've always fancied doing.'

He accepted it was probably a wise course. 'And after that?'

'I'll worry about that later. For now I need to try summat different.' A new positive note had crept into her voice.

He dropped a quick kiss on her forehead. 'Then I wish you lots of luck.'

She pulled away from his arms. 'Don't say anything else, Nick, or you'll start me off again. Just go!' She set off walking towards Mary Street then turned round. 'Will you cancel everything, Nick? I don't think I could bear to do it.'

'I will. And Sally, I think you're a great girl.' With a tortured look, she turned and walked away, leaving him amazed at her previously unrecognised strength of character.

Although Sally's news was welcome, he was also sad for her, that she'd lost the baby. She'd had nearly three months to get used to the idea and must have suffered, mentally as well as physically. He looked at his watch, saw it was still reasonably early and decided to go to the pub. One thing was for sure, he couldn't see Kathy, not yet. A decent space of time was needed for him to take stock of things.

The Long Pull was full of cheerful chatter coming at him in waves, along with the smoke pall that caught in his throat. He glanced round quickly at the groups of men – no women on this weekday night – and saw Bragger, standing a little apart, nursing a pint. Knowing the first move must come from him, he took a deep breath and said, 'Can I get you another pint, Brag?'

He looked up, startled and, seeing Nick beside him, his face lit up. 'Thanks, Nick.'

Once the pints were in his hands, Nick turned to Bragger and said, 'I've missed you, mate.'

'Me too.' Bragger swigged the remainder of his original pint, reached behind to put it on the bar and took the pint glass from Nick.

Both stood awkwardly for a minute before Nick said, 'Could have done with you beside me last week, Brag.'

Quick to pick up on the nuance behind Nick's words, Bragger said, 'Why, what happened?'

Nick related the incident at the cinema and how he'd missed having Bragger beside him as a witness.

'Bugger me!' he said. 'I wouldn't wish that on me worst enemy. How is Jud now?'

'Improving slowly. Been to see him tonight with Sally.'

'Which reminds me,' Bragger said, 'is it true that Sally's in the family way and the two of you are getting married?'

'You'd heard then?'

Bragger nodded and took another drink from his pint glass.

'It was true, right enough, but Sally herself has called off the wedding. She's had a miscarriage.'

Bragger grinned. 'Shouldn't say this but I bet that's a relief, isn't it?'

'In a way but it must have been hard for Sally.'

A brief silence followed then Bragger said, 'Look, Nick, I am really sorry about deceiving you. It weren't the smart thing to do.'

'Happen the least said about that the better.'

'How is Joyce?'

'Reconciled, I think. Best we don't discuss her, Dave.' Somehow the name slipped easily off his tongue.

'That's fine by me.' The other lad took another swig of his drink. 'By the way, Mac's trying to catch your eye.'

Nick turned and saw Mac sitting in his usual corner, a half-empty pint glass before him, and puffing on his pipe, looking his usual dependable, down-to-earth self. 'You coming over to chat to him?'

'No thanks but you go. I'll catch you later.'

'Sure thing.'

As Nick came up to him, Mac said, 'You look more pleased with life than you have recently.'

He leaned over the table. 'Let me get a pint, then I'll tell you all the latest. Can you manage another?'

Mac glanced at his own watch then said, 'A half'll do for me, thanks.'

Drinks in front of them, a cigarette in his hand, Nick related all that had happened that evening from the meeting with Jud to Sally's declaration that she was no longer pregnant.

'By the hell, Nick!' Mac said, putting his drink down on the table. 'That is good news – though I'm a bit sorry for Sally.'

'You're not on your own, Mac,' Nick said. 'I feel so damned guilty about it all.'

'You might want to think about working for me, after all.' Seeing Nick's puzzled look, Mac laughed and pointed his pipe at Nick. 'You hadn't thought about that, had you? That you can now take the job.'

'Bugger me, no! You're sure about that, Mac?'

'It's what I've wanted all along. We work well together.'

Nick raised his glass to him. 'Thanks, Mac. I'll look forward to that.'

* * *

It was Carole who'd suggested to Kathy they come to Rivington Hall Barn tonight. 'Do you good, get you out of yourself. You've been stuck at home long enough.'

'But what about Ian?' she'd asked but Carole had been adamant that he could do without her for one night. Now they stood in front of the speckled mirror in the cloakroom touching up their lipstick. The chill was only marginally less than it had been in the depths of winter but it was, after all, mid-October. Was it really only nine months since she and Carole had last come to the Barn? So much had happened since then. Inevitably, she was reminded of dancing with Nick and the closeness she'd felt even then. With the familiar thickening in her throat, she resolutely pushed all thoughts of Nick to the back of her mind. She wondered if she would feel any different after next week when he and Sally would be married. She doubted it. It would be another hurdle she'd have to overcome.

'Are you ready, Kathy?' Carole said, touching her arm.

She pulled her thoughts to the present. 'Yes. Let's face the hordes.'

The dance floor, when they pushed open the double doors, was a twirling mass of couples. She remembered that it had been a quickstep on that last occasion; this time it was the more graceful foxtrot. Even the tinny tune the mediocre band was playing reminded her of the laughter she and Nick had shared on that last occasion. She faltered then but with fierce determination, straightened her spine and linked her arm through Carole's. 'Let's show 'em what we're made of.'

Carole squeezed Kathy's arm to her side. 'Atta girl! Don't forget, we don't have to dance. We can just sit somewhere quietly and watch.'

'I can't not dance!' she said, her feet already tapping, as they sat down at a nearby table.

At one point, as the floor cleared momentarily, she thought she caught a glimpse of Nick coming through the door then shook her head, convinced that it was only because he was so much on her mind. In any case, whoever it had been had been wearing an ordinary suit, not a Teddy boy suit.

Carole was making some cutting remarks about the fashions some of the girls were wearing and making Kathy laugh, when a deep dark voice said in her ear, 'Do you want to dance, Kathy?'

With a sense of inevitability, she turned to face Nick, her heart pounding, her mouth suddenly dry. 'You've got a bloody nerve, Nick Roberts.'

'Please, Kathy, I need to talk to you.'

'I don't think there's anything else to say.'

'Don't make this any harder for me, Kathy.'

'Harder for you!' she snapped 'What about me? You're getting married in a few days – to someone else.'

'That's just it, I'm not.'

'What?'

Carole stood and said quietly, 'I'll be over there if you need me,' indicating with a nod of her head where she meant.

As she half rose to follow Carole, Nick grabbed her hand and pulled her back onto her seat. 'I know I've made a complete mess of things, Kathy, but I desperately want to sort them out, if I can.' His voice was quiet yet she could hear every word, despite the music, the noise of chattering groups around them, so heightened were her emotions. 'In the first place, it's Sally who's called off the wedding.'

'So you've come crawling back to me.' She tried to sound uncaring but deep inside a bubble of excitement was rising.

'It's not what you think, Kathy. She's had a miscarriage and feels it would be wrong to tie me down when she knows I don't love her.'

'Oh, poor Sally.' She meant it too. 'When did she tell you this?'

''Last Tuesday.'

'And today's Saturday. Not exactly in a hurry to come and see me, were you?'

'I needed time to think.'

'And what conclusion have you come to?' How he answered would be of vital importance to their future.

'That I love you more than I ever thought it possible to love someone.' He pondered for a moment. 'Sally said it were after seeing us together at Mac's flat that she knew she wanted a love like that and I wasn't the one to give it to her.'

When he paused, she waited in silence while he gathered his thoughts. 'I've changed, Kathy. I'll admit I were a bit of jack the lad, always out for a good time, but I know now there's more to life than drinking and dancing. You're the one who's made me see things differently.' He covered her hand with the warmth of his own and she thrilled to his touch. 'Because of all that's happened, I've learned what real love is. It's not feeling whole unless we're together. With you, I feel a sense of completeness. I'm not wrong in thinking you feel the same, am I?'

'No, you're not wrong.' That bubble of excitement was growing, filling her with anticipation. He'd described so perfectly her own feelings for him. 'I've learned a lot too. I thought stability and security were all I ever needed, that I'd found that in John. Now I know that those aren't the only things in life.' It was her turn to draw a deep breath. 'But something has come up that you should know about. I've been taken on as a trainee reporter by the Evening News.'

He grinned with obvious delight. 'That's brilliant news! I said you should think of it.'

'It means, though, I'm going to be a bit preoccupied with the training. There are another couple of trainees who are younger than me and probably very keen.'

'But you've got two years of practical experience on the newspaper to stand you in good stead,' he pointed out.

'I said that to the editor, when he interviewed me.'

He looked at her with those deep, dark eyes, his head to one side. 'Are you willing to give me a chance to prove meself?'

'It won't be easy. There's still my parents and the fact that you're a Teddy boy.'

'My Teddy boy days are over, love.' He indicated the ill-fitting new suit. 'It were meant to be me wedding suit. I'm hoping that wearing it will convince your parents that I'm now a responsible law-abiding member of society and that they'll be impressed by my new job as a motor mechanic.'

'You're taking the job Mac offered then?'

'No reason not to though it's a lot less money than I'm getting now. And you know I've been going for night classes at the Mechanics Institute. Who knows? In a few years, as Mac gets older, he might make me a partner.'

So absorbed had she been in what Nick was saying that she'd almost forgotten they were in Rivington Hall Barn, with a dance in full swing, and surrounded by noise and chatter. 'What made you choose here, of all places? It's not exactly the kind of place to have a heart to heart.'

'I could hardly turn up on your doorstep, could I? It were either here or the Fling and here seemed more appropriate somehow.'

'I can't leave Carole on her own for the rest of the evening.'

'I think you'll find she's taken care of.' He inclined his head to where Carole was standing with Ian now, smiling and giving a knowing wave.

'You had all this planned between you, didn't you?' she laughed but in her present euphoric state, she couldn't be cross with either of them.

He leaned towards her, looking deep into her eyes, and taking her face between his hands, his fingers tangling in her hair, pulled her gently towards him. 'Happen we can have that last dance together after all,' he whispered, as he touched her lips with his own.

To Kathy, his words, his touch, his kiss promised more than merely the last waltz.

EPILOGUE

Today should have been her wedding day.

With that thought, a sense of desolation swept over Sally, nearly causing her to miss her footing as she stepped off the train on to the platform of Blackpool Central station. She knew her solitude marked her out from her fellow passengers, who were either in family groups or gangs of lads and lasses. She was conscious that several of the lads were eyeing her up and, without thinking, straightened her spine, making her breasts, in a figure-hugging sweater, thrust forward and her bottom, covered by a tight black skirt, more pert. She was hoping someone would give her a hand with her suitcase, but no-one offered. Swapping her white handbag to the other hand, she picked up the case again, leaning to the side to compensate for the weight.

In white high heels, she staggered onto the main concourse of the station, amid all the hustle of a normal Saturday in busy Blackpool, mostly day trippers at this time of year, come for the famous Illuminations. Fighting clear of the crowds, she made her way out of the exit and on to the street at right angles to the Promenade, where she stopped to take in this first sight of her beloved Blackpool. She put her suitcase on the ground the better to absorb the sights, the sounds, the smells.

The Tower soared up, gigantic at such close quarters. If she looked to her left she could see the sea, seemingly stretching into infinity. The sharp saltiness of the air, the sweetness of candyfloss from a nearby rock stall filled her nostrils as she breathed in. Almost against her will, for the first time in several days, she felt the stirrings of anticipation and excitement. She was in Blackpool and she was at the beginning of a new life without the stifling presence of her family and, in particular, her brother. Gently, she placed both hands on her still-flat belly in a protective gesture. 'This is it, kid. It's you and me against the world.'

Author Notes

The film 'Blackboard Jungle' was actually shown in January not March 1956. It's the same with other films mentioned but always in same year, ie 1956.

The film 'Rock Around The Clock' never appeared in Bolton, having twice been turned down by the Local Authority, but I have used incidents which occurred in Burnley when the film was shown.

I have been unable to ascertain when the coffee bar, 'La Casa Blanca in' Bolton opened but it may well have been later than 1956.

Various items from Pathé Newsreels have been coalesced into one to give historical background. On checking the Pathé Newsreels online, it would seem that the only time Elvis appeared was when he was doing his military service in Germany.

The new front windows at the Mealhouse Lane Offices of the Bolton Evening News were not installed until 1960.

I have heard that the Passion Wagon was a non-corridor train but it suited my plot more to have a corridor train.

About The Author

Horwich is my home town in that I was born there, six months before WWII broke out. Following the death of my little sister in 1943, my mother took the decision to move away from Horwich and to go back into domestic service. When my father was demobbed in 1946, he joined us. Thus, most of my childhood was spent, with my parents, living in other people's houses, with my mother as cook-housekeeper, my father as chauffeur-gardener. Then, when I was thirteen, we moved back to Horwich for what proved to be the most formative years of my life, the 1950s. The mid-1950s was the period marking the transition from post-war austerity and a growing affluence. For me, it was a time of growing, learning, accepting and forming ideas and ideals that would see me throughout life.

As a child, I never actually played house with my dolls. Instead, I used to make up stories about them. Later, as I started becoming interested in boys, I would make up scenarios with myself as the heroine – who doesn't? When I first started work, I found the work I was doing (as a towel weaver) tedious and repetitious and used to scribble stuff onto the paper bag my break-time biscuits had been in. In the 1970s and 1980s, I wrote a couple of novels, now gathering dust on a shelf – probably the best place for them. Although I had a few articles published in the 1990s, it's only really been since I retired in 1998 that I've devoted more time to writing. I've had lots of success in getting family and social history articles published in national magazines but success with fiction has more or less eluded me. Now that anyone can self-publish, the Kindle version and this paperback is the end result.

If you have enjoyed 'A Suitable Young Man' follow Sally's story in 'Bittersweet,' to be published shortly.

You can reach me on lankyladyanne@gmail.com, @annelharvey1 on Twitter or check out www.annelharvey.blogspot.com

15181769R00150

Printed in Poland
by Amazon Fulfillment
Poland Sp. z o.o., Wrocław